072826

LP    Greene, Graham
        The confidential agent.

2C

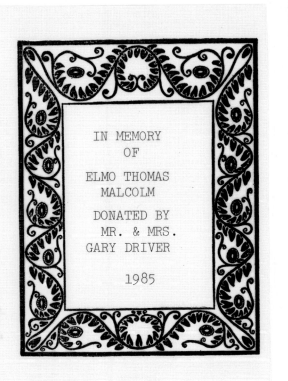

IN MEMORY
OF

ELMO THOMAS
MALCOLM

DONATED BY
MR. & MRS.
GARY DRIVER

1985

# THE CONFIDENTIAL AGENT

D. leaves his war-torn country to come to England on a mission of considerable importance: to obtain coal. But he is not alone in his mission; L. is on a similar mission on behalf of the rebel forces who will stop at nothing in their attempts to prevent D. from getting the coal. But it is not only his enemies that D. has to worry about. Distrust goes deep in wartime and he is constantly checked, tested, and watched by those purporting to be on his own side. Before long he has been disowned by his own Embassy and has the police on his trail for a string of crimes, including murder.

# THE CONFIDENTIAL AGENT

## GRAHAM GREENE

*A New Portway Large Print Book*

CHIVERS PRESS
BATH

First published 1939
by
William Heinemann Ltd
This Large Print edition published by
Chivers Press
by arrangement with William Heinemann Ltd
and in the U.S.A. with
The Viking Press (Viking Penguin Inc)
at the request of
The London & Home Counties Branch
of
The Library Association
1982

ISBN 0 85119 159 2

5.95    85 B 10 338

**British Library Cataloguing in Publication Data**

Greene, Graham
    The confidential agent.—Large print ed.—
    (A New Portway large print book)
    I. Title
    823'.912[F]            PR6013.R44

    ISBN 0–85119–159–2

# CONTENTS

TO
DOROTHY CRAIGIE

# PART ONE

# THE HUNTED

## I

THE gulls swept over Dover. They sailed out like flakes of the fog, and tacked back towards the hidden town, while the siren mourned with them: other ships replied, a whole wake lifted up their voices—for whose death? The ship moved at half speed through the bitter autumn evening. It reminded D. of a hearse, rolling slowly and discreetly towards the 'garden of peace,' the driver careful not to shake the coffin, as if the body minded a jolt or two. Hysterical women shrieked among the shrouds.

The third-class bar was jammed: a rugger team was returning home and they scrummed boisterously for their glasses, wearing striped ties. D. couldn't always understand what they were shouting: perhaps it was slang—or dialect: it would take a little time for his memory of English completely to return: he had known it very well once, but now his memories were rather literary. He tried to stand apart, a middle-aged man with a heavy moustache and a

1

scarred chin and worry like a habit on his forehead, but you couldn't go far in that bar—an elbow caught him in the ribs and a mouth breathed bottled beer into his face. He was filled with a sense of amazement at these people: you could never have told from their smoky good fellowship that there was a war on—not merely a war in the country from which he had come, but a war here, half a mile outside Dover breakwater. He carried the war with him. Wherever D. was, there was the war. He could never understand that people were not aware of it.

'Pass here, pass here,' a player screamed at the barman, and somebody snatched his glass of beer and shouted 'offside.' 'Scrum,' they all screamed together.

D. said, 'With your permission. With your permission,' edging out. He turned up the collar of his mackintosh and went up on to the cold and foggy deck where the gulls were mourning, blowing over his head towards Dover. He began to tramp—up and down beside the rail—to keep warm, his head down, the deck like a map marked with trenches, impossible positions, salients, deaths: bombing planes took flight from between his eyes, and in his brain the mountains shook with shell-bursts.

He had no sense of safety walking up and down on this English ship sliding imperceptibly into Dover. Danger was part of him. It wasn't

2

like an overcoat you sometimes left behind: it was your skin. You died with it: only corruption stripped it from you. The one person you trusted was yourself. One friend was found with a holy medal under the shirt, another belonged to an organisation with the wrong initial letters. Up and down the cold unsheltered third-class deck, into the stern and back, until his walk was interrupted by the little wooden gate with a placard: 'First-Class Passengers Only.' There had been a time when the class distinction would have read like an insult, but now the class divisions were too subdivided to mean anything at all. He stared up the first-class deck: there was only one man out in the cold like himself: collar turned up, he stood in the bow looking out towards Dover.

D. turned and went back into the stern, and again as regular as his tread the bombing planes took off. You could trust nobody but yourself, and sometimes you were uncertain whether after all you could trust yourself. *They* didn't trust you, any more than they had trusted the friend with the holy medal; they were right then, and who was to say whether they were not right now? You—you were a prejudiced party; the ideology was a complex affair: heresies crept in.... He wasn't certain that he wasn't watched at this moment. He wasn't certain that it wasn't right for him to be watched. After all, there were aspects of economic materialism

3

which, if he searched his heart, he did not accept. . . . And the watcher—was he watched? He was haunted for a moment by the vision of an endless distrust. In an inner pocket, a bulge over the breast, he carried what were called credentials, but credence no longer meant belief.

He walked slowly back—the length of his chain; through the fog a young female voice cried harshly and distinctly, 'I'm going to have one more. I *will* have one more': somewhere a lot of glass broke. Somebody was crying behind a lifeboat—it was a strange world wherever you were. He walked cautiously round the bow of the boat and saw a child, wedged in a corner. He stood and looked at it. It didn't mean a thing to him—it was like writing so illegible you didn't even try to decipher it. He wondered whether he would ever again share anybody's emotion. He said to it in a gentle dutiful way, 'What is the matter?'

'I bumped my head.'

He said, 'Are you alone?'

'Dad stood me here.'

'Because you bumped your head?'

'He said it wasn't any cause to take on.' The child had stopped crying; it began to cough, the fog in the throat: dark eyes stared out of their cave between boat and rail, defensively. D. turned and walked on; it occurred to him that he shouldn't have spoken: the child was probably

4

watched—by a father or a mother. He came up to the barrier—'First-Class Passengers Only'—and looked through. The other man was approaching through the fog, walking the longer length of his chain. D. saw first the pressed trousers, then the fur collar, and last the face. They stared at each other across the low gate. Taken by surprise they had nothing to say. Besides, they had never spoken to each other; they were separated by different initial letters, a great many deaths—they had seen each other in a passage years ago, once in a railway station and once on a landing field. D. couldn't even remember his name.

The other man was the first to move away; thin as celery inside his thick coat, tall, he had an appearance of nerves and agility: he walked fast on legs like stilts, stiffly, but you felt they might fold up. He looked as if he had already decided on some action. D. thought: he will probably try to rob me, perhaps he will try to have me killed. He would certainly have more helpers and more money and more friends. He would bear letters of introduction to peers and ministers—he had once had some kind of title himself, years ago, before the republic ... count, marquis ... D. had forgotten exactly what. It was a misfortune that they were both travelling on the same boat and that they should have seen each other like that at the barrier between the classes, two confidential agents wanting the same thing.

The siren shrieked again and suddenly out of the fog, like faces looking through a window, came ships, lights, a wedge of breakwater. They were one of a crowd. The engine went half speed and then stopped altogether. D. could hear the water slap, slap the side. They drifted, apparently, sideways. Somebody shouted invisibly—as though from the sea itself. They sidled forward and were there: it was as simple as all that. A rush of people carrying suitcases were turned back by sailors who seemed to be taking the ship to pieces. A bit of rail came off, as it were, in their hands.

Then they all surged over with their suitcases, labelled with Swiss Hotels and *pensions* in Biarritz. D. let the rush go by: he had nothing but a leather wallet containing a brush and comb, a tooth-brush, a few oddments. He had got out of the way of wearing pyjamas: it wasn't really worth while when you were likely to be disturbed twice in a night by bombs.

The stream of passengers divided into two for the passport examination: aliens and British subjects. There were not many aliens; a few feet away from D. the tall man from the first class shivered slightly inside his fur coat: pale and delicate, he didn't seem to go with this exposed and windy shed upon the quay. But he was wafted quickly through—one glance at his papers had been enough. Like an antique he was very well authenticated. D. thought without enmity: a museum piece. They all on that side seemed to him museum pieces—their lives led in big cold houses like public galleries hung with rather dull old pictures and with buhl cabinets in the corridors.

D. found himself at a standstill. A very gentle man with a fair moustache said, 'But do you mean that this photograph is—yours?'

D. said, 'Of course.' He looked down at it: it had never occurred to him to look at his own passport for—well, years. He saw a stranger's face—that of a man much younger and, apparently, much happier than himself: he was grinning at the camera. He said, 'It's an old photograph.' It must have been taken before he went to prison, before his wife was killed, and before the air raid of December 23 when he was buried for fifty-six hours in a cellar. But he could hardly explain all that to the passport officer.

'How old?'

'Two years perhaps.'

'But your hair is quite grey now.'

'Is it?'

The detective said, 'Would you mind stepping to one side and letting the others pass?' He was polite and unhurried. That was because this was an island. At home soldiers would have been called in: they would immediately have assumed that he was a spy, the questioning would have been loud and feverish and long drawn out. The detective was at his elbow. He said, 'I'm sorry to have kept you. Would you mind just coming in here a moment?' He opened the door of a room. D. went in. There was a table, two chairs and a picture of King Edward VII naming an express train 'Alexandra': extraordinary period faces grinned over high white collars: an engine-driver wore a bowler hat.

The detective said, 'I'm sorry about this. Your passport seems to be quite correct, but this picture—well—you know you've only to look at yourself, sir.'

He looked in the only glass there was: the funnel of the engine and King Edward's beard rather spoilt the view: but he had to confess that the detective was not unreasonable. He did look different now. He said, 'It never occurred to me—that I had changed so much.' The detective watched him closely. There was the old D.—he remembered now: it was just three years ago. He was forty-two, but a young forty-two. His wife had come with him to the studio: he had been going to take six months' leave from the university and travel—with her, of course. The civil war broke out exactly three days later. He had been six months in a military prison: his wife had been shot—that was a mistake, not an atrocity: and then. . . . He said, 'You know war changes people. That was before the war.' He

8

had been laughing at a joke—something about pineapples: it was going to be the first holiday together for years. They had been married for fifteen. He could remember the antiquated machine and the photographer diving under a hood; he could remember his wife only indistinctly. She had been a passion, and it is difficult to recall an emotion when it is dead.

'Have you got any more papers?' the detective asked. 'Or is there anyone in London who knows you? Your Embassy?'

'Oh no, I'm a private citizen—of no account at all.'

'You are not travelling for pleasure?'

'No. I have a few business introductions.' He smiled back at the detective. 'But they might be forged.'

He couldn't feel angry: the grey moustache, the heavy lines around the mouth—they were all new: and the scar on his chin. He touched it. 'We have a war on, you know.' He wondered what the other was doing now: he wouldn't be losing any time. Probably there was a car waiting. He would be in London well ahead of him—there might be trouble. Presumably he had orders not to allow anyone from the other side to interfere with the purchase of coal. Coal used to be called black diamonds before people discovered electricity. Well, in his own country it was more valuable than diamonds, and soon it would be as rare.

The detective said, 'Of course your passport's quite in order. Perhaps if you'd let me know where you are staying in London . . .'

'I have no idea.'

The detective suddenly winked at him. It happened so quickly D. could hardly believe it. 'Some address,' the detective said.

'Oh, well, there's a hotel, isn't there, called the Ritz?'

'There is, but I should choose something less expensive.'

'Bristol. There's always a Bristol.'

'Not in England.'

'Well, where do you suppose somebody like myself would stay?'

'Strand Palace?'

'Right.'

The detective handed back the passport with a smile. He said, 'We've got to be careful. I'm sorry. You'll have to hurry for your train.' Careful! D. thought. Was that what they considered careful in an island? How he envied them their assurance.

What with the delay D. was almost last in the queue at the customs: the noisy young men were presumably on the platform where the train would be waiting, and as for his fellow-countryman—he was convinced he hadn't waited for the train. A girl's voice said, 'Oh, I've got plenty to declare.' It was a harsh voice: he had heard it before demanding one more in the

10

bar. He looked at her without much interest; he had reached a time of life when you were either crazy or indifferent about women, and this one, very roughly speaking, was young enough to be his daughter.

She said, 'I've got a bottle of brandy here, but it's been opened.' He thought vaguely, waiting his turn, that she oughtn't to drink so much—her voice didn't do her justice: she wasn't that type. He wondered why she had been drinking in the third class; she was well dressed, like an exhibit. She said, 'And then there's a bottle of Calvados—but that's been opened too.' D. felt tired; he wished they'd finish with her and let him through. She was very young and blonde and unnecessarily arrogant; she looked like a child who has got nothing she wants and so is determined to obtain anything, whether she likes it or not.

'Oh yes,' she said, 'that's more brandy. I was going to tell you if you'd given me time, but you can see—that's been opened, too.'

'I'm afraid we shall have to charge,' the customs officer said, 'on some of these.'

'You've no right to.'

'You can read the regulations.'

The wrangle went interminably on: somebody else looked through D.'s wallet and passed it. 'The London train?' D. asked.

'It's gone. You'll have to wait for the seven-ten.' It was not yet a quarter to six.

11

'My father's a director of the line,' the girl said furiously.

'I'm afraid this is nothing to do with the line.'

'Lord Benditch.'

'If you want to take these drinks with you, the duty will be twenty-seven and six.'

So that was Benditch's daughter. He stood at the exit watching her. He wondered whether he would find Benditch as difficult as the customs man was finding his girl. A lot depended on Benditch; if he chose to sell his coal at a price they were able to pay, they could go on for years: if not, the war might be over before the spring.

She seemed to have got her own way, if that was any omen: she looked as if she were on top of the world as she came to the door which would let her out on to the bitter foggy platform. It was prematurely dark, a little light burned by a bookstall, and a cold iron trolley leant against a tin advertisement for Horlicks. It was impossible to see as far as the next platform, so that this junction for the great naval port—that was how D. conceived it—might have been a little country station planked down between the dripping fields which the fast trains passed.

'God!' the girl said, 'it's gone.'

'There's another,' D. said, 'in an hour and a half.' He could feel his English coming back to him every time he spoke: it seeped in like fog and the smell of smoke: any other language

12

would have sounded out of place.

'So they tell you,' she said. 'It will be hours late in this fog.'

'I've got to get to town to-night.'

'Who hasn't?'

'It may be clearer inland.'

But she'd left him and was pacing impatiently up the cold platform; she disappeared altogether beyond the bookstall, and then a moment later was back again eating a bun. She held one out to him, as if he were something behind bars. 'Like one?'

'Thank you.' He took it with a solemn face and began to eat: this was English hospitality.

She said, 'I'm going to get a car. Can't wait in this dull hole for an hour. It *may* be clearer inland' (so she had heard him). She threw the remains of her bun in the direction of the track: it was like a conjuring trick—a bun and then just no bun at all. 'Care for a lift?' she said. When he hesitated she went on, 'I'm as sober as a judge.'

'Thank you. I wasn't thinking that. Only what would be—most quick.'

'Oh, I shall be quickest,' she said.

'Then I'll come.'

Suddenly a face loomed oddly up at the level of their feet—they must have been standing on the very edge of the platform: an aggrieved face. A voice said, 'Lady, I'm not in a zoo.'

She looked down without surprise. 'Did I say

you were?' she said.

'You can't go—hurtling—buns like that.'

'Oh,' she said impatiently, 'don't be silly.'

'Assault,' the voice said. 'I could sue you, lady. It was a missile.'

'It wasn't. It was a bun.'

A hand and a knee came up at their feet: the face came a little nearer. 'I'd have you know . . .' it said.

D. said, 'It was not the lady who thew the bun. It was me. You can sue me—at the Strand Palace. My name is D.' He took What-was-her-name by the arm and moved her towards the exit. A voice wailed in disgust through the fog like a wounded sea animal, 'A foreigner.'

'You know,' the girl said, 'you don't really need to protect me like that.'

'You have my name now,' he said.

'Oh, mine's Cullen, if you want to know: Rose Cullen. A hideous name, but then, you see, my father's crazy about roses. He invented—is that right?—the Marquise Pompadour. He likes tarts too, you see. Royal tarts. We have a house called Gwyn Cottage.'

They were lucky over the car. The garage near the station was well lit up—it penetrated the fog for nearly fifty yards, and there was a car they could have, an old Packard. He said, 'I have business to do with Lord Benditch. It is an odd coincidence.'

'I don't see why. Everybody I ever meet has

14

business with him.'

She drove slowly in what she supposed was the direction of London, bumping over tramlines. 'We can't go wrong if we follow the tramlines.'

He said, 'Do you always travel third class?'

'Well,' she said, 'I like to choose my company. I don't find my father's business friends there.'

'I was there.'

She said, 'Oh, hell! the harbour,' and switched recklessly across the road and turned: the fog was full of grinding brakes and human annoyance. They moved uncertainly back the way they had come and began to climb a hill. 'Of course,' she said, 'if we'd been Scouts we'd have known. You always go down hill to find water.'

At the top of the hill the fog lifted a little; there were patches of cold grey afternoon sky, hedgerows like steel needles, and quiet everywhere. A lamb padded and jumped along the grass margin of the road, and two hundred yards away a light came suddenly out. This was peace. He said, 'I suppose you are very happy here.'

'Happy?' she said. 'Why?'

He said, 'All this—security.' He remembered the detective winking at him in a friendly way and saying, 'We've got to be careful.'

'It's not so rich,' she said in her immature

15

badly-brought-up voice.

'Oh yes,' he said. He explained laboriously, 'You see, I come from two years of war. I should go along a road like this very slowly, ready to stop and get into a ditch if I heard a plane.'

'Well, I suppose you're fighting for something,' she said. 'Or aren't you?'

'I don't remember. One of the things which danger does to you after a time is—well, to kill emotion. I don't think I shall ever feel anything again except fear. None of us can hate any more—or love. You know it's a statistical fact that very few children are being born in our country.'

'But your war goes on. There must be a reason.'

'You have to feel something to stop a war. Sometimes I think we cling to it because there is still fear. If we were without that, we shouldn't have any feeling at all. None of us will enjoy the peace.'

A small village appeared ahead of them like an island—an old church, a few graves, an inn. He said, 'I shouldn't envy us if I were you—with this.' He meant the casualness and quiet ... the odd unreality of a road you could follow over any horizon.

'It doesn't need a war to flatten things. Money, parents, lots of things are just as good as war.'

He said, 'After all, you are young ... very

16

pretty.'

'Oh, hell!' she said, 'are you going to start on me?'

'No. Of course not. I've told you ... I can't feel anything. Besides, I'm old.'

There was a sharp report, the car swerved and he flung his arms up over his face. The car came to a stop. She said, 'They've given us a dud tyre.' He put his arms down. 'I'm sorry,' he said. 'I do still feel that.' His hands were trembling. 'Fear.'

'There's nothing to be afraid of here,' she said.

'I'm not sure.' He carried the war in his heart: give me time, he thought, and I shall infect anything—even this. I ought to wear a bell like the old lepers.

'Don't be melodramatic,' she said. 'I can't stand melodrama.' She pressed the starter and they moved bumpingly forward. 'We shall hit a roadhouse or a garage or something before long,' she said; 'it's too cold to change the wretched thing here.' And a little later: 'The fog again.'

'Do you think you should go on driving? Without a tyre.'

'Don't be afraid,' she said.

He said apologetically, 'You see, I have important work to do.'

She turned her face to him—a thin worried face, absurdly young: he was reminded of a

17

child at a dull party. She couldn't be more than twenty. That was young enough to be his daughter. She said, 'You lay on the mystery with a trowel. Do you want to impress me?'

'No.'

'It's such a stale gag.' The conjuror had not come off.

'Have so many people tried it with you?'

'I couldn't count them,' she said. It seemed to him immeasurably sad that anyone so young should have known so much fraud. Perhaps because he was middle-aged it seemed to him that youth should be a season of—well, hope. He said gently, 'I'm nothing mysterious. I am just a business man.'

'Do you stink of money, too?'

'Oh no. I am the representative of a rather poor firm.'

She smiled at him suddenly, and he thought, without emotion, one could call her beautiful. 'Married?'

'In a way.'

'You mean separated?'

'Yes. That is to say, she's dead.'

The fog turned primrose ahead of them; they slowed down and came bumpingly into a region of voices and tail lights. A high voice said, 'I told Sally we'd get here.' A long glass window came into view; there was soft music: a voice, very hollow and deep, sang, 'I know I knew you only when you were lonely.'

'Back in civilisation,' the girl said gloomily.

'Can we get the tyre changed here?'

'I should think so.' She opened the door, got out and was submerged at once in fog and light and other people. He sat alone in the car: now the engine wasn't running it was bitterly cold. He tried to think what his movements should be. First he had been directed to lodge at a number in a Bloomsbury street. Presumably the number had been chosen so that his own people could keep an eye on him. Then he had an appointment the day after next with Lord Benditch; they were not beggars:they could pay a fair price for the coal, and a profiteer's bonus when the war was over. Many of the Benditch collieries were closed down: it was a chance for both of them. He had been warned that it was inadvisable to bring in the Embassy—the Ambassador and the First Secretary were not trusted, although the Second Secretary was believed to be loyal. It was a hopelessly muddled situation—it was quite possible that really it was the Second Secretary who was working for the rebels. Anyway, the whole affair was to be managed quietly; nobody had expected the complication he had encountered on the Channel boat. It might mean anything—from a competitive price for the coal shipments to robbery or even murder. Well, he was somewhere in the fog ahead.

D. suddenly felt an inclination to turn off the

lights of the car. Sitting in the dark he transferred his credentials from his breast pocket, he hesitated with them in his hand and then stuffed them down into his sock. The door of the car was pulled open and the girl said, 'Why on earth did you turn out the lights? I had an awful business finding you.' She switched them on again and said, 'There's nobody free at the moment—but they'll send a man . . .'

'We've got to wait?'

'I'm hungry.'

He came cautiouly out of the car, wondering whether it was his duty to offer her dinner: he grudged every inessential penny he spent. He said, 'Can we get dinner?'

'Of course we can. Have you got enough? I spent my last sou on the car.'

'Yes. Yes. You will have dinner with me?'

'That was the idea.'

He followed her into the house . . . hotel . . . whatever it was. This sort of thing was new since the days when he came to England as a youth to read at the British Museum. An old Tudor house—he could tell it was genuine Tudor—it was full of arm-chairs and sofas, and a cocktail bar where you expected a library. A man in a monocle took one of the girl's hands, the left one and wrung it. 'Rose. Surely it's Rose.' He said, 'Excuse me. I think I see Monty Crookham,' and slid rapidly sideways.

'Do you know him?' D. said.

20

'He's the manager. I didn't know he was down this way. He used to have a place on Western Avenue.' She said with contempt, 'This is fine, isn't it? Why don't you go back to your war?'

But that wasn't necessary. He had indeed brought the war with him: the infection was working already. He saw beyond the lounge—sitting with his back turned at the first table inside the restaurant—the other agent. His hand began to shake just as it always shook before an air raid: you couldn't live six months in prison expecting every day to be shot and come out at the end of it anything else but a coward. He said, 'Can't we have dinner somewhere else? Here—there are so many people.' It was absurd, of course, to feel afraid, but watching the narrow stooping back in the restaurant he felt as exposed as if he were in a yard with a blank wall and a firing squad.

'There's nowhere else. What's wrong with it?' She looked at him with suspicion. 'Why not a lot of people? Are you going to begin something after all?'

He said, 'No. Of course not.... It only seemed to me...'

'I'll get a wash and find you here.'

'Yes.'

'I won't be a minute.'

As soon as she had gone, he looked quickly round for a lavatory: he wanted cold water, time

21

to think. His nerves were less steady than they had been on the boat—he was worried by little things like a tyre bursting. He pursued the monocled manager across the lounge; the place was doing good business in spite of—or because of—the fog. Cars came yapping distractedly in from Dover and London. He found the manager talking to an old lady with white hair. He was saying, 'Just so high. I've got a photograph of him here—if you'd like to see. I thought of your husband at once . . .' All the time he kept his eye open for other faces; his words had no conviction: his lean brown face carved into the right military lines by a few years' service in the army was unattached, like an animal's in a shop window. D. said, 'Excuse me a moment.'

'Of course I wouldn't sell him to anyone.' He swivelled round and switched on a smile as he would a cigarette lighter. 'Let me see where have we met?' He held a snapshot of a wire-haired terrier in his hand. He said, 'Good lines. Stands square. Teeth . . .'-

'I just wanted to know . . .'

'Excuse me, old man, I see Tony,' and he was off and away. The old lady said suddenly and brusquely, 'No use asking him anything. If you want the W.C. it's downstairs.'

The lavatory was certainly not Tudor: it was all glass and black marble. He took off his coat and hung it on a peg—he was the only man in the place—and filled a basin with cold water.

22

That was what his nerves needed: cold water on the base of the neck worked with him like an electric charge. He was so on edge that he looked quickly round when someone else came in—as if it could be anyone he knew: it was just a chauffeur from one of the cars. D. plunged his head down into the cold water and lifted it dripping. He felt for a towel and got the water out of his eyes. His nerves felt better now. His hand didn't shake at all when he turned and said, 'What are you doing with my coat?'

'What do you mean?' the chauffeur said. 'I was hanging up my coat. Are you trying to put something on me?'

'It seemed to me,' D. said, 'that you were trying to take something off me.'

'Call a policeman then,' the chauffeur said.

'Oh, there were no witnesses.'

'Call a policeman or apologise.' The chauffeur was a big man—over six feet. He came forward threateningly across the glassy floor. 'I got a good mind to knock your block off. A bloody foreigner coming over here, taking our bread, thinking you can do what . . .'

'Perhaps,' D. said gently, 'I was mistaken.' He was puzzled: the man, after all, might be only an ordinary sneak thief . . . no harm was done.

'*Per*haps you were mistaken. *Per*haps I'll knock your bloody block off. Call that an apology?'

'I apologise,' D. said, 'in any way you like.'
War doesn't leave you the sense of shame.

'Haven't even got the guts to fight,' the
chauffeur said.

'Why should I? You are the bigger man. And
younger.'

'I could take on any number of you bloody
dagos...'

'I daresay you could.'

'Are you saucing me?' the chauffeur said. One
of his eyes was out of the straight: it gave him an
effect of talking always with one eye on an
audience ... and perhaps, D. thought, there
was an audience....

'If it seems so to you, I apologise again.'

'Why, I could make you lick my boots...'

'I shouldn't be at all surprised.' Had the man
been drinking—or had he perhaps been told by
someone to pick a quarrel? D. stood with his
back to the wash-basin. He felt a little sick with
apprehension. He hated personal violence: to
kill a man with a bullet, or to be killed, was a
mechanical process which conflicted only with
the will to live or the fear of pain. But the fist
was different: the fist humiliated; to be beaten
up put you into an ignoble relationship with the
assailant. He hated the idea as he hated the idea
of promiscuous intercourse. He couldn't help it:
this made him afraid.

'Saucing me again.'

'I did not intend that.' His pedantic English

24

seemed to infuriate the other. He said, 'Talk English or I'll smash your bloody lip.'

'I am a foreigner.'

'You won't be much of anything when I've finished.' The man came nearer, his fists hung down ready at his side like lumps of dried meat: he seemed to be beating himself into an irrational rage. 'Come on,' he said, 'put up your fists. You aren't a coward, are you?'

'Why not?' D. said. 'I'm not going to fight you. I should be glad if you would allow me. . . . There is a lady waiting for me upstairs.'

'She can have what's left,' the man said, 'when I've finished with you. I'm going to show you you can't go about calling honest men thieves.' He seemed to be left-handed, for he began to swing his left fist.

D. flattened himself against the basin. The worst was going to happen now: he was momentarily back in the prison yard as the warder came towards him, swinging a club. If he had had a gun he would have used it; he would have been prepared to answer any charge to escape the physical contact. He shut his eyes and leant back against the mirror: he was defenceless. He didn't know the first thing about using his fists.

The manager's voice said, 'I say, old chap. Not feeling well?' D. straightened himself. The chauffeur was hanging back with a look of self-conscious righteousness. D. said gently with his

25

eyes on the man, 'I get taken sometimes with—what is it you call it—giddiness?'

'Miss Cullen sent me to find you. Shall I see if there's a doctor about?'

'No. It's nothing at all.'

D. checked the manager ouside the lavatory. 'Do you know that chauffeur?'

'Never seen him before, but one can't keep a check on the retainers, old man. Why?'

'I thought he went for my pockets.'

The eye froze behind he monocle. 'Most improbable, old man. Here, you know, we get—well, I don't mean to be snobbish, only the best people. Must have been mistaken. Miss Cullen will bear me out.' He said with false indifference, 'You an old friend of Miss Cullen's?'

'No. I would not say that. She was good enough to give me a lift from Dover.'

'Oh, I see,' the manager said icily. He detached himself briskly at the top of the stairs. 'You'll find Miss Cullen in the restaurant.'

He passed in: somebody in a high-necked jumper was playing a piano and a woman was singing, very deep down in the throat and melancholy. He went stiffly by the table where the other sat. 'What's up?' the girl said. 'I thought you'd walked out on me. You look as if you'd seen a ghost.'

Where he sat he couldn't see L.—the name came back to him now. He said softly, 'I was attacked—that is to say, I was going to be attacked—in the lavatory.'

'Why do you tell stories like that?' she said. 'Making yourself out mysterious. I'd rather have the Three Bears.'

'Oh, well,' he said, 'I had to make some excuse, hadn't I?'

'You don't really believe it, do you?' she asked anxiously. 'I mean, you haven't got shell-shock?'

'No. I don't think so. I am just not a good friend to know.'

'If only you wouldn't be funny. You say these melodramatic things. I've told you—I don't like melodrama.'

'Sometimes it just happens that way. There's a man sitting facing this way at the first table inside the door. Don't look yet. I will make a bet with you. He is looking at us. Now.'

'He is, but what of it?'

'He is watching me.'

'There's another explanation, you know. That he's just watching me.'

'Why you?'

'My dear, people often do.'

'Oh yes, yes,' he said hurriedly. 'Of course. I can understand that.' He sat back and watched her: the sullen mouth, transparent skin. He felt an unreasonable dislike for Lord Benditch: if he had been her father he wouldn't have allowed her to go this way. The woman with the deep

27

voice sang an absurd song about unrequited love:

> 'It was just a way of talking—I hadn't learned.
> It was just day-dreaming—but my heart burned.
> You said 'I love you'—and I thought you meant it.
> You said 'My heart is yours'—but you'd only lent it.'

People set down their wine and listened—as if it were poetry. Even the girl stopped eating for a while. The self-pity of it irritated him: it was a vice nobody in his country on either side the line had an opportunity of indulging.

> 'I don't say you lie: it's just the modern way.
> I don't intend to die: in the old Victorian way.'

He supposed it represented the 'spirit of the age,' whatever that meant: he almost preferred the prison cell, the law of flight, the bombed house, his enemy by the door. He watched the girl moodily: there was a time in his life when he would have tried to write her a poem—it would have been better stuff than this.

'It was just day-dreaming—I begin to
   discern it:
It was just a way of talking—and I've
   started to learn it.'


She said, 'It's muck, isn't it? But it has a sort
of appeal.'

A waiter came over to their table. He said,
'The gentleman by the door asked me to give
you this, sir.'

'For somebody who's just landed,' she said,
'you make friends quickly.'

He read it: it was short and to the point,
although it didn't specify exactly what was
wanted. 'I suppose,' he said, 'you wouldn't
believe me if I told you I had just been offered
two thousand pounds.'

'Why should you tell me if you had?'

'That's true.' He called a waiter. 'Can you tell
me if that gentleman has a chauffeur—a big man
with something wrong about his eye?'

'I'll find out, sir.'

'You play it fine,' she said, 'fine. The mystery
man.' It occurred to him that she'd been
drinking too much again. He said, 'We'll never
get up to London if you do not go carefully.'

The waiter came back and said, 'That's his
chauffeur, sir.'

'A left-handed man?'

'Oh, stop it,' she said, 'stop it.'

He said gently, 'I'm not showing off. This has

nothing to do with you. Things are going so
fast—I had to be sure.' He gave the waiter a tip.
'Give the gentleman back his note.'

'Any reply, sir?'

'No reply.'

'Why not be a gentleman,' she said, 'and
write "Thank you for the offer"?'

'I wouldn't want to give him a specimen of my
handwriting. He might forge it.'

'I give up,' she said. 'You win.'

'Better not drink any more.' The singing
woman had shut down—like a wireless set the
last sound was a wail and a vibration; a few
couples began to dance. He said, 'We have a
long drive in front.'

'What's the hurry? We can always stay the
night here.'

'Of course,' he said. 'You can—but I must get
to London somehow.'

'Why?'

'My employers,' he said, 'wouldn't
understand the delay.' They would have time-
tabled his movements, he knew for certain, with
exactly this kind of situation in mind—the
meeting with L. and the offer of money. No
amount of service would ever convince them
that he hadn't got, at some level, a price. After
all, he recognised sadly, *they* had their price: the
people had been sold out over and over again by
their leaders. But if the only philosophy you had
left was a sense of duty, that knowledge didn't

30

prevent you going on. . . .

The manager was swinging his monocle at Rose Cullen and inviting her to dance; this, he thought gloomily, was going on all night—he would never get her away. They moved slowly round the room to the sad stiff tune: the manager held her firmly with one large hand splayed out on her spine, the other was thrust, with rather insulting insouciance it seemed to D., in his pocket. He was talking earnestly, and looking every now and then in D.'s direction. Once they came into earshot and D. caught the word 'careful.' The girl listened attentively, but her feet were awkward: she must be more drunk than he had imagined.

D. wondered whether anybody had changed that tyre. If the car was ready, perhaps after this dance he could persuade her. . . . He got up and left the restaurant; L. sat over a piece of veal, he didn't look up, he was cutting the meat up into tiny pieces—his digestion must be rotten. D. felt less nervous; it was as if the refusal of the money had put him into a stronger position than his opponent. As for the chauffeur, it was unlikely that he'd start anything now.

The fog was lifting a little: he could see the cars in the courtyard—half a dozen of them—a Daimler, a Mercédès, a couple of Morrises, their old Packard and a little scarlet cad car. The tyre had been fixed.

He thought, if only we could leave now, at

once, while L. is at his dinner, and then heard a voice which could only be L.'s speaking to him in his own language. He was saying, 'Excuse me. If we could have a few words together . . .'

D. felt a little envious of him as he stood there in the yard among the cars—he looked established. Five hundred years of inbreeding had produced him, set him against an exact background, made him at home, and at the same time haunted—by the vices of ancestors and the tastes of the past. D. said, 'I don't think there's much to talk about.' But he recognised the man's charm: it was like being picked out of a party by a great man to be talked to. 'I can't help thinking,' L. said, 'that you don't understand the position.' He smiled deprecatingly at his own statement, which might sound impertinent after two years of war. 'I mean—you really belong to us.'

'It didn't feel like that in prison.'

The man had an integrity of a kind: he gave an impression of truth. He said, 'You probably had a horrible time. I have seen some of our prisons. But, you know, they are improving: the beginning of a war is always the worst time. After all, it is no good at all our talking atrocities to each other. You have seen your own prisons. We are both guilty. And we shall go on being guilty, here and there, I suppose, until one of us has won.'

'That is a very old argument. Unless we

surrender we are just prolonging the war. That's how it goes. It's not a good argument to use to a man who has lost his wife . . .'

'That was a horrible accident. You probably heard—we shot the commandant. What I want to say'—he had a long nose like the ones you see in picture galleries in old brown portraits: thin and worn, he ought to have worn a sword as supple as himself—'is this. If you win, what sort of a world will it be for people like you? They'll never trust you—you are a bourgeois—I don't suppose they even trust you now. And you don't trust them. Do you think you'll find among those people—the ones who destroyed the National Museum and Z.'s pictures—anyone interested in your work?' He said gently—it was like being recognised by a State academy—'I mean the Berne MS.'

'I'm not fighting for myself,' D. said. It occurred to him that if there had not been a war he might have been friends with this man: the aristocracy did occasionally fling up somebody like this thin tormented creature interested in scholarships or the arts, a patron.

'I didn't suppose you were,' he said. 'You are more of an idealist than I am. My motives, of course, are suspect. My property has been confiscated. I believe—' he gave a kind of painful smile which suggested that he knew he was in sympathetic company—'that my pictures have been burnt—and my manuscript

33

collection. I had nothing, of course, which was in your line—but there was an early manuscript of Augustine's "City of God" . . .' It was like being tempted by a devil of admirable character and discrimination. He couldn't find an answer. L. went on, 'I'm not really complaining. These horrible things are bound to happen in war—to the things one loves. My collection and your wife.'

It was amazing that he hadn't seen his mistake. He waited there for D.'s assent—the long nose and the too sensitive mouth, the tall thin dilettante body. He hadn't the faintest conception of what it meant to love another human being: his house—which they had burnt—was probably like a museum, old pieces of furniture, cords drawn on either side the picture gallery on days when the public were admitted. He appreciated the Berne MS. very likely, but he had no idea that the Berne MS. meant nothing at all beside the woman you loved. He went fallaciously on, 'We've both suffered.' It was difficult to remember that he had for a moment sounded like a friend. It was worth killing a civilisation to prevent the government of human beings falling into the hands of—he supposed they were called the civilised. What sort of a world would that be? a world full of preserved objects labelled 'Not to be touched': no religious faith, but a lot of Gregorian chants and picturesque ceremonies.

Miraculous images which bled or waggled their heads on certain days would be preserved for their quaintness: superstition was interesting. There would be excellent libraries, but no new books. He preferred the distrust, the barbarity, the betrayals ... even chaos. The Dark Ages, after all, had been his 'period.'

He said, 'It isn't really any good our talking. We have nothing in common—not even a manuscript.' Perhaps this was what he had been painfully saved from by death and war; appreciation and scholarship were dangerous things: they could kill the human heart.

L. said, 'I wish you would listen.'

'It would waste our time.'

L. gave him a smile. 'I'm so glad,' he said, 'at any rate, that you finished your work on the Berne MS. before this—wretched—war.'

'It doesn't seem to me very important.'

'Ah,' L. said, 'now that is treachery.' He smiled—wistfully; it wasn't that war in his case had killed emotion: it was that he had never possessed more than a thin veneer of it for cultural purposes. His place was among dead things. He said whimsically, 'I give you up. You won't blame me, will you?'

'What for?'

'For what happens now.' Tall and brittle, courteous and unconvincing, he disengaged himself—like a patron leaving an exhibition of pictures by somebody he has decided is, after all, not quite good enough: a little sad, the waspishness up the sleeve.

D. waited a moment and then went back into the lounge. Through the double glass doors of the restaurant he could see the narrow shoulders bent again over the veal.

The girl wasn't at her table. She'd joined another party: a monocle flashed near her ear: the manager was imparting a confidence. He could hear their laughter—and the harsh childish voice he had heard from the bar in the third class, 'I want another. I will have another.' She was set for hours. Her kindness was something which meant nothing at all: she gave you a bun on a cold platform: offered you a lift and then left you abandoned half-way: she had the absurd mind of her class—which would give a pound note to a beggar and forget the misery of anybody out of sight. She belonged really, he thought, with L.'s lot, and he remembered his own, at this moment queuing up for bread or trying to keep warm in unheated rooms.

He turned abruptly on his heel; it was untrue that war left you no emotions except fear: he could still feel a certain amount of anger and disappointment. He came back into the yard, opened the door of the car; an attendant came round the bonnet and said, 'Isn't the lady . . . ?'

'Miss Cullen's staying the night,' D. said. 'You can tell her I'll leave the car—to-morrow—at Lord Benditch's.' He drove away.

He drove carefully, not too fast; it would never do to be stopped by the police and arrested for driving without a licence. A finger-post read, 'London, 45 miles.' With any luck he would be in well before midnight. He began to wonder what L.'s mission was. The note had given nothing away; it had simply said: 'Are you willing to accept two thousand pounds?'; on the other hand, the chauffeur had searched his coat. If they were after his credentials they must know what it was he had come to England to get—without those papers he would have no standing at all with the English coal-owners. But there were only five people at home concerned in this affair—and every one of them was a Cabinet Minister. Yes, the people were certainly sold out by their leaders. Was it the old Liberal, he wondered, who had once protested at the executions? or was it the young pushing Minister of the Interior who perhaps saw more scope for himself under a dictatorship? But it might be any of them. There was no trust anywhere. All over the world there were people like himself who didn't believe in being corrupted—simply because it made life impossible—as when a man or woman cannot tell the truth about anything. It wasn't so much a question of morality as a question of simply existing.

A signpost said 40 miles.

But was L. simply here to stop the

purchase—or did the other side need the coal as badly? They had possession of the mines in the mountains, but suppose the rumour was true that the workmen had refused to go down the pits? He became aware of a headlamp behind him—he put out his hand and waved the car on. It drew level—a Daimler; then he saw the driver. It was the chauffeur who had tried to rob him in the lavatory.

D. stepped on his accelerator: the other car refused to give way: they raced side by side recklessly through the thin fog. He didn't know what it was all about: were they trying to kill him? It seemed improbable in England, but for two years now he had been used to the improbable: you couldn't be buried in a bombed house for fifty-six hours and emerge incredulous of violence.

The race only lasted two minutes: his needle went up to sixty: he strained the engine on to sixty-two, sixty-three, for a moment he hit sixty-five, but the old Packard was no match for the Daimler—the other car hesitated, for the fraction of a minute allowing him to edge ahead: then, as it were, it laid back its ears and raced on at eighty miles an hour. It was in front of him: it went ahead into the edge of the fog and slid across the road, blocking his way. He drew up: it wasn't probable, but it seemed to be true— they were going to kill him. He thought carefully, sitting in his seat, waiting for them, trying to find some way of fixing responsibility—the publicity would be appalling for the other side; his death might be far more valuable than his life had ever been. He had once brought out a scholarly edition of an old Romance poem—this would certainly be more worth while.

A voice said, 'Here's the beggar.' To his surprise it was neither L. nor his chauffeur who stood at the door, it was the manager. But L. was there—he saw his thin celery shape wavering at the edge of the fog. Could the manager be in league? ... the situation was crazy. He said, 'What do you want?'

'What do I want? This is Miss Cullen's car.'

No; after all, this was England—no violence: he was safe. Just an unpleasant explanation. What did L. expect to get out of this? Or did they mean to take him to the police? Surely she wouldn't charge him. At the worst it meant a few hours' delay. He said gently, 'I left a message for Miss Cullen—that I'd leave the car at her father's.'

'Your bloody dago,' the manager said. 'Did you really think you could walk off with a girl's bags just like that? A fine girl like Miss Cullen. And her jewellery.'

'I forgot about the bags.'

'I bet you didn't forget about the jewellery. Come on. Get out of there.'

There was nothing to be done. He got out.

Two or three cars were hooting furiously somewhere behind. The manager shouted, 'I say, old man, do you mind clearing the road now? I've got the beggar.' He grasped D. by the lapel of his coat.

'That isn't necessary,' D. said. 'I'm quite ready to explain to Miss Cullen—or to the police.'

The other cars went by. The chauffeur loomed up a few yards away. L. stood by the Daimler talking to somebody through the window.

'You think you're damned smart,' the manager said. 'You know Miss Cullen's a fine girl—wouldn't charge you.'

His monocle swung furiously: he thrust his face close to D.'s and said, 'Don't think you can take advantage of her.' One eye was a curious dead blue: it was like a fish's eye: it recorded none of the emotion. He said, 'I know your sort. Worm your way in on board a boat. I spotted you from the first.'

D. said, 'I'm in a hurry. Will you take me to Miss Cullen—or to the police?'

'You foreigners,' the manager said, 'come over here, get hold of our girls . . . you are going to learn a lesson . . .'

'Surely your friend over there is a foreigner too?'

'He's a gentleman.'

'I don't understand,' D. said, 'what you

40

propose to do?'

'If I had my way, you'd go to gaol—but Rose—Miss Cullen—won't charge you.' He had been drinking a lot of whisky: you could tell that from the smell. 'We'll treat you better than you deserve—give you a thrashing, man to man.'

'You mean—assault me?' he asked incredulously. 'There are three of you.'

'Oh, we'll let you fight. Take off your coat. You called this chap here a thief—you bloody thief! He wants a crack at you.'

D. said with horror, 'If you want to fight, can't we get—pistols—the two of us?'

'We don't go in for that sort of murder here.'

'And you don't fight your own battles either.'

'You know very well,' he said, 'I've got a gammy hand.' He drew it out of his pocket and waggled it—a gloved object with stiff formalised fingers like a sophisticated doll's.

'I won't fight,' D. said.

'That's as you like.' The chauffeur came edging up without a cap. He had taken off his overcoat, but hadn't troubled about his jacket— tight, blue and vulgar. D. said, 'He's twenty years younger.'

'This isn't the Sporting Club,' the manager said. 'This is a punishment.' He let go of D.'s collar and said, 'Go on. Take off your coat.' The chauffeur waited with his fists hanging down. D. slowly took off his overcoat, all the horror of

41

the physical contact was returning: the club swung: he could see the warder's face—this was degradation. Suddenly he became aware of a car coming up behind; he darted into the middle of the road and began to wave. He said, 'For God's sake . . . these men . . .'

It was a small Morris. A thin nervous man sat at the wheel with a grey powerful woman at his side. She looked at the odd group in the road with complacent disapproval. 'I say—I say,' the man said. 'What's all this about?'

'Drunks,' his wife said.

'That's all right, old man,' the manager said; he had his monocle back over the fish-like eye. 'My name's Captain Currie. you know—the Tudor Club. This man stole a car.'

'Do you want us to fetch the police for you?' the woman said.

'No. The owner—a fine girl, one of the best—doesn't want to charge. We're just going to teach him a lesson.'

'Well, you don't want us,' the man said. 'I don't intend to be mixed up . . .'

'One of these foreigners,' the manager explained. 'Glib tongue, you know.'

'Oh, a foreigner,' the woman said with tight lips. 'Drive on, dear . . .' The car ground into gear and moved forward into the fog.

'And now,' the manager said, 'are you going to fight?' He said with contempt, 'You needn't be afraid. You'll get fair play.'

42

'We better go into the field,' the chauffeur said. 'Too many cars here.'

'I won't move,' D. said.

'All right, then.' The chauffeur struck him lightly on the cheek, and D.'s hands automatically went up in defence. Immediately the chauffeur struck again on the mouth, all the time looking elsewhere, with one eye: it gave him an effect of appalling casualness, as if he only needed half a mind in order to destroy. He followed up without science at all, smashing out—not seeking a quick victory so much as just pain and blood. D.'s hands were useless: he made no attempt to hit back (his mind remained a victim of the horror and indignity of the physical conflict), and he didn't know the right way to defend himself. The chauffeur battered him; D. thought with desperation—they'll have to stop soon: they don't want murder. He went down under a blow. The manager said, 'Get up, you skunk, no shamming,' and as he got to his feet he thought he saw his wallet in L.'s hands. Thank God, he thought, I hid the papers: they can't batter the socks off me. The chauffeur waited till he got up, and then knocked him against the hedge. He took a step back and waited, grinning. D. could see with difficulty and his mouth was full of blood; his heart was jumping and he thought with reckless pleasure—the damned fools, they *will* kill me. That would be worth while, and with his last vitality he came back out of the hedge and struck out at the chauffeur's belly. 'Oh, the swine,' he heard the manager cry, 'hitting below the belt. Go on. Finish him.' He went down again before a fist which felt like a steel-capped boot. He had an odd impression that someone was saying 'seven, eight, nine.'

One of them had undone his coat: for a moment he believed he was at home, buried in the cellar with the rubble and a dead cat. Then he remembered—and his mind retained a stray impression of fingers which lingered round his shirt, looking for something. Sight returned and he saw the chauffeur's face very big and very close. He had a sense of triumph: it was he really who had won this round. He smiled satirically up at the chauffeur.

The manager said, 'Is he all right?'

'Oh, he's all right, sir,' the chauffeur said.

'Well,' the manager said, 'I hope it's been a lesson to you.' D. got, with some difficulty, on to his feet; he realised with surprise that the manager was embarrassed—he was like a prefect who has caned a boy and finds the situation afterwards less clear-cut. He turned his back on D. and said, 'Come on. Let's get going. I'll take Miss Cullen's car.'

'Will you give me a lift?' D. said.

'A lift! I should damn well think not. You can hoof it.'

'Then perhaps your friend will give me back

44

my coat.'

'Go and get it,' the manager said.

D. walked up to the ditch to where his coat lay; he couldn't remember leaving it there near L.'s car—and his wallet too. He stooped and as he painfully straightened again he saw the girl— she had been sitting all the time in the back of L.'s Daimler. Again he felt suspicion widen to include the whole world—was she an agent too? But, of course, it was absurd; she was still drunk: she hadn't an idea of what it all meant any more than the absurd Captain Currie. The zip-fastener of his wallet was undone; it always stuck when pulled open, and whoever had been looking inside had not had time to close it again. He held the wallet up to the window of the car and said, 'You see. These people are very thorough. But they haven't got what they wanted.' She looked back at him through the glass with disgust; he realised that he was still bleeding heavily.

The manager said, 'Leave Miss Cullen alone.'

He said gently, 'It's only a few teeth gone. A man of my age must expect to lose his teeth. Perhaps we shall meet at Gwyn Cottage.' She looked hopelessly puzzled, staring back at him. He put his hands to his hat—but he had no hat: it must have dropped somewhere in the road. He said, 'You must excuse me now. I have a long walk ahead. But I do assure you—quite seriously—you ought to be careful of these people.' He began to walk towards London: he could hear Captain Currie exclaiming indignantly in the darkness behind, the word 'infernal.' It seemed to him that it had been a long day, but on the whole a successful one.

It had not been an unexpected day: this was the atmosphere in which he had lived for two years; if he had found himself on a desert island, he would have expected to infect even the loneliness somehow with violence. You couldn't escape a war by changing your country: you only changed the technique—fists instead of bombs: the sneak thief instead of the artillery bombardment. Only in sleep did he evade violence; his dreams were almost invariably made up of peaceful images from the past—compensation? wish-fulfilment? he was no longer interested in his own psychology. He dreamed of lecture rooms, his wife, sometimes of food and wine, very often of flowers.

He walked in the ditch to escape cars; the world was blanketed in white silence. Sometimes he passed a bungalow dark among chicken coops. The chalky cutting of the road took headlamps like a screen. He wondered what L.'s next move would be; he hadn't much time left, and to-day had got him nowhere at all. Except that by now he certainly knew about the appointment with Benditch: it had been indiscreet to mention it to Benditch's daughter, but he hadn't imagined then this meeting between the two. Practical things began to absorb him, to the exclusion of weariness or pain. The hours went quite rapidly by: he moved automatically: only when he had thought long enough did he begin to consider his feet, the chance of a lift. Presently he heard a lorry grinding up a hill behind him and he stepped into the road and signalled—a battered middle-aged figure who carried himself with an odd limping sprightliness.

## II

THE early morning trams swung round the public lavatory in Theobald's Road in the direction of Kingsway. The lorries came in from the eastern counties aiming at Covent Garden. In a big leafless Bloomsbury square a cat walked homewards from some alien roof-top. The city, to D., looked extraordinarily exposed and curiously undamaged; nobody stood in a queue: there was no sign of a war—except himself. He carried his infection past the closed shops, a tobacconist's, a twopenny library. He knew the number he wanted, but he put his hand in his pocket to check it—the notebook was gone. So they had got something for their trouble, but it had contained nothing but his address that was of any significance to them—a recipe he had

47

— noticed in a French paper for making the most of cabbage; a quotation he had found somewhere from an English poet of Italian origin which had expressed a mood connected with his own dead:

> ' . . . the beat
>   Following her daily of thy heart and feet,
>  How passionately and irretrievably
> In what fond flight, how many ways and days.'

There was also a letter from a French quarterly on the subject of the Song of Roland, referring to an old article of his own. He wondered what L. or his chauffeur would make of the quotation. Perhaps they would look for a code: there was no limit to the credulity and also the mistrust inherent in human beings.

Well, he remembered the number—35. He was a little surprised to find that it was a hotel—not a good hotel. The open outer door was a sure mark of its nature in every city in Europe. He took stock of his surroundings—he remembered the district very slightly. It had attached to it a haze of sentiment from his British Museum days, days of scholarship and peace and courtship. The street opened at the end into a great square—trees blackened with frost: the fantastic cupolas of a great inexpensive hotel: an advertisement for Russian baths. He went in and rang at the glass inner door. Somewhere a

48

clock struck six.

A peaky haggard face looked at him: a child, about fourteen. He said, 'I think there is a room waiting for me. The name is D.'

'Oh,' the child said, 'we were expecting you last night.' She was struggling with the bow of an apron; sleep was still white at the corners of her eyes: he could imagine the cruel alarm clock dinning in her ears. He said gently, 'Just give me the key and I'll go up.' She was looking at his face with consternation. He said, 'I had a little accident—with a car.'

She said, 'It's number twenty-seven. Right at the top. I'll show you.'

'Don't bother,' he said.

'Oh, it's no bother. It's the "short times" that are the bother. In and out three times in a night.' She had all the innocence of a life passed since birth with the guilty. For the first two flights there was a carpet: afterwards just wooden stairs; a door opened and an Indian in a gaudy dressing-gown gazed out with heavy and nostalgic eyes. His guide plodded up ahead; she had a hole in one heel which slipped out of the trodden shoe. If she had been older she would have been a slattern, but at her age she was only sad.

He asked, 'Have there been any messages left for me?'

She said, 'A man called last night. He left a note.' She unlocked a door. 'You'll find it on the washstand.'

The room was small: an iron bedstead, a table covered with a fringed cloth, a basket chair, a blue-patterned cotton bedspread, clean and faded and spider-thin. 'Do you want some hot water?' the child asked gloomily.

'No, no, don't bother.'

'And what will you be wanting for breakfast?—most lodgers take kippers or boiled eggs.'

'I won't want any this morning. I will sleep a little.'

'Would you like me to call you later?'

'Oh no,' he said. 'These are such long stairs. I am quite used to waking myself. You needn't bother.'

She said passionately, 'It's good working for a gentleman. Here they are all 'short time'—you know what I mean—or else they're Indians.' She watched him with the beginning of devotion, she was of an age when she could be won by a single word for ever. 'Haven't you any bags?'

'No.'

'It's lucky as how you were introduced. We don't let rooms to people without luggage—not if they're by themselves.'

There were two letters waiting for him, propped against the tooth-glass on the washstand. The first he opened contained letter-paper headed The Entrenationo Language

Centre: a typed message—'Our charge for a course of thirty lessons in Entrenationo is six guineas. A specimen lesson has been arranged for you at 8.45 o'clock to-morrow (the 16th inst.), and we very much hope that you will be encouraged to take a full course. If the time arranged is for any reason inconvenient, will you please give us a ring and have it altered to suit your requirements?' The other was from Lord Benditch's secretary confirming the appointment.

He said, 'I've got to be going out again very soon. I shall just take a nap.'

'Would you like a hot bottle?'

'Oh no, I shall do very well.'

She hovered anxiously at the door. 'There's a gas meter for pennies. Do you know how they work?' How little London altered. He remembered the ticking meter with its avidity for coins and its incomprehensible dial: on a long evening together they had emptied his pocket and her purse of coppers, until they had none left and the night got cold and she left him till morning. He was suddenly aware that, outside, two years of painful memories still waited to pounce. 'Oh yes,' he said quickly, 'I know. Thank you.' She absorbed his thanks passionately: he was a gentleman. Her soft closing of the door seemed to indicate that, in her eyes at any rate, one swallow made a whole summer.

D. took off his shoes and lay down on the bed, not waiting to wash the blood off his face. He told his subconscious mind, as if it were a reliable servant who only needed a word, that he must wake at eight-fifteen, and almost immediately was asleep. He dreamed that an elderly man with beautiful manners was walking beside him along a river bank; he was asking for his views on the Song of Roland, sometimes arguing with great deference. On the other side of the river there was a group of tall cold beautiful buildings like pictures he had seen of the Rockefeller Plaza in New York and a band was playing. He woke exactly at eight-fifteen by his own watch.

He got up and washed the blood from his mouth; the two teeth he had lost were at the back: it was lucky, he thought grimly, for life seemed determined to make him look less and less like his passport photograph. He was not so bruised and cut as he had expected. He went downstairs. In the hall there was a smell of fish from the dining-room, and the little servant ran blindly into him carryng two boiled eggs. 'Oh,' she said, 'I'm sorry.' Some instinct made him stop her. 'What is your name?'

'Else.'

'Listen, Else. I have locked the door of my room. I want you to see that nobody goes in while I am away.'

'Oh, nobody would.'

He put his hand gently on her arm. 'Somebody might. You keep the key, Else. I trust you.'

'I'll see to it. I won't let anybody,' she swore softly while the eggs rolled on the plate.

The Entrenationo Language Centre was on the third floor of a building on the south side of Oxford Street: over a bead shop, an insurance company, and the offices of a magazine called *Mental Health*. An old lift jerked him up: he was uncertain of what he would find at the top. He pushed open a door marked 'Inquiries' and found a large draughty room with several arm-chairs, two filing cabinets, and a counter at which a middle-aged woman sat knitting. He said, 'My name is D. I have come for a specimen lesson.'

'I'm so glad,' she said, and smiled at him brightly: she had a wizened idealist's face and ragged hair and she wore a blue woollen jumper with scarlet bobbles. She said, 'I hope you will soon be quite an old friend,' and rang a bell. What a country, he thought with reluctant and ironic admiration. She said, 'Dr. Bellows always likes to have a word with new clients.' Was it Dr. Bellows, he wondered, whom he had to see? A little door opened behind the counter into a private office. 'Would you just step through?' the woman said, lifting the counter.

No, he couldn't believe that it was Dr. Bellows. Dr. Bellows stood in the little tiny inner room, all leather and walnut stain, and the smell of dry ink, and held out both hands. He had smooth white hair and a look of timid hope. He said something which sounded like 'Me tray joyass.' His gestures and his voice were more grandiloquent than his face, which seemed to shrink from innumerable rebuffs. He said, 'The first words of the Entrenationo Language must always be ones of welcome.'

'That is good of you,' D. said. Dr. Bellows closed the door. He said, 'I have arranged that your lesson—I hope I shall be able to say 'lessons'—will be given by a compatriot. That is always, if possible, our system. It induces sympathy and breaks the new world order slowly. You will find Mr. K. is quite an able teacher.'

'I'm sure of it.'

'But first,' Dr. Bellows said, 'I always like to explain just a little of our ideals.' He still held D. by the hand, and he led him gently on towards a leather chair. He said, 'I always hope that a new client has been been brought here by love.'

'Love?'

'Love of all the world. A desire to be able to exchange—ideas—with—everybody. All this hate,' Dr. Bellows said, 'these wars we read about in the newspapers, they are all due to misunderstanding. If we all spoke the same language ...' He suddenly gave a little

54

wretched sigh which wasn't histrionic. He said, 'It has always been my dream to help.' The rash unfortunate man had tried to bring his dream to life, and he knew that it wasn't good—the little leather chairs and the draughty waiting-room and the woman in a jumper knitting. He had dreamt of universal peace—and he had two floors on the south side of Oxford Street. There was something of a saint about him, but saints are successful.

D. said, 'I think it is a very noble work.'

'I want everyone who comes here to realise that this isn't just a—commercial—relationship. I want you all to feel my fellow-workers.'

'Of course.'

'I know we haven't got very far yet ... But we have done better than you may think. We have had Spaniards, Germans, a Siamese, one of your own countrymen—as well as English people. But of course it is the English who support us best. Alas, I cannot say the same of France.'

'It is a question of time,' D. said. He felt sorry for the old man.

'I have been at it now—for thirty years. Of course the War was our great blow.' He suddenly sat firmly up and said, 'But the response this month has been admirable. We have given five sample lessons. You are the sixth. I mustn't keep you any longer away from Mr. K.' A clock struck nine in the waiting-

55

room. 'Lahora sonas,' Dr. Bellows said with a frightened smile and held out his hand.'That is—the clock sounds.' He held D's hand again in his, as if he were aware of more sympathy than he was accustomed to . 'I like to welcome an intelligent man . . . it is possible to do so much good.' He sid, 'May I hope to have another interesting talk with you?'

'Yes. I am sure of it.'

Dr. Bellows clung to him a little longer in the doorway. "I ought perhaps to have warned you. We teach by the direct method. We trust—to your honour—not to speak anything but Entrenationo.' He shut himself back in his little room. The woman in the jumper said, 'Such an interesting man, don't you think, Dr. Bellows?'

'He has great hopes.'

'One must—don't you think?' She came out from behind the counter and led him back to the lift. 'The tuition rooms are on the fourth floor. Just press the button. Mr. K. will be waiting.' He rattled upwards. He wondered what Mr. K. would look like—surely he wouldn't fit in here if he belonged—well, to the ravaged world he had himself emerged from.

But he did fit in—with the building if not with the idealism—a little shabby and ink-stained, he was any underpaid language master in a commercial school. He wore steel spectacles and economised on razor blades. He opened the lift door and said 'Bona matina.'

'Bona matina,' D. said, and Mr. K. led the way down a pitchpine passage walnut-stained: one big room the size of the waiting-room below had been divided into four. He couldn't help wondering whether he was not wasting time—somebody might have made a mistake—but then, who could have got his name and address? Or had L. arranged this to get him out of the hotel while he had his room searched? But that, too, was impossible. L. had had no means of knowing his address until he had the pocket-book.

Mr. K. ushered him into a tiny cubicle warmed by a tepid radiator. Double windows shut out the air and the noise of the traffic far below in Oxford Street. On one wall was hung a simple child-like picture on rollers—a family sat eating in front of what looked like a Swiss chalet: the father had a gun, and one lady an umbrella; there were mountains, a forest, a waterfall; the table was crammed with an odd mixture of food—apples, an uncooked cabbage, a chicken, pears, oranges and raw potatoes, a joint of meat. A child played with a hoop, and a baby sat up in a pram drinking out of a bottle. On the other wall was a clockface with movable hands. Mr. K. said, 'Tablo' and rapped on the table. He sat down with emphasis on one of the two chairs, and said, 'Essehgo.' D. followed suit. Mr. K. said, 'El timo es...' he pointed at the clock, 'neuvo.' He began to take a lot of little boxes out of his pocket. He said, 'Attentio.'

D. said, 'I'm sorry. There must be some mistake...'

Mr. K. piled the little boxes one on top of the other, counting as he did so, 'Una, Da, Trea, Kwara, Vif.' He added in a low voice, 'We are forbidden by the rules to talk anything but Entrenationo. I am fined one shilling if I am caught. So please speak low except in Entrenationo.'

'Somebody arranged a lesson for me...'

'That is quite right. I have had instructions.' He said, 'Que son la?' pointing at the boxes and replied to his own question, 'La son castes.' He lowered his voice again and said, 'What were you doing last night?'

'Of course I want to see your authority.'

Mr. K. took a card from his pocket and laid it in front of D. He said, 'Your boat was only two hours late and yet you were not in London last night.'

'First I missed my train—delay at the passport control—then a woman offered me a lift: the tyre burst, and I was delayed—at a roadhouse. L. was there.'

'Did he speak to you?'

'He sent me a note offering me two thousand pounds.'

An odd expression came into the little man's eyes—it was like envy or hunger. He said, 'What did you do?'

58

'Nothing, of course.'

Mr. K. took off the old steel-rimmed spectacles and wiped the lenses. He said, 'Was the girl connected with L.?'

'I think it's unlikely.'

'What else happened?' He said suddenly, pointing at the picture, 'La es un famil. Un famil gentilbono.' The door opened and Dr. Bellows looked in. 'Excellente. Excellente,' he said, smiling gently and closed the door again. Mr. K. said, 'Go on.'

'I took her car. She was drunk and wouldn't go on. The manager of the roadhouse—a Captain Currie—followed me in his car. I was beaten up by L.'s chauffeur. I forgot to tell you he tried to rob me in the lavatory—the chauffeur, I mean. They searched my coat, but of course found nothing. I had to walk. It was a long time before I got a lift.'

'Is Captain Currie...'

'Oh no. Just a fool, I think.'

'It's an extraordinary story.'

D. allowed himself to smile. 'It seemed quite natural at the time. If you disbelieve me— there's my face. Yesterday I was not quite so battered.'

The little man said, 'To offer so much money... Did he say what—exactly—for?'

'No.' It suddenly occurred to D. that the man didn't know what he had come to London to do—it would be just like the people at home to

59

send him on a confidential mission and set other people whom they didn't trust with a knowledge of his object to watch him. Distrust in civil war went to fantastic lengths; it made wild complications; who could wonder if it sometimes broke down more seriously than trust? It needs a strong man to bear distrust: weak men live up to the character they are allotted. It seemed to D. that Mr. K. was a weak man. He said, 'Do they pay you much here?'

'Two shillings an hour.'

'It isn't much.'

Mr. K. said, 'Luckily I do not have to live on it,' But from his suit, his tired evasive eyes, it wasn't probable that he had much more to live on from another source. Looking down at his fingers—the nails bitten close to the quick—he said, 'I hope you have—everything—arranged?' One nail didn't meet with his approval: he began to bite it down to match the rest.

'Yes. Everything.'

'Everyone you want is in town?'

'Yes.'

He was fishing, of course, for information, but his attempts were pathetically inefficient: they were probably right not to trust Mr. K. on the salary they paid him.

'I have to send in a report,' Mr. K. said. 'I will say you have arrived safely, that your delay seemed to have been accounted for . . .' It was ignominious to have your movements checked up by a man of Mr. K.'s calibre. 'When will you be through?'

'A few days at most.'

'I understand that you should be leaving London at latest on Monday night.'

'Yes.'

'If anything delays you, you must let me know. If nothing does, you must leave not later than the eleven-thirty train.'

'So I understand.'

'Well,' Mr. K. said wearily, 'you can't leave this place before ten o'clock. We had better go on with the lesson.' He stood up beside the wall picture, a little weedy and undernourished figure—what had made them choose him? Did he conceal somewhere under his disguise a living passion for his party? He said, 'Un famil tray gentilbono,' and pointing to the joint, 'Vici el carnor.' Time went slowly by. Once D. thought he heard Dr. Bellows pass down the passage on rubber-soled shoes. There wasn't much trust even in the centre of internationalism.

In the waiting-room he fixed another appointment—for Monday—and paid for a course of lessons. The elderly lady said, 'I expect you found it a teeny bit hard?'

'Oh, I feel I made progress,' D. said.

'I am so glad. For advanced students, you know, Dr. Bellows runs little soirées. Most interesting. On Saturday evenings—at eight.

They give you an opportunity to meet people of all countries—Spanish, German, Siamese—and exchange ideas. Dr. Bellows doesn't charge— you only have to pay for coffee and cake.'

'I feel sure it is very good cake,' D. said, bowing courteously.

He went out into Oxford Street: there was no hurry now: nothing to be done until he saw Lord Benditch. He walked, enjoying the sense of unreality—the shop windows full of goods, no ruined houses anywhere, women going into Buzzard's for coffee. It was like one of his own dreams of peace. He stopped in front of a bookshop and stared in—people had time to read books—new books. There was one called *A Lady in Waiting at the Court of King Edward*, with a photograph on the paper jacket of a stout woman in white silk with ostrich feathers. It was incredible. And there was *Safari Days*, with a man in a sun helmet standing on a dead lioness. What a country, he thought again with affection. He went on. He couldn't help noticing how well clothed everybody was. A pale winter sun shone, and the scarlet buses stood motionless all down Oxford Street: there was a traffic block. What a mark, he thought, for enemy planes. It was always about this time that they came over. But the sky was empty—or nearly empty. One winking glittering little plane turned and dived on the pale clear sky, drawing in little puffy clouds, a slogan: 'Keep Warm with Ovo.' He reached Bloomsbury—it occurred to him that he had spent a very quiet morning: it was almost as if his infection had met a match in this peaceful and preoccupied city. The great leafless square was empty, except for two Indians comparing lecture notes under the advertisements for Russian baths. He entered his hotel.

A woman whom he supposed was the manageress was in the hall—a dark bulky woman with spots round her mouth. She gave him an acute commercial look and called: 'Else! Else! Where are you, Else?' harshly.

'It's all right,' he said. 'I will find her on my way up.'

'The key ought to be here on its hook,' the woman said.

'Never mind.'

Else was sweeping the passage outside the room. She said, 'Nobody's been in.'

'Thank you. You are a good watcher.'

But as soon as he was inside he knew that she hadn't told the truth. He had placed his wallet in an exact geometrical relationship to other points in the room, so that he could be sure. . . . It had been moved. Perhaps Else had been dusting. He zipped the wallet open—it contained no papers of importance, but their order had been altered. He called 'Else!' gently. Watching her come in, small and bony with that expression of fidelity she wore awkwardly like her apron, he wondered whether there was anybody in the world who couldn't be bribed. Perhaps he could be bribed himself—with what? He said, 'Somebody *was* in here.'

'Only me and—'

'And who?'

'The manageress, sir. I didn't think you'd mind *her*.' He felt a surprising relief at finding that, after all, there was a chance of discovering honesty somewhere. He said, 'Of course you couldn't keep *her* out, could you?'

'I did my best. She said as I didn't want her to see the untidiness. I said you'd told me—no one. She said, "Give me that key." I said, "Mr. D. put this in my hands and said I wasn't to let anybody in." Then she snatched it. I didn't mean her to come in. But afterwards I thought, well, no harm's done. I didn't see how you'd ever know.' She said, 'I'm sorry. I didn't ought to 'ave let her in.' She had been crying.

'Was she angry with you?' he asked gently.

'She's given me the sack.' She went on hurriedly, 'It don't matter. It's slavery here—but you pick up things. There's ways of earning more—I'm not going to be a servant all my life.'

He thought: the infection's still on me after all. I come into this place, breaking up God knows what lives. He said, 'I'll speak to the manageress.'

'Oh, I won't stay—not after this. She'—the confession came out like a crime—'slapped my face.'

'What will you do?'

Her innocence and her worldly knowledge filled him with horror. 'Oh, there's a girl who used to come here. She's got a flat of her own now. She always said as how I could go to her—to be her maid. I wouldn't have anything to do with the men, of course. Only open the door.'

He exclaimed: 'No. No.' It was as if he had been given a glimpse of the guilt which clings to all of us without our knowing it. None of us knows how much innocence we have betrayed. He would be responsible. ... He said, 'Wait till I've talked to the manageress.'

She said with a flash of bitterness, 'It's not very different what I do here, is it?' She went on, 'It wouldn't be like being a servant at all. Me and Clara would go to cinemas every afternoon. She wants company, she says. She's got a Pekinese, that's all. You can't count men.'

'Wait a little. I'm sure I can help you—somehow.' He had no idea, unless perhaps Benditch's daughter ... but that was unlikely after the episode of the car.

'Oh, I won't be leaving for a week.' She was preposterously young to have such complete theoretical knowledge of vice. She said, 'Clara's got a telephone which fits into a doll. All dressed up as a Spanish dancer. And she always gives her maid the chocolates, Clara says.'

'Clara,' he said, 'can afford to wait.' He

seemed to be getting a very complete picture of that young woman; she probably had a kind heart, but so, he believed, had Benditch's daughter. She had given him a bun on a platform: it had seemed at the time a rather striking gesture of heedless generosity.

A voice outside said, 'What are you doing here, Else?' It was the manageress.

'I called her in,' D. said, 'to ask who had been in here.'

He hadn't yet had time to absorb the information the child had given him—was the manageress another of his, as it were, collaborators, like K., anxious to see that he followed the narrow and virtuous path, or had she been bribed by L.? Why, in that case, should he have been sent to this hotel by the people at home? His room had been booked; everything had been arranged for him, so that they should never lose contact. But that, of course, might all have been arranged by whoever it was gave information to L.—if anybody had. There was no end to the circles in this hell.

'Nobody,' the manageress said, 'has been in here but myself—and Else.'

'I told Else to let nobody in.'

'You ought to have spoken to me.' She had a square strong face ruined by ill-health. 'Besides, there's nobody would go into your room— except those with business there.'

'Somebody seemed to take an interest in these papers of mine.'

'Did you touch them, Else?'

'Of course I didn't.'

She turned her big square spotty face to him like a challenge: an old keep still capable of holding out. 'You see, you *must* be wrong—if you believe the girl.'

'I believe *her*.'

'Then there's no more to be said—and no harm done.' He said nothing: it wasn't worth saying anything—she was either one of his own or one of L.'s party. It didn't matter which, for she had found nothing of interest, and he couldn't move from the hotel: he had his orders. 'And now perhaps you'll let me say what I came up here to say—there's a lady wants to speak to you on the telephone. In the hall.'

He said with surprise, 'A lady?'

'It's what I said.'

'Did she give her name?'

'She did not.' He saw Else watching him with anxiety: he thought—good God, surely not another complication, calf-love? He touched her sleeve as he went out of the door and said, 'Trust me.' Fourteen was a dreadfully early age at which to know so much and be so powerless. If this was civilisation—the crowded prosperous streets, the women trooping in for coffee at Buzzard's, the lady-in-waiting at King Edward's court, and the sinking, drowning child—he

67

preferred barbarity, the bombed streets and the food queues: a child there had nothing worse to look forward to than death. Well, it was for *her* kind that he was fighting: to prevent the return of such a civilisation to his own country.

He took off the receiver. 'Hullo. Who's that, please?'

An impatient voice said, 'This is Rose Cullen.' What on earth, he thought, does that mean? Are they going to try to get at me, as in the story-books, with a girl? 'Yes?' he said. 'Did you get home safely the other night—to Gwyn Cottage?' There was only one person who could have given her his address, and that was L.

'Of course I got home. Listen.'

'I'm sorry I had to leave you in such questionable company.'

'Oh,' she said, 'Don't be a fool. Are you a thief?'

'I began stealing cars before you were born.'

'But you *have* got an appointment with my father.'

'Did he tell you so?'

An exclamation of impatience came up the wire. 'Do you think father and I are on speaking terms? It was written down in your diary. You dropped it.'

'And this address too?'

'Yes.'

'I'd like to have that back. The diary, I mean. It has sentimental associations—with my other

68

robberies.'

'Oh, for God's sake,' the voice said, 'if only you wouldn't try . . .'

He stared gloomily away across the little hotel hall: an aspidistra on stilts, an umbrella rack in the form of a shell-case. He thought: we could make an industry out of that, with all the shells we have at home. Empty shell-cases for export. Give a tasteful umbrella stand this Christmas from one of the devastated cities. 'Have you gone to sleep?' the voice asked.

'No, I'm just waiting to hear what you want. It is—you see—a little embarrassing. Our last meeting was—odd.'

'I want to talk to you.'

'Well?' He wished he could make up his mind as to whether she was L.'s girl or not.

'I don't mean on the 'phone. Will you have dinner with me to-night?'

'I haven't, you know, got the right clothes.' It was strange—her voice sounded extraordinarily strained. If she was L.'s girl, of course they might be getting anxious—time was very short. His appointment with Benditch was for to-morrow at noon.

'We'll go anywhere you like.'

It didn't seem to him as if there would be any harm in their meeting as long as he didn't take his credentials with him, even in his socks. On the other hand, his room might be searched again: it was certainly a problem. He said,

'Where should we meet?'

She said promptly, 'Outside Russell Square Station—at seven.' That sounded safe enough. He said, 'Do you know anyone who wants a good maid? You or your father, for instance?'

'Are you crazy?'

'Never mind. We'll talk about that to-night. Good-bye.'

He walked slowly upstairs. He wasn't going to take any chances; the credentials had got to be hidden. He had only to get through twenty-four hours, and then he would be a free man—to return to his bombed and starving home. Surely they were not going to throw a mistress at his head—people didn't fall for that sort of thing except in melodrama. In melodrama a secret agent was never tired or uninterrested or in love with a dead woman. But perhaps L. read melodramas—he represented, after all, the aristocracy—the marquises and generals and bishops—who lived in a curious formal world of their own jingling with medals that they awarded to each other: like fishes in a tank, perpetually stared at through glass, and confined to a particular element by their physiological needs. They might take their ideas of the other world—of professional men and working people—partly from melodrama. It was wrong to underestimate the ignorance of the ruling class. Marie Antoinette had said of the poor: 'Can't they eat cake?'

The manageress had gone: perhaps there was an extension and she had been listening to his conversation on another 'phone. The child was still cleaning the passage with furious absorption. He stood and watched her for a while. One had to take risks sometimes. He said, 'Would you mind coming into my room for just a moment?' He closed the door behind them both. He said, 'I want to speak low—because the manageress mustn't hear.' Again he was startled by that look of devotion—what on earth had he done to earn it? a middle-aged foreigner with a face from which he had only recently cleaned the blood, scarred.... He had given her half a dozen kind words: in her environment were they so rare that they evoked automatically—this? He said, 'I want you to do something for me.'

'Anything,' she said. She was devoted too, he thought, to Clara. What a life when a child had to fix her love on an old foreigner and a prostitute for want of anything better.

He said, 'Nobody at all must know. I have some papers people are looking for. I want you to keep them for me until to-morrow.'

She asked, 'Are you a spy?'

'No. No.'

'I wouldn't mind,' she said, 'what you are.' He sat down on the bed and took off his shoes: she watched him with fascination. She said, 'That lady on the 'phone...'

He looked up with a sock in one hand and the papers in the other. 'She mustn't know. You and me only.' Her face glowed: he might have given her a jewel; he changed his mind quickly about offering her money. Later—perhaps—when he was leaving—some present she could turn into money if she chose, but not the brutal and degrading payment. 'Where will you keep them?' he said.

'Where you did.'

'And nobody must know.'

'Cross my heart.'

'Better do it now. At once.' He turned his back and looked out of the window: the hotel sign in big gilt letters was strung just below: forty feet down the frosty pavement and a coal cart going slowly by. 'And now,' he said, 'I'm going to sleep again.' There were enormous arrears of sleep to make up.

'Won't you have some lunch?' she asked. 'It's not so bad to-day. There's Irish stew and treacle pudding. It keeps you warm.' She said, 'I'll see you get big helpings—when *her* back's turned.'

'I'm not used yet,' he said, 'to your big meals. Where I've come from, we've got out of the way of eating.'

'But you have to eat.'

'Oh,' he said, 'we've found a cheaper way. We look at pictures of food—in the magazines—instead.'

'Go on,' she said. 'I don't believe you. You've

got to eat. If it's the money . . .'

'No,' he said, 'it's not the money. I promise you I'll eat well to-night. But just now it's sleep I want.'

'Nobody'll come in this time,' she said. 'Nobody.' He could hear her moving in the passage outside like a sentry: a flap, flap, flap: she was probably pretending to dust.

He lay down again on his bed in his clothes. No need this time to tell his sub-conscious mind to wake him. He never slept for more than six hours at a time. That was the longest interval there ever was between raids. But this time he couldn't sleep at all—never before had he let those papers out of his possession. They had been with him all across Europe: on the express to Paris, to Calais, Dover: even when he was being beaten up, they were there, under his heel, a safeguard. He felt uneasy without them. They were his authority and now he was nothing—just an undesirable alien, lying on a shabby bed in a disreputable hotel. Suppose the girl should boast of his confidence: but he trusted her more than he trusted anyone else. But she was simple: suppose she should change her stockings and leave his papers lying about, forgotten. . . . L., he thought grimly, would never have done a thing like that. In a way the whole future of what was left of his country lay in the stockings of an underpaid child. They were worth at least £2,000 on the nail—that had been proved. They would probably pay a great deal more if you gave them credit. He felt powerless, like Samson with his hair shorn. He nearly got up and called Else back. But if he did, what should he do with the papers? There was nowhere in the little bare room to hide them. In a way, too, it was suitable that the future of the poor should depend upon the poor.

The hours passed slowly. He supposed that this was resting. There was silence in the passage after a while: she hadn't been able to spin out her dusting any longer. If only I had a gun, he thought, I shouldn't feel so powerless; but it had been impossible to bring one: it was to risk too much at the customs. Presumably here there were ways of obtaining a revolver secretly, but he didn't know them. He discovered that he was a little frightened: time was so short—they were certain to spring something on him soon. If they began with a beating up, their next attempt was likely to be drastic. It felt odd, lonely, terrifying to be the only one in danger; as a rule he had the company of a whole city. Again his mind returned to the prison and the warder coming across the asphalt: he had been alone then. Fighting was better in the old days. Roland had companions at Roncesvalles— Oliver and Turpin: the whole chivalry of Europe was riding up to help him. Men were united by a common belief. Even a heretic would be on the side of Christendom against the

Moors: they might differ about the persons of the Trinity, but on the main issue they were like rock. Now there were so many varieties of economic materialism, so many initial letters.

A few street cries came up through the cold air—old clothes and a man who wanted chairs to mend. He had said that war killed emotion: it was untrue. Those cries were an agony. He buried his head in the pillow as a young man might have done. They brought back the years before his marriage with intensity. They had listened to them together. He felt like a young man who has given all his trust and found himself mocked, cuckolded, betrayed. Or who has himself in a minute of lust spoilt a whole life together. To live was like perjury. How often they had declared that they would die within a week of each other—but he hadn't died: he had survived prison, the shattered house. The bomb which had wrecked four floors and killed a cat had left him alive. Did L. really imagine that he could trap him with a woman? and was this what London—a foreign peaceful city—had in store for him, the return of feeling, despair?

The dusk fell: lights came out like hoar frost. He lay on his back again with his eyes open. Oh, to be home. Presently he got up and shaved. It was time to be gone. He buttoned his overcoat round the chin as he stepped out into the bitter night. An east wind blew from the City: it had the stone-cold of big business blocks and banks.

You thought of long passages and glass doors and a spiritless routine. It was a wind to take the heart out of a man. He walked up Guilford Street—the after-office rush was over and the theatre traffic hadn't begun. In the small hotels dinners were being laid, and oriental faces peered out from bedsitting rooms with gloomy nostalgia.

As he turned up a side street he heard a voice behind him, cultured, insinuating, weak: 'Excuse me, sir. Excuse me.' He stopped. A man dressed very oddly in a battered bowler and a long black overcoat from which a fur collar had been removed bowed with an air of excessive gentility; he had a white stubble on his chin, his eyes were bloodshot and pouchy, and he carried in front of him a thin worn hand as if it were to be kissed. He began at once to apologise in what remained of a university—or a stage—accent: 'I felt sure you wouldn't mind my addressing you, sir. The fact of the matter is, I find myself in a predicament.'

'A predicament?'

'A matter of a few shillings, sir.' D. wasn't used to this: their beggars at home in the old days had been more spectacular, with lumps of rotting flesh uplifted at the doors of churches.

The man had an air of badly secreted anxiety. 'I wouldn't have addressed you, sir, naturally, if I hadn't felt that you were—well, of one's own kind.' Was there really a snobbery in begging—

or was it just a method of approach which had proved workable? 'Of course, if it's inconvenient at the moment, say no more about it.'

D. put his hand into his pocket. 'Not here, if you don't mind, sir, in the full light of day, as it were. If you would just step into this mews. I confess to a feeling of shame—asking a complete stranger for a loan like this.' He sidled nervously sideways into the empty mews: 'You can imagine my circumstances.' One car stood here, big green closed gates: nobody about. 'Well,' D. said, 'here's half a crown.'

'Thank you, sir.' He grabbed it. 'Perhaps one day I shall be able to repay . . .' he was off with lanky strides, out of the mews, into the street, out of sight. D. began to follow: there was a small scraping sound behind him, and a piece of brick suddenly flew out of the wall and struck him sharply on the cheek. Memory warned him: he ran. In the street there were lights in windows, a policeman stood at a corner, he was safe. He knew that somebody had fired at him with a gun fitted with a silencer. Ignorance. You couldn't aim properly with a silencer.

The beggar, he thought, must have waited for me outside the hotel, acted as decoy into the mews: if they had hit him the car was there ready to take his body. Or perhaps they only meant to maim him. Probably they hadn't made up their own minds which, and that was another reason why they had missed, just as in billiards if you have two shots in mind, you miss both. But how had they known the hour at which he would be leaving the hotel? He quickened his step, and came up Bernard Street, with a tiny flame of anger at his heart. The girl, of course, would not be at the station.

But she was.

He said, 'I didn't really expect to find you here. Not after your friends had tried to shoot me.'

'Listen,' she said, 'there are things I won't and can't believe. I came here to apologise. About last night. I don't believe you meant to steal that car, but I was drunk, furious.... I never thought they meant to smash you as they did. It was that fool Currie. But if you start being melodramatic again.... Is it a new kind of confidence trick? Is it meant to appeal to the romantic female heart? Because you'd better know, it doesn't work.'

He said, 'Did L. know you were meeting me here at seven-thirty?'

She said, with a faint uneasiness, 'Not L.; Currie did.' The confession surprised him: perhaps, after all, she *was* innocent. 'He'd got your notebook, you see. He said it ought to be kept—in case you tried anything more on. I spoke to him on the telephone today—he was in town. I said I didn't believe you meant to steal that car and that I was going to meet you. I

78

wanted to give it back to you.'

'He let you have it?'

'Here it is.'

'And perhaps you told him where, what time?'

'I may have done. We talked a lot. He argued. But it's no use you telling me Currie shot at you—I don't believe it.'

'Oh no. Nor do I. I suppose he happened to meet L. and told him.'

She said, 'He was having lunch with L.' She exclaimed furiously, 'But it's fantastic. How could they shoot at you in the street—here? What about the police, the noise, the neighbours? Why are you here at all? Why aren't you at the police station?'

He said gently, 'One at a time. It was in a mews. There was a silencer. And as for the police station, I had an appointment here—with you.'

'I don't believe it. I won't believe it. Don't you see that if things like that happened life would be quite different? One would have to begin over again.'

He said, 'It doesn't seem odd to me. At home we live with bullets. Even here you'd get used to it. Life goes on much the same.' He took her by the hand like a child and led her down Bernard Street, then into Grenville Street. He said, 'It will be quite safe. He won't have stayed.' They came to the mews. He picked up a scrap of brick

79

at the entrance. He said, 'You see, this was what he hit.'

'Prove it. Prove it,' she said fiercely.

'I don't suppose that's possible.' He began to dig with his nail at the wall, looking for something: the bullet might have wedged. . . . He said, 'They are getting desperate. There was the business in the lavatory yesterday—and then what you saw. To-day somebody has searched my room—but that may be one of my own people. But this—to-night—is going pretty far. They can't do much more now than kill me. I don't think they'll manage that, though. I'm horribly hard to kill.'

'Oh, God,' she said suddenly, 'it's true.' He turned. She held a bullet in her hand: it had ricocheted off the wall. She said, 'It's true. So we've got to do something. The police . . .'

'I saw nobody. There's no evidence.'

'You said last night that note offered you money.'

'Yes.'

'Why don't you take it?' she asked angrily. 'You don't want to be killed.'

It occurred to him that she was going to be hysterical. He took her arm and pushed her in front of him into a public-house. 'Two double brandies,' he said. He began to talk cheerfully and quickly, 'I want you to do me a favour. There's a girl at the hotel where I'm staying— she's done me a service and got the sack for it.

80

She's a good little thing—only wild. God knows what mightn't happen to her. Couldn't you find her a job? You must have hundreds of smart friends.'

'Oh, stop,' she said, 'being so damned quixotic. I want to hear more about all this.'

'There's not much I can tell you. Apparently they don't want me to see your father.'

'Are you,' she said with a kind of angry contempt, 'what they call a patriot?'

'Oh no, I don't think so. It's they, you know, who are always talking about something called our country.'

'Then why don't you take their money?'

He said, 'You've got to choose some line of action and live by it. Otherwise nothing matters at all. You probably end with a gas-oven. I've chosen certain people who've had the lean portion for some centuries now.'

'But your people are betrayed all the time.'

'It doesn't matter. You might say it's the only job left for anyone—sticking to a job. It's no good taking a moral line—my people commit atrocities like the others. I suppose if I believed in a God it would be simpler.'

'Do you believe,' she said, 'that *your* leaders are any better than L.'s?' She swallowed her brandy and began to tap the counter nervously with the little metal bullet.

'No. Of course not. But I still prefer the people they lead—even if they lead them all

81

wrong.'

'The poor, right or wrong.' she scoffed.

'It is no worse—is it?—than my country, right or wrong. You choose your side once for all—of course, it may be the wrong side. Only history can tell that.' He took the bullet out of her hand and said, 'I'm going to eat something. I haven't had anything since last night.' He took a plate of sandwiches and carried them to a table. 'Go on,' he said, 'eat a little. You are always drinking on an empty stomach when I meet you. It's bad for the nerves.'

'I'm not hungry.'

'I am.' He took a large bite out of a ham sandwich. She began to squeak her finger up and down on the shiny china top. 'Tell me,' she said, 'about what you were—before all this started.'

'I was a lecturer,' he said, 'in medieval French. Not an exciting occupation.' He smiled. 'It had its moment. You've heard of the Song of Roland?'

'Yes.'

'It was I who discovered the Berne MS.'

'That doesn't mean a thing to me,' she said. 'I'm bone-ignorant.'

'The best MS. was the one your people had at Oxford—but it was too corrected—and there were gaps. Then there was the Venice MS. That filled in some of the gaps not all ... it was very inferior.' He said proudly, 'I found the Berne

MS.'

'You did, did you?' she said gloomily, with her eyes on the bullet in his hand. Then she looked up at the scarred chin and the bruised mouth. He said, 'You remember the story—of that rearguard in the Pyrenees, and how Oliver, when he saw the Saracens coming, urged Roland to blow his horn and fetch back Charlemagne.'

She seemed to be wondering about the scar. She began to ask, 'How?...'

'And Roland wouldn't blow—swore that no enemy could ever make him blow. A big brave fool. In war one always chooses the wrong hero. Oliver should have been the hero of that song—instead of being given second place with the blood-thirsty bishop Turpin.'

She said, 'How did your wife die?' but he was determined to keep the conversation free from the infection of his war.

He said, 'And then, of course, when all his men are dead or dying, and he himself is finished, he says he'll blow the horn. And the song-writer makes—what is your expression?—a great dance about it. The blood streams from his mouth, the bones of his temple are broken. But Oliver taunts him. He had had his chance to blow his horn at the beginning and save all those lives, but for his own glory he would not blow. Now because he is defeated and dying he will blow and bring disgrace on his race

83

and name. Let him die quietly and be content with all the damage his heroism has done. Didn't I tell you Oliver was the real hero?'

'Did you?' she said. She was obviously not following what he said. He saw that she was nearly crying, and ashamed of it: self-pity, probably. It was a quality he didn't care for, even in an adolescent.

He said. 'That's the importance of the Berne MS. It re-establishes Oliver. It makes the story tragedy, not just heroics. Because in the Oxford version Oliver is reconciled, he gives Roland his death-blow by accident, his eyes blinded by wounds. The story, you see, has been tidied up to suit. . . . But in the Berne version he strikes his friend down with full knowledge—because of what he has done to his men: all the wasted lives. He dies hating the man he loves—the big boasting courageous fool who was more concerned with his own glory than with the victory of his faith. But you can see how that version didn't appeal—in the castles—at the banquets, among the dogs and reeds and beakers: the jongleurs had to adapt it, to meet the tastes of the medieval nobles who were quite capable of being Rolands in a small way—it only needs conceit and a strong arm—but couldn't understand what Oliver was at.'

'Give me Oliver,' she said, 'any day.' He looked at her with some surprise. She said, 'My father, of course, would be like one of your barons—all for Roland.'

He said, 'After I had published the Berne MS. the war came.'

'And when it's over,' she said, 'what will you do then?'

It had never occurred to him to wonder that. He said, 'Oh, I don't suppose I shall see the end.'

'Like Oliver,' she said, 'you'd have stopped it if you could, but as it's happened . . .'

'Oh, I'm not an Oliver any more than the poor devils at home are Rolands. Or L. a Ganelon.'

'Who was Ganelon?'

'He was the traitor.'

She said, 'You are sure about L.? He seemed to me pleasant enough.'

'They know how to be pleasant. They've cultivated that art for centuries.' He drank his brandy down. He said, 'Well, I'm here. Why should we talk business? You asked me to come and I've come.'

'I just wished I could help you, that's all.'

'Why?'

She said, 'After they'd beaten you up last night I was sick. Of course Currie thought it was the drink. But it was your face. Oh,' she exlaimed, 'you ought to know how it is—there's no trust anywhere. I'd never seen a face that looked medium honest. I mean about everything. My father's people—they're honest about—well, food and love perhaps—they have stuffy contented wives anyway—but where coal is concerned—or the workmen...' She said, 'If you hope for anything at all from them, for God's sake don't breathe melodrama—or sentiment. Show them a cheque-book, a contract—let it be a cast-iron one.'

In the public bar across the way they were throwing darts with enormous precision. He said, 'I haven't come to beg.'

'Does it really matter a lot to you?'

'Wars to-day are not what they were in Roland's time. Coal can be more important than tanks. We've got more tanks than we want. They aren't much good, anyway.'

'But Ganelon can still upset everything?'

'It's not so easy for him.'

She said, 'I suppose they'll all be there when you see my father. There's honour among thieves. Goldstein and old Lord Fetting, Brigstock—and Forbes. You better know what you'll be up against.'

He said. 'Be careful. After all. They are *your* people.'

'I haven't got a people. My grandfather was a workman, anyway.'

'You're unlucky,' he said. 'You are in No Man's Land. Where I am. We just have to choose our side—and neither side will trust us, of course.'

'You can trust Forbes,' she said, 'about coal, I

mean. Not of course all round the clock. He's dishonest about his name—he was a Jew called Furtstein. And he's dishonest in love. He wants to marry me. That's how I know. He keeps a mistress in Shepherd's Market. A friend of his told me.' She laughed. 'We have fine friends.'

For the second time that day D. was shocked. He remembered the child in the hotel. You learned too much in these days before you came of age. His own people knew death before they could walk: they got used to desire early—but this savage knowledge, that ought to come slowly, the gradual fruit of experience. . . . In a happy life the final disillusionment with human nature coincided with death. Nowadays they seemed to have a whole lifetime to get through somehow after it . . .

'You are not going to marry him?' he asked anxiously.

'I may. He's better than most of them.'

'Perhaps it's not true about the mistress.'

'Oh yes. I put detectives on to check up.'

He gave it up: this wasn't peace. When he landed in England, he had felt some envy . . . there had been a casualness . . . even a certain sense of trust at the passport control, but there was probably something behind that. He had imagined that the suspicion which was the atmosphere of his own life was due to civil war, but he began to believe that it existed everywhere: it was part of human life. People were united only by their vices: there was honour among adulterers and thieves. He had been too absorbed in the old days with his love and with the Berne MS. and the weekly lecture on Romance Languages to notice it. It was as if the whole world lay in the shadow of abandonment. Perhaps it was still propped up by ten just men—that was a pity: better scrap it and begin again with newts. 'Well,' she said, 'let's go.'

'Where?'

'Oh, anywhere. One must do something. It's early yet. A cinema?'

They sat for nearly three hours in a kind of palace—gold-winged figures, deep carpets, and an endless supply of refreshments carried round by girls got up to kill: these places had been less luxurious when he was last in London. It was a musical play full of curious sacrifice and suffering: a starving producer and a blonde girl who had made good. She had her name up in neon lights on Piccadilly, but she flung up her part and came back to Broadway to save him. She put up the money—secretly—for a new production and the glamour of her name gave it success. It was a revue all written in no time and the cast was packed with starving talent. Everybody made a lot of money: everybody's name went up in neon lights—the producer's too: the girl's, of course, was there from the first. There was a lot of suffering—gelatine tears pouring down the big blonde features—and a lot of happiness. It was curious and pathetic: everybody behaved nobly and made a lot of money. It was as if some code of faith and morality had been lost for centuries, and the world was trying to reconstruct it from the unreliable evidence of folk memories and subconscious desires—and perhaps some hieroglyphics upon stone.

He felt her hand rest on his knee. She wasn't romantic, she had said: this was an automatic reaction, he supposed, to the deep seats and the dim lights and the torch songs, as when Pavlov's dogs saliva'd. It was a reaction which went through all social levels like hunger, but he was short-circuited. He laid his hand on hers with a sense of pity—she deserved something better than a Jew called Furtstein who kept a girl in Shepherd's Market. She wasn't romantic, but he could feel her hand cold and acquiescent under his. He said gently, 'I think we've been followed.'

She said, 'It doesn't matter. If that's how the world is I can take it. Is somebody going to shoot or a bomb go off? I don't like sudden noises. Perhaps you'll warn me.'

'It's only a man who teaches Entrenationo. I'm sure I saw his steel glasses in the lobby.'

The blonde heroine wept more tears—for people predestined for success by popular choice they were all extraordinarily sad and obtuse. If *we* lived in a world, he thought, which guaranteed a happy ending, should we be as long discovering it? Perhaps that's what the saints were at with their incomprehensible happiness—they had seen the end of the story when they came in and couldn't take the agonies seriously. Rose said, 'I can't stand this any more. Let's go. You can see the ending half an hour away.'

They got out with difficulty into the gangway; he discovered he was still holding her hand. He said, 'I wish—sometimes—I could see *my* ending.' He felt extraordinarily tired; two long days and the beating had weakened him.

'Oh,' she said, 'I can tell you that. You'll go on fighting for people who aren't worth fighting for. Some day you'll be killed. But you won't hit back at Roland—not intentionally. The Berne MS. is all wrong there.'

They got into a taxi. She said to the driver, 'The Carlton Hotel, Gabitas Street.' He looked back through the little window: there was no sign of Mr. K. Perhaps it had been a coincidence—even Mr. K. must sometimes relax and watch the gelatine tears. He said more to himself than her, 'I can't believe they'll really give up, so soon. After all, to-morrow—it's defeat. The coal is as good as a whole fleet of the latest bombers.' They came slowly down Guilford Street. He said, 'If only I had a gun . . .'

'They'd never dare, would they?' she said. She put her hand through his arm, as if she wanted him to stay with her in the taxi, safely anonymous. He remembered that he had momentarily thought she was one of L.'s agents: he regretted that. He said, 'My dear, it's just like a sum in mathematics. It might cause diplomatic trouble—but then, that might not be so bad for them as if we got the coal. It's a question of addition—which adds up to most.'

'Are you afraid?'

'Yes.'

'Why not stay somewhere else? Come back with me. I can give you a bed.'

'I've left something here. I can't.' The taxi stopped. He got out. She followed him and stood on the pavement at his side. She said. 'Can't I come in with you ... in case ...'

'Better not.' He held her hand. It was an excuse to linger and make sure the street was empty. He wondered whether the manageress was his friend or not: Mr. K.... He said: 'Before you go, I meant to ask again ... could you find a job for this girl here? She's a good thing ... trustworthy.'

She said sharply, 'I wouldn't lift a finger if she were dying.' It was that voice he had heard ages ago in the bar of the Channel steamer, making her demands to the steward—'I want one more. I will have one more'—the disagreeable child at the dull party. She said, 'Let go of my hand.' He

91

dropped it quickly. She said, 'You damned quixote. Go on. Get shot, die ... you're out of place.'

He said, 'You have it all wrong. The girl's young enough to be my...'

'Daughter,' she said. 'Go on. So am I. Laugh. This is what always happens. I know. I told you. I'm not romantic. This is what's called a father-fixation. You hate your own father—for a thousand reasons, and then you fall for a man the same age.' She said, 'It's grotesque. Nobody can pretend there's any poetry in it. You go telephoning, making apppointments...'

He watched her uneasily, aware of that awful inability to feel anything but fear, a little pity.... Seventeenth-century poets wrote as if you could give away your heart for ever. That wasn't true according to modern psychologists, but you could feel such grief and such despair that you flinched away from the possibility of ever feeling again. He stood hopelessly in front of the open door of the shabby hotel to which 'short-timers' came, inadequate....

He said, 'If only this war was over...'

'It won't be over ever—you've said it—for you.'

She was lovely; he had never, when he was young, known anyone so lovely—certainly not his wife: she had been quite a plain woman. That hadn't mattered. All the same, it ought to be possible to feel desire with the help of a little beauty. He took her tentatively in his arms like an experiment. She said, 'Can I come up?'

'Not here.' He let her go: it hadn't worked.

'I knew there was something wrong with me when you came up to the car last night. Dithering. Polite. I felt sick when I heard them beating you—I thought I was drunk, and then when I woke up this morning it still went on. You know, I've never been in love before. They have a name for it—haven't they—calf-love.'

She used an expensive scent: he tried to feel more than pity. After all, it was a chance for a middle-aged ex-lecturer in the Romance Languages. 'My dear,' he said.

She said, 'It doesn't last, does it? But then, it won't have to last long. You'll be killed—won't you?—as sure as eggs is eggs.'

He kissed her unconvincingly. He said: 'My dear, I'll be seeing you ... to-morrow. All this—business will be over then. We'll meet ... celebrate...' He knew he was acting not very effectively, but this wasn't an occasion for honesty. She was too young to stand honesty.

She said, 'Even Roland, I suppose, had a woman...' But he remembered that *she*—her name was Alda—had fallen dead when they brought the news. Life didn't go on in a legend, after the loved one died, as his had done. It was taken for granted—the jongleur only gave her a few formal lines. He said, 'Good night.'

'Good night.' She went back up the street

93

towards the black trees. he thought to himself that, after all, L. might have had a worse agent. He discovered in himself a willingness to love which was like treachery—but what was the use? Tomorrow everything would be settled, and he would return.... He wondered whether, in the end, she would marry Furtstein.

He pushed the glass inner door: it was ajar—he flashed his hand automatically to his pocket, but of course he had no gun. The light was out, but somebody was there; he could hear the breathing, not far from the aspidistra. He himself was exposed in front of the door, with the street lamp beyond. It was no good moving: they could always fire first. He took his hand out of his pocket again, with his cigarette case in it. He tried to stop his fingers shaking, but he was afraid of pain. He put a cigarette in his mouth and felt for a wax match—they mightn't expect the sudden flash on the wall. He moved a little way forward and suddenly struck with the match sideways. It scraped against a picture frame and flared up. A white childish face sailed like a balloon out of the darkness. He said, 'Oh, God, Else, you gave me a fright. What are you doing there?'

'Waiting for you,' the thin immature voice whispered. The match went out.

'Why?'

'I thought you might be bringing her in here. It's my job,' she said, 'to see that clients get

94

their rooms.'

'That's nonsense.'

'You kissed her, didn't you?'

'It wasn't a good kiss.'

'But it's not that. You've got a right. It's what *she* said.'

He wondered whether he had made a mistake in giving her his papers—suppose she destroyed them, out of jealousy? He asked, 'What did she say?'

'She said they'd kill you, sure as eggs is eggs.'

He laughed with relief. 'Well, we've got a war on at home. People do get killed. But she doesn't *know*.'

'And *here . . .*' she said, 'they're after you too.'

'They can't do much.'

'I knew something awful was happening,' she said. 'They're upstairs now, talking.'

'Who?' he asked sharply.

'The manageress—and a man.'

'What sort of a man?'

'A little grey man—with steel spectacles.' He must have slipped out of the cinema before them. She said, 'They were asking *me* questions.'

'What questions?'

'If you'd said anything to me. If I'd seen anything—papers. Of course I was "mum." Nothing *they* could do would make me talk.' He was moved with pity by her devotion—what a

95

world to let such qualities go to waste. She said passionately, 'I don't mind their killing me.'

'There's no danger of that.'

Her voice came shivering out from beside the aspidistra: '*She*'d do anything. She acts mad sometimes—if she's crossed. I don't mind. I won't let you down. You're a gentleman.' It was a horribly inadequate reason. She went mournfully on, 'I'd do anything that girl'll do.'

'You are doing much more.'

'Is she going back with you—there?'

'No, no.'

'Can I?'

'My dear,' he said, 'you don't know what it's like there.'

He could hear a long whistling sigh. 'You don't know what it's like here.'

'Where are they now?' he said. 'The manageress and her friend?'

'The first-floor front,' she said. 'Are they your—deadly foes?' God knew out of what twopenny trash she drew her vocabulary.

'I think they're my friends. I don't know. Perhaps I'd better find out before they know I'm here.'

'Oh, they'll know by now. *She* hears everything. What's said on the roof, she hears in the kitchen. She told me not to tell you.' He was shaken by a doubt: could this child be in danger? But he couldn't believe it. What could they do to her? He went cautiously up the unlighted stair: once a board creaked. The staircase made a half-turn and he came suddenly upon the landing. A door stood open: an electric globe, under a pink frilly silken shade, shone on the two figures waiting for him with immense patience.

D. said gently, 'Bona matina. You didn't teach me the word for night.'

The manageress said, 'Come in—and shut the door.' He obeyed her—there was nothing else to do: it occurred to him that never once yet had he been allowed the initiative. He had been like a lay figure other people moved about, used as an Aunt Sally. 'Where have you been?' the manageress said. It was a bully's face; she should have been a man, with that ugly square jaw, the shady determination, the impetigo.

He said, 'Mr. K. will tell you.'

'What were you doing with the girl?'

'Enjoying myself.' He looked curiously round at the den—that was the best word for it; it wasn't a woman's room at all, with its square unclothed table, its leather chairs, no flowers, no frippery, a cupboard for shoes; it seemed made and furnished for nothing but use. The cupboard door was open full of heavy, low-heeled, sensible shoes.

'She knows L.'

'So do I.' Even the pictures were masculine—of a kind. Cheap coloured pictures of women, all silk stockings and lingerie. It seemed to him the

97

room of an inhibited bachelor. It was dimly horrifying, like timid secret desires for unattainable intimacies. Mr. K. suddenly spoke. He was like a feminine element in the male room: there were traces of hysteria. He said, 'When you were out—at the cinema—somebody rang up—to make you an offer.'

'Why did they do that? They should have known I was out.'

'They offered you your own terms not to keep your appointment to-morrow.'

'I haven't made any terms.'

'They left the message with me,' the manageress said.

'They were quite prepared, then, that everybody should know? You and K.'

Mr. K. squeezed his bony hands together. 'We wanted to make sure,' he said, 'that you still have the papers.'

'You were afraid I might have sold them already. On my way home.'

'We have to be careful,' he said, as if he were listening for Dr. Bellows's rubber soles. He was dreadfully under the domination even here of the shilling fine.

'Are you acting on instructions?'

'Our instructions are so vague. A lot is left to our discretion. Perhaps you would show us the papers.' The woman didn't talk any more—she let the weak ones have their rope.

'No.'

He looked from one to the other—it seemed to him that at last the initiative was passing into his hands; he wished he had more vitality to take it, but he was exhausted. England was full of tiresome memories which made him remember that this wasn't really his job: he should be at the Museum now reading Romance Literature. he said: 'I accept the fact that we have the same employers. But I have no reason to trust you.' The little grey man sat as if condemned with his eyes on his own bitten finger-tips: the woman faced him with that square dominant face— which had nothing to dominate except a shady hotel. He had seen many people shot on both sides of the line for treachery: he knew you couldn't recognise them by their manners or faces: there was no Ganelon type. He said, 'Are you anxious to see that you get your cut out of the sale? But there won't be a cut—or a sale.'

'Perhaps, then, you'll read this letter,' the woman suddenly said: they had used up their rope.

He read it slowly. There was no doubt at all of its genuineness: he knew the signature and the notepaper of the ministry too well to be deceived. This, apparently, was the end of his mission—the woman was empowered to take over from him the necessary papers—for what purpose wasn't said.

'You see,' the woman said, 'they don't trust you.'

'Why not have shown me this when I arrived?'

'It was left to my discretion. To trust you or not.'

The position was fantastic. He had been entrusted with the papers as far as London: Mr. K. was told to check up on his movements before he reached the hotel but was not trusted with the secret of his mission: this woman seemed to have been trusted with both the secret and the papers—but only as a last resort—if his conduct were suspicious. He said suddenly, 'Of course you know what these papers are.'

She said stubbornly, 'Naturally.' But he was sure that, after all, she didn't—he could read that in her face—the obstinate poker features. There was no end to the complicated work of half-trust and half-deceit. Suppose the ministry had made a mistake ... suppose, if he handed the papers over, they should sell them to L. He knew he could trust himself. He knew nothing else. There was a horrid smell of cheap scent in the room—it was apparently her only female characteristic—and it was disturbing like scent on a man.

'You see,' she said, 'you can go home now. Your job is finished.'

It was all too easy and too dubious. The ministry didn't trust him or them or anybody. They didn't trust each other. Only each individual knew that one person was true or false. Mr. K. knew what Mr. K. meant to do with those papers. The manageress knew what she intended. You couldn't answer for anybody but yourself. He said, 'Those orders were not given to me. I shall keep the papers.'

Mr. K.'s voice became shrill. He said, 'If you go behind our backs...' His underpaid jumpy Entrenationo eyes gave away unguardedly secrets of greed and envy.... What could you expect on that salary? How much treachery is always nourished in little overworked centres of somebody else's idealism. The manageress said, 'You are a sentimental man. A bourgeois. A professor. Probably romantic. If you cheat us you'll find—oh, I can think up things.' He couldn't face her; it was really like looking into the pit—she had imagination: the impetigo was like the relic of some shameful act from which she had never recovered. He remembered Else saying, 'She acts like mad.'

He said, 'Do you mean if I cheat you—or cheat our people at home?' He was genuinely uncertain of her meaning. He was lost and exhausted among potential enemies: the further you got away from the open batttle the more alone you were. He felt envy of those who were now in the firing line. Then suddenly he was back there himself—a clang of bells, the roar down the street—fire engine, ambulance? The raid was over and the bodies were being uncovered; men picked over the stones carefully for fear they might miss a body; sometimes a pick wielded too carelessly caused agony.... The world misted over—as in the dust which hung for an hour about a street. He felt sick and shaken; he remembered the dead tom-cat close to his face: he couldn't move: he just lay there with the fur almost on his mouth.

The whole room began to shake. The manageress's head swelled up like a blister. He heard her say, 'Quick! Lock the door,' and tried to pull himself together. What were they going to do to him? Enemies ... friends.... He was on his knees. Time slowed up. Mr. K. moved with appalling slowness towards the door. The manageress's black skirt was close to his mouth, dusty like the cat's fur. He wanted to scream, but the weight of human dignity lay like a gag over his tongue—one didn't scream, even when the truncheon struck. He heard her say, 'Where are the papers?' leaning down on him. Her breath was all cheap scent and nicotine—half female and half male.

He said apologetically, 'Fight yesterday. Shot at to-day.' A thick decisive thumb came down towards his eyeballs: he was involved in a nightmare. He said, 'I haven't got them.'

'Where are they?' It hovered over his right eye; he could hear Mr. K. fiddling at the door. Mr. K. said, 'It doesn't lock.' He felt horror as if her hand as well as her face carried infection.

'You turn it the other way.' He tried to heave

himself upwards, but a thumb pushed him back. A sensible shoe trod firmly upon his hand. Mr. K. protested about something in low tones. A scared determined voice said. 'Was it you who rang, ma'am?'

'Of course I didn't ring.'

D. raised himself carefully. He said, 'I rang, Else. I felt ill. Nothing much. Ambulance outside. I was buried once in a raid. If you'll give me your arm, I can get to bed.' The little room swung clearly back—the boot cupboard and the epicene girls in black silk stockings and the masculine chairs. He said, 'I'll lock my door to-night or I'll be walking in my sleep.'

They climbed slowly up to the top floor. He said, 'You came just in time. I might have done something silly. I think after to-morrow morning we'll go away from here.'

'Me, too?'

He promised rashly, as if in a violent world you could promise anything at all, beyond the moment of speaking. 'Yes. You, too.'

## III

THE cat's fur and the dusty skirt stayed with him all the night. The peace of his usual dreams was hopelessly broken: no flowers or quiet rivers or old gentlemen talking of lectures. He

103

had always, after that worst raid, been afraid of suffocation. He was glad the other side shot their prisoners and didn't hang them—the rope round the neck would bring nightmare into life. Day came without daylight: a yellow fog outside shut visibility down to twenty yards. While he was shaving Else came in with a tray, a boiled egg and a kipper, a pot of tea.

'You shouldn't have bothered,' he said. 'I would have come down.'

'I thought,' she said, 'it would be a good excuse. You'll be wanting the papers back.' She began to haul off a shoe and a stocking. She said, 'O Lord, what would they think if they came in now?' She sat on the bed and felt for the papers in the instep.

'What's that?' he said, listening hard. He found he dreaded the return of the papers: responsibility was like an unlucky ring you preferred to hand on to strangers. She sat up on the bed and listened too; then the footsteps creaked on the stairs going down.

'Oh,' she said, 'that's only Mr. Muckerji—a Hindu gentleman. He's not like the other Indian downstairs. Mr. Muckerji's very respectful.'

He took the papers—well, he'd be free of them very soon now. She put on her stocking again. She said, 'He's inquisitive. That's the only thing. Asks such questions.'

'What sort of questions?'

'Oh, everything. Do I believe in horoscopes?

104

Do I believe in newspapers? What do I think of Mr. Eden? And he writes down the answers too. I don't know why.'

'Odd.'

'Do you think it'll get me into trouble? When I'm in the mood I say such things—about Mr. Eden, anything. For fun, you know. But sometimes it gets me scared to think that every word is written down. And then I look up sometimes and there he is watching me like I was an animal. But always respectful.'

He gave it up: Mr. Muckerji didn't concern him. He sat down to his breakfast. But the child didn't go; it was as if she had a reservoir of speech saved up for him—or Mr. Muckerji. She said, 'You meant what you said last night about us going away?'

'Yes,' he said. 'Somehow I'll manage it.'

'I don't want to be a burden to you.' The novelette was on her tongue again. 'There's always Clara.'

'We'll do better for you than Clara.' He would appeal to Rose again: last night she had been a little hysterical.

'Can't I go back with you?'

'It wouldn't be allowed.'

'I've read,' she said, 'about girls who dressed up . . .'

'That's only in books.'

'I'd be afraid to stay here any more—with *her*.'

'You won't have to,' he assured her.

A bell began to ring furiously down below. She said, 'Oh, he's rightly called Row.'

'Who is?'

'The Indian on the second floor.' She moved reluctantly to the door. She said, 'It's a promise, isn't it? I won't be here to-night?'

'I promise.'

'Cross your heart.' He obeyed her. 'Last night,' she said, 'I couldn't sleep. I thought she'd do something—awful. You should 'ave seen her face when I came in. "Was it you who rung?" I said. "Of course it wasn't ," she said and looked—oh, daggers. I tell you I locked my door when I left you. What was it she was up to in there?'

'I don't know for certain. She couldn't do much. She's like the devil, you know—more brimstone than bite. She can't do us any harm if we don't get scared.'

'Oh,' she said, 'I tell you I'll be glad—to be off from here.' She smiled at him from the door with joy: she was like a child on her birthday. 'No more Mr. Row,' she said, 'or the "short-timers"—no Mr. Muckerji—no more of *her* for ever. It's my lucky day all right.' It was as if she were paying an elaborate farewell to a whole way of life.

He stayed in his room with the door locked until the time came to start for Lord Benditch's. He was taking no chances at all now. He put the

106

papers ready in the breast pocket of his jacket, and wore his overcoat fastened up to the neck. No pickpocket, he was certain, could get at them: as for violence, he had to risk that. They would all know now that he had the papers with him; he had to trust London to keep him safe. Lord Benditch's house was like home to a boy playing hide-and-seek in an elaborate and unfamiliar garden. In three-quarters of an hour, he thought, as a clock told eleven-fifteen, everything would be decided one way or another. They would probably try and take some advantage of the fog.

This was to be his route: up Bernard Street to Russell Square Station—they could hardly attempt anything in the Tube—then from Hyde Park Corner to Chatham Terrace—about ten minutes' walk in this fog. He could, of course, ring up a taxi and go the whole way by car, but it would be horribly slow; traffic-blocks, noise and fog gave opportunities to really driven men—and he was beginning to think that they were driven hard by now. Besides, it was not beyond their ingenuity to supply a taxi themselves. If he had to take a taxi to Hyde Park Corner, he would take one from a rank.

He came downstairs with his heart knocking; he told himself in vain that nothing could possibly happen in daylight, in London: he was safe. But he was glad, nevertheless, when the Indian looked out of his room on the second floor: he was still wearing his frayed and gaudy dressing-gown. It was almost like having a friend at your back to have any witness at all. He would have liked to leave visible footprints wherever he walked, to put it incontestably on record that he had been here.

The carpet began: he walked gently, he had no wish to advertise his departure to the manageress. But he couldn't escape without seeing her. She was there in her masculine room, sitting at the table with the door open, the same musty black dress of his nightmare. He paused at the door and said, 'I'm off now.'

She said, 'You know best why you haven't obeyed instructions.'

'I shall be back here in a few hours. I shan't be staying another night.'

She looked at him with complete indifference: it startled him. It was as if she knew more of his plans than he knew himself, as if everything had been provided for, a long time ago, in her capacious brain. 'I imagine,' he said, 'that you have been paid for my room.'

'Yes.'

'What isn't provided for—in my expenses—is a week's wages for the maid. I'll pay that myself.'

'I don't understand.'

'Else is leaving, too. You've given the child a fright. I don't know what motive . . .'

Her face became positively interested—not

angry at all: it was almost as though he had given her an idea for which she was grateful. 'You mean, you are taking the girl away?' He was touched by uneasiness: it hadn't been necessary to tell her that; somebody seemed to be warning him—'Be careful.' He looked round: of course there was nobody there; in the distance a door closed: it was like a premonition. He said unguardedly, 'Be careful how you frighten that child again.' He found it hard to tear himself away; he had the papers safe in his pocket, but he felt that he was leaving something else behind which needed his care. It was absurd: there could be no danger. He stared belligerently back at the square spotty veined face. He said, 'I'll be back very soon. I shall ask her if you . . .'

He hadn't noticed last night how big her thumbs were. She sat placidly there with them hidden in the large pasty fists—it was said to be a mark of neurosis—she wore no rings. She said firmly and rather loudly, 'I still don't understand,' and at the same time her face contorted—a lid dropped, she gave him an enormous crude wink full of an inexplicable amusement. He had an impression that she wasn't worried now any more, that she was mistress of the situation. He turned away, his heart still knocking in its cage, as if it were trying to transmit a message, a warning, in a code he didn't understand. It was the fault of the intellectual, he thought, always to talk too much. He could have told her all that when he returned. Suppose he didn't return? Well, the girl wasn't a slave, she couldn't be made to suffer. This was the best policed city in the world.

As he came down into the hall a rather too-humble voice said, 'Would you do me the greatest favour...?' It was an Indian with large brown impervious eyes, an expression of docility, he wore a shiny blue suit with rather orange shoes, it must be Mr. Muckerji. He said, 'If you would answer me just one question? How do you save money?'

Was he mad? He said, 'I never save money.' Mr. Muckerji had a large open soft face which fell in deep folds around the mouth. He said anxiously, 'Literally not? I mean, that there are those who put aside all their copper coins—or Victorian pennies. There are the building societies and national savings.'

'I never save.'

'Thank you,' Mr. Muckerji said, 'that is exactly what I wished to know,' and began to write something in a notebook. Behind Mr. Muckerji Else appeared, watching him go. Again he felt irrationaly glad, even for the presence of Mr. Muckerji. He wasn't leaving her alone with the manageress. He smiled at her across Mr. Muckerji's bent studious back, and gave her a small wave of the hand. She smiled in

110

return uncertainly. It might have been a railway station full of good-byes and curiosities, of curtailed intimacies, the embarrassments of lovers and parents, the chance for strangers, like Mr. Muckerji, to see, as it were, into the interior of private houses. Mr. Muckerji, looked up and said a little too warmly, 'Perhaps we may meet again for another interesting talk.' He put forward a hand and then too quickly withdrew it, as if he were afraid of a rebuff; then he stood gently, humbly smiling, as D, walked out—into the fog.

Nobody ever knows how long a parting is for, otherwise we would pay more attention to the smile and the formal words. The fog came up all round him: the train had left the station: people would wait no longer on the platform: an arch will cut off the most patient waving hand.

He walked quickly, listening hard. A girl carrying an attache case passed him, and a postman zigzagged off the pavement into obscurity. He felt like an Atlantic flier who is still over the traffic of the coast before the plunge. . . . It couldn't take more than half an hour. Everything would have to be decided soon. It never occurred to him that he might not come to terms with Benditch: they were ready to go to almost any price for coal. The fog clouded everything; he listened for footsteps and heard only his own feet tapping on stone. The silence was not reassuring. He overtook people and only became aware of them when their figures broke the fog ahead. If he was followed he would never be aware of it, but could they follow him in this blanketed city? Somehow, somewhere, they would have to strike.

A taxi drew slowly alongside him. The driver said, 'Taxi, sir?' keeping pace with him along the pavement. He forgot his decision to take a taxi only from the rank. He said, 'Gwyn Cottage, Chatham Terrace,' and got in. They slid away into impenetrable mist; backed, turned. He thought with sudden uneasiness, 'This isn't the way. What a fool I've been.' He said, 'Stop!' but the taxi went on. He couldn't see where they were: only the big back of the driver and the fog all around. He hammered on the glass, "Let me out," and the taxi stopped. He thrust a shilling into the man's hand and dived on to the pavement. He heard an astonished voice say, 'What the bloody hell?'— the man had probably been quite honest. His nerve was horribly shaken. He ran into a policeman 'Russell Square Station?'

'You are going the wrong way.' He said, 'Turn round, take the first to the left along the railings.'

He came, after what seemed a long while, to the station. He waited for the lift and suddenly realised that this needed more nerve than he had thought—this going underground. He had never been below the surface of a street since the house had caved in on him—now he watched air raids from a roof. He would rather die quickly than slowly suffocate with a dead cat beside him. Before the lift doors closed he stood tensely—he wanted to bolt for the entrance. It was a strain his nerves could hardly stand; he sat down on the only bench and the walls sailed up all round him. He put his head between his hands and tried not to see or feel the descent. It stopped. He was underground.

A voice said, 'Like a hand? Give the gentleman your hand, Conway.' He found himself urged to his feet by a small, horribly sticky fist. A woman with a bit of fur round a scrawny neck said, 'Conway used to be taken that way in the lifts, didn't you, duck?' A pasty child of about seven held his hand glumly. He said, 'O, I think I shall be all right now,' still tense at the white below-ground passage, the dry stale wind and the rumble of a distant train.

The woman said, 'You going west? We'll put you off at the right station. You're a foreigner, aren't you?'

'Yes.'

'Oh, I've nothing against foreigners.'

He found himself led down the long passage. The child was clothed hideously in corduroy shorts, a lemon-yellow jumper and a school cap, all chocolate and mauve stripes. The woman said, 'I got quite worried about Conway. The doctor said it was just his age, but his father had duodenal ulcers.' There was no escape; they herded him onto the train between them. She said, 'All that's wrong with him now's he snuffles. Shut your mouth, Conway. The gentleman doesn't want to see your tonsils.'

There were not many people in the carriage. He certainly hadn't been followed into the train. Would something happen at Hyde Park Corner? or was he exaggerating the whole thing? This was England. But he remembered the chauffeur coming at him with a look of greedy pleasure on the Dover road, the bullet in the mews. The woman said, 'The trouble with Conway is he won't touch greens.'

An idea struck him. He said, 'Are you going far west?'

"High Street, Kensington. We got to go to Barkers. That boy wears out clothes so quick...'

'Perhaps you would let me give you a lift in a taxi from Hyde Park Corner...'

'Oh, we wouldn't bother you. It's quicker by underground.'

They pulled in and out of Piccadilly and he sat tense as they roared again into a tunnel. It was the same sound that reached you blowing back from where a high-explosive bomb had fallen, a wind full of death and the noise of pain,

He said, 'I thought perhaps the boy... Conway...'

'It's a funny name, isn't it? but we were at the

pictures seeing Conway Tearle just before he came. My husband fancied the name. More than I did. He said, "That's the one if it's a boy." And when it happened that night it seemed— well, an omen.'

'Wouldn't he perhaps—like the ride?'

'Oh, a taxi makes him sick. He's funny that way. A bus is all right—and a tube. Though there *were* times when I'd be ashamed to be with him in lift. It wasn't nice for the others. He'd look at you and then—before you could say Jack Robinson—it was like a conjuring trick.'

It was hopeless. Anyway, what could happen? They had shot their bolt. You couldn't go further than attempted murder. Except, of course, a murder which succeeded. He couldn't imagine L. being concerned in that, but then he would have a marvellous facility for disengaging himself from the unpleasant fact. 'Here you are,' she said. 'This is your station. It's been pleasant having a chat. Give the gentleman your hand, Conway.' He shook perfunctorily the sticky fingers and went up into the yellow morning.

There were cheers in the air: everyone was cheering: it might have been a great victory. The Knightsbridge pavement was crowded; over the road the tops of the Hyde Park gates appeared above the low fog: in another direction a chariot spurred behind four tossing horses above the dingy clouds. All round St. George's

115

Hospital the buses were held up, vanishing gradually like alligators into the marshy air. Somebody was blowing on a whistle: a Bath-chair slowly emerged trundled by its invalid while with the other hand he played a pipe, a painful progress along the gutter. The tune never got properly going; it whistled out, like the air from a rubber pig, and then started again with an effort. On a blackboard the man had written, 'Gassed in 1917. One lung gone.' The yellow air fumed round him and people were cheering.

A Daimler drew out of the traffic block, women squealed, several men took off their hats. D. was at a loss; he had seen religious processions in the old days, but nobody here seemed to be kneeling. The car moved slowly in front of him: two very small girls stiffly dressed in tailored coats and wearing gloves peered through the pane with pasty indifference. A woman screamed, 'Oh, the darlings. They're going to shop at Harrods.' It was an extraordinary sight: the passage of a totem in a Daimler. A voice D. knew said sharply, 'Take off your hat, sir.'

It was Currie.

For a moment he thought: he's followed me. But the embarrassment when Currie recognised him was too genuine. He grunted and sidled and swung his monocle. 'Oh, sorry. Foreigner.' D. might have been a woman with whom he had

had shameful relations. You couldn't cut her, but you tried to pass on.

'I wonder,' D, said, 'if you'd mind telling me the way to Chatham Terrace.'

Currie flushed, 'You going there—to Lord Benditch's?'

'Yes.' The piper in the gutter began again brokenly. The buses moved ponderously on, and everybody scattered.

'Look here,' Currie said. 'I seem to have made a fool of myself the other night. Apologise.'

'That's all right.'

'Thought you were one of these confidence men. Stupid of me. But I've been caught that way myself, and Miss Cullen's a fine girl.'

'Yes.'

'I bought a sunken Spanish galleon once. One of Armada fleet, you know. Paid a hundred pounds in cash. Of course, there wasn't a galleon.'

'No.'

'Look here. I'd like to show there's no ill-feeling. I'll walk you along to Chatham Terrace. Always glad to be of use to foreigners. Expect you'd do the same if I came to your country. Of course, that's not likely.'

'It's very good of you,' D, said. He meant it: it was a great relief. This was the end of the battle; if they had planned a last desperate throw in the fog, they had been out-fortuned. He could hardly call it outwitted. He put his hand up to his breast and felt through the overcoat the comforting bulge of his credentials.

'Of course,' Captain Currie went on, explaining too much, 'an experience like that—well, it makes you chary.'

'Experience?'

'The Spanish Galleon. The fellow was so plausible—gave me fifty pounds to hold while he cashed my cheque. I wouldn't hear of it, but he insisted. Said *he* had to insist on cash, so it was only fair.'

'So you were only fifty pounds down?'

'Oh, they were dud notes. I suppose he saw I was a Romantic. Of course, it gave me an idea. You learn by your mistakes.'

'Yes?' It was an immense pleasure to have this man prattling at his elbow down Knightsbridge.

'You've heard of the Spanish Galleon?'

'No—I don't think so.'

'It was my first roadhouse. Near Maidenhead. But I had to sell out in the end. You know—the west—it's losing caste a bit. Kent's better—or Essex even. On the west you get a rather—popular—element, on the way to the Cotswolds, you know.' Violence seemed more than ever out of place in this country of complicated distinctions and odd taboos. Violence was too simple. It was a breach of taste. They turned to the left out of the main road: fantastic red towers and castellations emerged from the fog.

Captain Currie said, 'Seen any good shows?'

'I have been rather busy.'

'Mustn't overdo it.'

'And I've been learning Entrenationo.'

'Good God, what for?'

'An international language.'

'When you get down to it,' Captain Currie said, 'most people talk a bit of English.' He said, 'Well, I'll be damned. Do you know whom we just passed?'

'I didn't see anyone.'

'That chauffeur—what's his name? The one you had the bout with.'

'I never saw him.'

'He was in a doorway. The car was there, too. What do you say we go back and have a word with him?' He laid his unmaimed hand on D.'s sleeve. 'There's heaps of time. Chatham Terrace is just ahead.'

'No. No time.' He felt panic. Was this a trap after all? The hand was urging him gently, remorselessly. . . .

'I have an appointment with Lord Benditch.'

'Won't take a moment. After all, it was fair fight and no favour. Ought to shake hands and show there's no ill-feeling. Customary. It was *my* mistake, you know.' He babbled breezily into D.'s ear, tugging at his sleeve: there was was a slight smell of whisky.

'Afterwards,' D. said. 'After I've seen Lord Benditch.'

'I wouldn't like to think there was any bad blood. My fault.'

'No,' D. said, 'no.'

'When's your appointment?'

'Noon.'

'It's not five to. Shake hands all round and have a drink.'

'No.' He shook off the strong persistent hand: somebody whistled just behind him. He turned desperately at bay with his fists up. It was only a postman. He said, 'Could you show me Gwyn Cottage?'

'You're almost on the doorstep,' the postman said. ''This way.' He had a glimpse of Captain Currie's astonished and rather angry face. Afterwards he thought that he had probably been wrong—Captain Currie was merely anxious that everything should be smoothed away.

It was like an all-clear signal seeing the big Edwardian door swing open upon the fantastic hall. He was able to smile again at a mineowner's fondness for the mistresses of kings. There was a huge expanse of fake panelling, and all round the walls reproductions of famous paintings—Nell Gwyn sported in the place of honour above the staircase, among a number of cherubs who had all been granted peerages. What a lot of noble blood was based on the sale of oranges. He detected the Pompadour and Mme de Maintenon; there was also—startlingly pre-war in black silk stockings and black gloves—Mlle Gaby Deslys. It was an odd taste.

'Coat, sir?'

He let the manservant take his overcoat. There was an appalling mixture of Chinoiserie, Louis Seize and Stuart in the furniture—he was fascinated. An odd haven of safety for a confidential agent. He said, 'I'm afraid I'm a little early.'

'His lordship gave orders that you were to go straight in.'

Most curious of all was the thought that somehow Rose had been produced among these surroundings—this vicarious sensuality. Did they represent the day-dreams of an ambitious working-man's son? Money meant women. The manservant, too, was unbelievably exaggerated: very tall with a crease that seemed to begin at the waist and to be maintained unimpaired only by an odd stance, by leaning back like the Tower of Pisa. He had always felt a faint distaste for menservants: they were so conservative, so established, such parasites, but this man made him want to laugh. He was a caricature. He was reminded of an actor-manager's house he had once dined in; there had been liveried footmen there.

The man swept open a door. 'Mr. D.' He found himself in an enormous parqueted room. It seemed to be hung with portraits—they could hardly be family ones. Some arm-chairs were grouped round a big log fire. They had high backs. It was difficult to see whether they were occupied. He advanced tentatively. The room would have been more effective, he thought, if he were someone else. It was meant to make you aware of the frayed sleeve, the shabbiness, the insecurity of your life, but, as it happened, he had been born without the sense of snobbery. He simply didn't mind his shabbiness. He hummed gently to himself, proceeding at a leisurely pace across the parquet. He was far too happy to be here at all to care about anything.

Somebody rose up from the central chair—a big man with a bullet head and a mass of grey-black hair and the jaw of an equestrian statue. He said, 'Mr. D.?'

'Lord Benditch?'

He waved his hand at three other chairs—'Mr. Forbes, Lord Fetting, Mr. Brigstock,' He said, 'Mr. Goldstein could not come.'

D. said. 'I think you know the object of my visit.'

'We had a letter,' Lord Benditch said, 'a fortnight ago warning us.' He flapped his hand towards a big desk of inlaid wood—it was a mannerism to use his hand like a signpost. 'You will forgive me if we get to business straight away. I'm a busy man.'

'I should like it.'

Another man emerged from an arm-chair. He was small and dark and sharp-featured with a quick doggish air. He began to arrange chairs behind the desk with an air of importance. 'Mr. Forbes,' he said, 'Mr. Forbes.' Mr. Forbes came into view: he wore tweeds and carried very successfully the air of a man just up from the country; only the shape of the skull disclosed the Furtstein past. He said, 'Coming, Brigstock,' with a faint air of mockery.

'Lord Fetting.'

'I should let Fetting sleep,' Mr. Forbes said. 'Unless, of course, he snores.' They ranged themselves on one side of the desk, Lord Benditch in the middle. It was like the final viva voce examination for a degree. Mr. Brigstock, D. thought, would be the one who gave you the bad time: he would hang on to a question like a terrier.

'Sit down, won't you?' Lord Benditch said heavily.

'I would,' D. said, 'if there were a chair on this side of the frontier.' Forbes laughed. Lord Benditch said sharply, 'Brigstock.'

Brigstock swarmed round the desk and pushed up a chair. D. sat down. There was a horrible air of unreality about everything. This was the moment, but he could hardly believe it—in the fake house, among the fake ancestors and the dead mistresses; he couldn't even see Lord Fetting. This wasn't the sort of place where you expected a war to be decided. He said, 'You know the amount of coal we require between now and April?'

'Yes.'

'Can it be supplied?'

Lord Benditch said, 'Granted I am satisfied and Forbes and Fetting...' He added, 'and Brigstock,' as an afterthought.

'A question of price?'

'Of course. And confidence.'

'We will pay the highest market price—and a bonus of twenty-five per cent when delivery is completed.'

Brigstock asked, 'In gold?'

'A proportion in gold.'

'You can't expect us to take notes,' Brigstock said, 'which may be valueless by the spring—or goods which you may not be able to get out of the country.'

Lord Benditch leant back in his chair and left it all to Brigstock: Brigstock had been trained to bring back the game. Mr. Forbes was drawing little Aryan faces on the paper in front of him—girls with big circular goo-goo eyes, wearing bathing shorts.

'If we get this coal there is no question of the exchange falling. We've maintained an even level now for two years of war. This coal may mean the complete collapse of the rebels.'

'We have other information,' Brigstock said.

'I don't think it can be reliable.'

Somebody suddenly snored—out of sight behind a chair-back.

'We must insist on gold,' Brigstock said. 'Shall I wake Fetting?'

'Let him sleep,' Mr. Forbes said.

'We will meet you half-way on that point,' D. said. 'We are prepared to pay the market price in gold, if you will accept the bonus in notes—or goods.'

'Then it must be thirty-five per cent.'

'That's very high.'

Brigstock said, 'We take a lot of risk. The ships have to be insured. A lot of risk.' Behind his back was a picture by—was it Etty? flesh and flowers in a pastoral landscape.

'When would you start delivery?'

'We have certain stocks ... we could begin next month, but for the quantity you need we shall have to reopen several mines. That takes time—and money. There will have been depreciation of machinery. And the men will not be first-class workers any longer. They depreciate quicker than tools.'

D. said, 'Of course you hold a pistol to our heads. We must have the coal.'

'Another point,' Brigstock said. 'We are business men: we are not politicians—or crusaders.' Lord Fetting's voice came sharply from the fire, 'My shoes. Where are my shoes?' Mr. Forbes smiled again, drawing goo-goo eyes, putting in the long lashes: was he thinking of the girl in Shepherd's Market? He had a look of healthy sensuality: sex in tweeds with a pipe.

Lord Benditch said heavily and contemptuously, 'Brigstock means that we may get a better offer elsewhere.'

'You may, but there's the future to think of. If they win they will cease to be your customers. They have other allies . . .'

'That is looking very far ahead. What concerns us is the immediate profit.'

'You may find their gold is less certain than our paper. After all, it's stolen. We should bring an action. . . . And there's your own government. To send coal to the rebels might prove illegal.'

Brigstock said sharply, 'If we come to terms—we should be prepared to take thirty per cent in notes at the rate prevailing on the last day of shipment—you must understand that any commission must come from your side. We have gone as far as we can towards meeting you.'

'Commission? I don't quite understand.'

'Your commission, of course, on the sale. Your people must look after that.'

'I was not proposing,' D. said, 'to ask for a commission. Is it the usual thing? I didn't know, but in any case I wouldn't ask for it.'

Benditch said, 'You are an unusual agent,' and loured at him as if he had expressed a heresy, had been found guilty of some sharp practice. Brigstock said, 'Before we draw up the contract we had better see your credentials.'

D. put his hand to his breast pocket. They

were gone: it was incredible.

He began in panic-stricken haste to search all his pockets ... there was nothing there. He looked up and saw the three men watching him: Mr. Forbes had stopped drawing and was gazing at him with interest. D. said, 'It's extraordinary. I had them here in my breast pocket...'

Mr. Forbes said gently, 'Perhaps they are in your overcoat.'

'Brigstock,' Lord Benditch said, 'ring the bell.' He said to the manservant, 'Fetch this gentleman's coat.' It was just a ceremony: he knew they wouldn't be there, but how had they gone? Could Currie possibly? No, it wasn't possible. Nobody had had a chance except... The manservant came back with the coat over his arm. D. looked up at the trusty paid impassive eyes as if he might read there some hint ... but they would take a bribe as they would take a tip without registering any feeling at all.

'Well?' Brigstock asked sharply.

'They are not there.'

A very old man appeared suddenly on his feet in front of the fire. He said, 'When's this man going to turn up, Benditch? I've been waiting a very long time.'

'He's here now.'

'Somebody should have told me.'

'You were asleep.'

'Nonsense.' One after the other, D. searched the pockets: he searched the lining: of course there was nothing. It was no more than a rather theatrical gesture—to convince them that he had once had the credentials. He felt himself that his acting was poor, that he wasn't really giving the impression that he expected to find them.

'Was I asleep, Brigstock?'

'Yes, Lord Fetting.'

'Well, what if I was? I feel all the fresher for it. I hope nothing is settled.'

'No, nothing, Lord Fetting.' Brigstock looked smug and satisfied; he seemed to be saying, "I suspected all the time..."

'Do you really mean,' Lord Benditch said, 'that you've come out without your papers? It's very odd.'

'I had them with me. They were stolen.'

'Stolen! When?'

'I don't know. On the way to this room.'

'Well,' Brigstock said, 'that's that.'

'What's what?' Lord Fetting asked sharply. He said, 'I shall not give my signature to anything any of you have decided.'

'We've decided nothing.'

'Quite right,' Lord Fetting said. 'It needs thinking over.'

'I know,' D. said, 'you have only my word for this—but what possibly have I to gain?'

Brigstock leant across the desk and said sharply, venomously, 'There was the

128

commission, wasn't there?'

'Oh come, Brigstock,' Forbes said, 'he refused the commission.'

'Yes, when he saw that it was usless to expect it.'

Lord Benditch said, 'There's no point in arguing, Brigstock. This gentleman is either genuine or not genuine. If he is genuine—and can prove it—I am quite prepared to sign a contract.'

'Certainly,' Forbes said. 'So am I.'

'But you, sir, will understand—as a business man—that no contract can be signed with an unaccredited agent.'

'And you will also understand,' Brigstock said, 'that there's a law in this country against trying to obtain money on false pretences.'

'We'd better sleep on it,' Lord Fetting said. 'We'd better all sleep on it.'

What am I to do now? he thought, what am I to do now? He sat in his chair, beaten. He had evaded every trap but one ... that was no comfort. There remained only the long pilgrimage back—the Channel boat, the Paris train. Of course at home they would never believe his story. It would be odd if he had escaped—with no effort on his part—the enemy's bullets to fall against a cemetery wall on his own side of the line. They carried out their executions at the cemetery to avoid the trouble of transporting bodies...

'Well,' Lord Benditch said, 'I don't think there's any more to be said. If, when you get to your hotel, you find your credentials, you had better telephone at once. We have another client ... we can't hold matters up indefinitely.'

Forbes asked, 'Is there nobody in London who would answer for you?'

'Nobody.'

Brigstock said, 'I don't think we need keep him any longer.'

D. said, 'I suppose it's useless telling you that I expected this. I've been here less than three days—my rooms have been searched—I have been beaten up.' He put his hand to his face: 'You can see the bruises. I have been shot at.' He remembered, while he watched their faces, what Rose had warned him—no melodrama. It was like the putting up of shutters at night to guard—well, the Royal mistresses and the Etty. Benditch, Fetting, Brigstock—they all became expressionless as if he had told a dirty story in unsuitable company. Lord Benditch said, 'I'm prepared to believe you may have *lost* the papers ...'

'This is a waste of time,' Brigstock said. 'This *shows*.'

Lord Fetting said, 'It's nonsense. There's the police.'

D. got up. He said, 'One thing more, Lord Benditch. Your daughter knows I was shot at. She has seen the place. She found the bullet.'

Lord Fetting began to laugh. 'Oh, that young woman,' he said, 'that young woman. The scamp...' Brigstock looked nervously sideways at Lord Benditch: he looked as if he wanted to speak and dared not. Lord Benditch said, 'What my daughter may say is not evidence—in this house.' He frowned, staring down at his big hands, hairy on the knuckles. D. said, 'I must say good-bye, then. But I haven't finished. I do implore you not to be rash.'

'We are never rash,' Lord Fetting said.

D. went the long way back across the cold room: it was like the beginning of a retreat—nobody could say whether a stand was possible before the cemetery wall. In the hall L. was waiting; it was a small satisfaction to feel that he had been kept a few minutes like someone of no account. He stood there rather too deliberately aloof, examining Nell Gwyn among the cherubs. He didn't turn his head; he was the former patron forced by cruel circumstances to administer the cut direct: he leant closely to the canvas and inspected the backside of the Duke of St. Albans.

D. said, 'I should go carefully. Of course, you have a lot of agents, but two can play at your game.'

He turned sadly away from the cherub to face a man with no social sense. He said, 'I suppose you'll be catching the first boat back—but I shouldn't go further than France.'

'I'm not leaving England.'

'What good can you do here?'

D. was silent—he had no ideas at all. His silence seemed to disconcert L. He said earnestly, 'I do advise you...' Then there must be some angle from which he was still dangerous. Was it the simplest of all? He said, 'You've made mistakes. That beating-up—Miss Cullen will never support you that I had stolen the car. And then the shooting—I didn't find the bullet. Miss Cullen did. I am going to bring a charge...'

A bell rang; the manservant appeared too quickly and too silently. 'Lord Benditch will see you now, sir.'

L. took no notice of him at all (that in itself was significant enough). He said, 'If only you would give your word ... there would be no more unpleasantness.'

'I give you my word that my address for the next few days will be London.' His confidence began to come back; the defeat had not been final: L. was shaken—about something. He seemed prepared to plead; he had some knowledge which D. did not possess. Then a bell rang, the servant opened the front door, and Rose came into her home like a stranger. She said, 'I wanted to catch...' and then saw L. She said, 'What a gathering!'

D. said, 'I have been persuading him that I

didn't steal your car.'

'Of course you didn't.'

L. bowed. He said, 'I mustn't keep Lord Benditch waiting,' the servant opened the door, and he was engulfed in the big room.

'Well,' she said, 'you remember what you said—about celebrating.' She faced him with bogus bravado: it couldn't be easy—your first meeting again after telling a man you loved him; he wondered whether she would introduce some reason—'I've got such a head. Was I very drunk?' But she had an appalling honesty. She said, 'You haven't forgotten about last night?'

He said, 'I remember everything if you do. But there's nothing to celebrate. They got my papers.'

She asked quickly, 'They didn't hurt you?'

'Oh, they did it painlessly. Is the man who opened the door new here?'

'I don't know.'

'Surely . . .'

She said, 'You don't think, do you, that I live in this place?' But she swept that subject aside. 'What did you tell them?'

'The truth.'

'All the melodrama?'

'Yes.'

'I warned you. How did Furt take it?'

'Furt?'

'Forbes. I always call him Furt.'

'I don't know. Brigstock did most of the

133

talking.'

'Furt's honest,' she said, 'in his way.' Her mouth was hard—as if she were considering his way. He felt again an immense pity for her, standing harshly in her father's house with a background of homelessness, private detectives and distrust. She was so young she had been a child when he married. It takes such a short time to make appalling changes: in the same period they had both travelled too far for happiness. She said, 'Isn't there anybody who'll answer for you at your Embassy?'

'I don't think so. We don't trust them—expect perhaps the Second Secretary.'

She said. 'It's worth trying. I'll get Furt. He's not a fool.' She rang the bell and said to the servant, 'I want to see Mr. Forbes.'

'I'm afraid, madam, he's in conference.'

'Never mind. Tell him I want to speak to him urgently.'

'Lord Benditch gave orders . . .'

'You don't know who I am, do you? You must be new. It's not my business to know your face, but you'd better know mine. I'm Lord Benditch's daughter.'

'I'm very sorry, miss. I didn't know . . .'

'Go in and take that message.' She said, 'So he's new.'

When the door opened they could hear Fetting's voice, 'No hurry. Better sleep . . .' She said, 'If he stole your papers . . .'

'I'm sure of it.'

She said furiously, 'I'll see he starves. There won't be a registry office in England...' Mr. Forbes came out. She said, 'Furt, I want you to do something for me.' He closed the door behind him and said, 'Anything.' He was like an oriental potentate in plus-fours, ready to promise the most fantastic riches. She said, 'Those fools don't believe him.' His eyes were moist when he looked at her—whatever the detectives reported, he was a man hopelessly in love. He said to D., 'Excuse me—but it *is* a tall story.'

'I found the bullet,' Rose said.

Away from the others, standing up, he looked more Jewish—there was the shape of the paunch as well as the shape of the head. He replied, 'I said a tall story, not an impossible one.' Very far back in the past was the desert, the dead salt sea, the desolate mountains and the violence on the road from Jericho. He had a basis of belief.

'What are they doing in there?' Rose asked.

'Not much. Old Fetting is a wonderful brake—and so is Brigstock.' He said to D., 'Don't think you are the only man Brigstock distrusts.'

Rose said, 'If we can prove to you that we are not lying...'

'We?'

'Yes, we.'

'If I'm satisfied,' Forbes said, 'I'll sign a

135

contract for as much as I can supply. It won't be all you need, but the others will follow.' He watched them anxiously, as if he were afraid of something: perhaps the man lived in perpetual fear of the announcement to the press—'A marriage has been arranged,' or of the ugly rumour: 'Have you heard about Benditch's daughter?'

'Will you come to the Embassy now?' she asked.

'I thought you told us . . .'

'This isn't my idea,' D. said. 'I don't think it will be any use. You see, at home they don't trust the Ambassador. . . . But there's always a chance.'

They drove in silence, slowly, through the fog. Once Forbes said, 'I'd like to get the pits started. It's a rotten life for the men there.'

'Why should it bother you, Furt?'

He grinned painfully across the car at her, 'I don't like being disliked.' Then his dark raisin eyes stared out again into the yellow day with some of the patience of Jacob who served seven years. . . . After all, D. thought, it was possible that even Jacob kept some consolation in a tent. Could you blame him? He felt almost envious of Forbes: it was something to be in love with a living woman, even if you got nothing from it but fear, jealousy, pain. It wasn't an ignoble emotion.

At the door of the Embassy he said, 'Ask for

the Second Secretary.... There's a chance.'

They were shown into a waiting-room. The walls were hung with pre-war pictures. D. said, 'That's the place where I was born.' A tiny village died out against the mountains. He said, '*They* hold it now.' He walked slowly round the room, leaving Forbes alone, as it were, with Rose. They were very bad pictures, very picturesque, full of thick cloud effects and heavy flowers. There was the university where he used to lecture ... empty and cloistered and untrue. The door opened. A man like a mute in a black morning coat and a high white collar said, 'Mr. Forbes?'

D. said, 'Pay no attention to me. Ask what questions you like.' There was a bookshelf: the books all looked unused in heavy uniform bindings: the national dramatist, the national poet.... He turned his back on the others and pretended to study them.

Mr. Forbes said, 'I've come to make some inquiries. On behalf of myself and Lord Benditch...'

'Anything we can help you in ... we shall be so pleased.'

'We have been seeing a gentleman who claims to be an agent of your government. In connection with the sale of coal.'

The stiff Embassy voice said, 'I don't think we have any information ... I will ask the Ambassador, but I am quite certain...' His

137

voice took on more and more assurance as he spoke.

'But I suppose it's possible that you would not be informed,' Mr. Forbes said. 'A confidential agent.'

'It is most improbable.'

Rose said sharply, 'Are you the Second Secretary?'

'No, madam, I'm afraid he is on leave. I am the First Secretary.'

'When will he be returning?'

'He will not be returning here.'

So that, probably, was the end of things. Mr. Forbes said, 'He claims that his credentials were stolen.'

'Well ... I'm afraid ... we know nothing ... it seems, as I say, very improbable.'

Rose said, 'This gentleman is not completely unknown. He is a scholar ... attached to a university ...'

'In that case we could easily tell you.'

What a fighter she was, he thought with admiration: she picked the right point every time.

'He is an authority on the Romance languages. He edited the Berne MS. of the Song of Roland. His name is D.'

There was a pause. Then the voice said, 'I'm afraid ... the name's completely unfamiliar to me.'

'Well, it might be, mightn't it? Perhaps you

aren't interested in the Romance languages.'

'Of course,' he said with a small self-assured laugh, 'but if you will wait two minutes, I will look the name up in a reference book.'

D. turned away from the bookshelf. He said to Mr. Forbes, 'I'm afraid we are wasting your time.'

'Oh,' Mr. Forbes said, 'I don't value my time as much as all that.' He couldn't keep his eyes off the girl; he followed every move she made with a tired sad sensuality. She was standing by the bookcase now, looking at the works of the national poet and the national dramatist. She said, 'I wish you didn't have so many consonants in your language. So gritty.' She picked a book out of a lower shelf and began to turn the pages. The door opened again. It was the secretary.

He said, 'I have looked up the name, Mr. Forbes. There is no such person. I'm afraid you have been misled.'

Rose turned on him furiously. She said, 'You are lying, aren't you?'

'Why should I be, Miss . . . Miss . . . ?'

'Cullen.'

'My dear Miss Cullen, a civil war flings up these plausible people.'

'Then why is his name printed here?' She had a book open. She said, 'I can't read what it says, but here it is. . . . I can't mistake the name. Here's the word Berne too. It seems to be a reference book.'

'That's very odd. Can I see? Perhaps if you don't know the language...'

D. said, 'But, as I do, may I read it out? It gives the dates of my appointment as lecturer at the University of Zed. It refers to my book on the Berne MS. Yes, it's all here.'

'You are the man?'

'Yes.'

'May I see that book?' D. gave it him. He thought, by God! she's won. Forbes watched her with admiration. The secretary said, 'Ah, I am sorry. It was your pronunciation of the name, Miss Cullen, which set me wrong. Of course we know D. One of our most respected scholars....' He let the words hang in the air; it was like a complete surrender, but all the time he kept his eyes on the girl, not on the man concerned. Somewhere there was a snag: there must be a snag. 'There,' the girl said to Forbes, 'you see.'

'But,' the secretary went gently on, 'he is no longer alive. He was shot by the rebels in prison.'

'No,' D. said, 'that's untrue. I was exchanged. Here—I have my passport.' He was thankful that he hadn't kept it in the same pocket as his papers. The secretary took it. D. said, 'What will you say now? That it's forged?'

'Oh no,' the secretary said, 'I think this is a genuine passport. But it isn't yours. You have only to look at the photograph.' He held it out to them: D. remembered the laughing stranger's face he had seen in the passport office at Dover. Of course, nobody would believe... He said hopelessly, 'War and prison change a man.'

Mr. Forbes said gently, 'There's a strong resemblance, of course.'

'Of course,' the secretary said. 'He would hardly choose...'

The girl said furiously, 'It's his face. I know it's his face. You've only to look...' but he could read the doubt somewhere behind which whipped up anger only to convince herself.

'How he got it,' the secretary said, 'one doesn't know.' He turned on D. and said, 'I shall see you are properly punished... Oh yes, I shall see to it.' He lowered his voice respectfully, 'I am sorry, Miss Cullen, but he was one of our finest scholars.' He was extraordinarily convincing. It was like hearing yourself praised behind your back. D. felt an odd pleasure: it was, in a way, flattering.

Mr. Forbes said, 'Better let the police get to the bottom of this. It's beyond me.'

'If you will excuse me I will ring them up at once.' He sat down at a table and took the 'phone.

D. said, 'For a man who's dead I seem to be accumulating a lot of charges.'

The secretary said, 'Is that Scotland Yard?' He began to give the name of the Embassy.

'First there was stealing your car.'

The secretary said, 'The passport is stamped Dover: two days ago. Yes, that's the name.'

'Then Mr. Brigstock wanted to have me up for trying to obtain money on false pretences—I don't know why.'

'I see,' the secretary said, 'it certainly seems to fit in. Yes, we'll keep him here.'

'And now I'm to be charged with using a false passport.' He said, 'For a university lecturer it's a dark record.'

'Don't joke,' the girl said. 'This is crazy. You are D. I know you are D. If you aren't honest, then the whole putrid world...'

The secretary said, 'The police were already looking for this fellow. Don't try to move. I have a gun in my pocket. They want to ask you a few questions.'

'Not so few,' D. said. 'A car ... false pretences ... passport.'

'And about the death of a girl,' the secretary said.


IV


THE nightmare was back: he was an infected man. Violence went with him everywhere. Like a typhoid-carrier he was responsible for the deaths of strangers. He sat down on a chair and

142

said, 'What girl?'

'You'll know very soon,' the secretary said.

'I think,' Mr. Forbes said, 'we'd better go.'
He looked puzzled, out of his depth.

'I would much rather you stayed,' the
secretary said. 'They will probably want an
account of his movements.'

Rose said, 'I shan't go. It's fantastic,
mad . . .' She said, 'You can tell them where
you've been all day?'

'Oh yes,' he said. 'I've got witnesses for every
minute of the day.' Despair began to lose its
hold: this was a mistake, and his enemies
couldn't afford many mistakes. But then, he
remembered that somebody, somewhere, must
be dead: that couldn't be a mistake. He felt
more pity than horror; one got so accustomed to
the deaths of strangers.

Rose said, 'Furt, you don't believe all this?'
He could read doubt again in her exclamation.

'Well,' Forbes said, 'I don't know. It's very
odd.'

But she was on again to the right fact, at the
right moment: 'If he's a fraud, why should
anyone take the trouble to shoot at him?'

'If they did.'

The secretary sat by the door with a polite air
of not listening.

'But I found the bullet myself, Furt.'

'A bullet, I suppose, can be planted.'

'I won't believe it.' She no longer said, D.

143

noticed, that she didn't believe it. She turned back to him, 'What else are they going to try now?'

Mr. Forbes said, 'You'd better go.'

'Where?' she asked.

'Home.'

She laughed—hysterically. Nobody else said a thing; they all just waited. Mr. Forbes began to look at the pictures carefully, one after the other, as if they were important. Then the front-door bell rang. D. got to his feet. The secretary said, 'Stay where you are. The officers will be coming through.' Two men entered; they lookd like a shopkeeper and his assistant. The middle-aged one said, 'Mr. D.?'

'Yes.'

'Would you mind coming along to the station to answer a few questions?'

'I can answer any you like here,' D. said.

'As you please, sir.' He stood and waited silently for the others to go. D. said, 'I have no objection to these people being present. If it's a case of wanting to know my movements, they'll be of use to you.'

Rose said, 'How can he have done a thing? He can bring witnesses any moment of the day . . .'

The detective said with embarrassment, 'This is a serious matter, sir. It would be better for all of us if you came to the station . . .'

'Arrest me, then.'

'I can't arrest you here, sir. Besides . . . we

144

haven't got that far.'

'Go on, then. Ask your questions.'

'I believe, sir, you are acquainted with a Miss Crole?'

'I have never even heard of her.'

'Oh yes, you have. You are staying at the hotel where she worked.'

'You don't mean, Else?' He got up and advanced towards the officer with his hands out, imploring him. 'They haven't done anything to her, have they?'

'I don't know who "they" are, sir, but the girl's dead.'

He said, 'O God, it's my fault.'

The officer went gently on, like a doctor with a patient. 'I ought to warn you, sir, that anything you say . . .'

'It was murder.'

'Technically perhaps, sir.'

'What do you mean? Technically?'

'Never mind that now, sir. All that concerns us at the moment is—the girl seems to have jumped out of a top-floor window.' He remembered the look of the pavement far away below, between the shreds of fog. He heard Rose saying, 'You can't implicate him. He's been at my father's since noon.' He remembered how the news of his wife's death had come to him; he thought that news of that kind would never hurt him again. A man who has been burnt by fire doesn't heed a scald. But this was like the death of an only child. How scared she must have been before she dropped. Why, why, why?

'Were you intimate with the girl, sir?'

'No. Of course not. Why, she was a child.' They were all watching him closely; the police officer's mouth seemed to stiffen under the respectable shopkeeper's moustache. He said to Rose, 'You had better go, ma'am. This isn't a case for lady's ears.'

She said, 'You're all wrong. I know you're all wrong.' Mr. Forbes took her arm and led her out. The detective said to the secretary, 'If you would stay, sir. The gentleman may want to be represented by his Embassy.'

D. said, 'This isn't my embassy. Obviously. Never mind that now. Go ahead.'

'There is an Indian gentleman, a Mr. Muckerji, staying in your hotel. He has made a statement that he saw the girl in your room this morning, undressing.'

'It's absurd. How could he?'

'He makes no bones about that, sir. He was peeping. He said he was getting evidence—I don't know what for. He said the girl was on your bed, taking down her stocking.'

'Of course. I see now.'

'Do you still deny intimacy?'

'Yes.'

'What was she doing, then?'

'I had given her some valuable papers the

146

night before to hide for me. She carried them in her instep under her stocking. You see, I had reason to suppose that my room might be searched—or I might be attacked.'

'What sort of papers, sir?'

'Papers from my Government establishing my position as their agent, giving me power to conclude certain business.'

The detective said, 'But this gentleman denies that you are—in fact—Mr. D. He suggests that you are travelling with the passport of a dead man.'

D. said, 'Oh yes, he has his reasons.' The toils were round him now all right; he was inextricably tied.

The detective said, 'Could I see those papers?'

'They were stolen from me.'

'Where?'

'In Lord Benditch's house.' It was, of course, an incredible story. He said, with a kind of horrified amusement at the whole wild tale, 'By Lord Benditch's manservant.' There was a pause: nobody said anything: the detective didn't even trouble to make a note. His companion pursed his lips and stared mildly round as if he was no longer interested in the tales criminals told. The detective said, 'Well, to come back to the girl.' He paused as if to give D. time to reconsider his story. He said, 'Can you throw any light on this—suicide?'

'It wasn't suicide.'

'Was she unhappy?'

'Not to-day.'

'Had you threatened to leave her?'

'I wasn't her lover, man. I don't pursue children.'

'Had you, by any chance, suggested that you should both kill yourselves?' The cat was out of the bag now: a suicide pact: that was what the detective had meant by 'technically murder.' They imagined he had brought her to that pitch and then climbed down himself: the worst kind of coward. What, in heaven's name, had put them on that track? He said wearily, 'No.'

'By the way,'the detective said, looking away at the bad pictures on the walls, 'why were you staying at this hotel?'

'I had my room booked before I came.'

'So you knew the girl before?'

'No, no, I haven't been in England for nearly eighteen years.'

'You chose a curious hotel.'

'My employers chose it.'

'Yet you gave the Strand Palace as your address to the passport officer at Dover.'

He felt like giving up; everything he had done since he landed seemed to add a knot to the cord. He said stubbornly, 'I thought that was a formality.'

'Why?'

'The officer winked at me.'

The detective sighed, uncontrollably, and

seemed inclined to shut his notebook. He said,
'Then you can throw no light on this—suicide?'

'She was murdered—by the manageress and a
man called K.'

'What motive?'

'I'm not sure yet.'

'Then it would surprise you, I suppose, to
hear that she left a statement?'

'I do not believe it.'

The detective said, 'It would make things
easier for all of us if you would make a proper
statement yourself.' He said with contempt,
'These suicide pacts are not hanging matters. I
only wish they were.'

'Can I see the girl's statement?'

'I don't mind reading you a few extracts—if
it'll help you to make up your own mind.' He
leant back in his chair and cleared his throat as if
he were going to read a poem or an essay of his
own composition. D. sat with his hands hanging
down and his eyes on the secretary's face:
treachery darkened the whole world. He
thought, this is the end. They can't kill a young
child like that. He remembered the long drop to
the cold pavement: how long did two seconds
seem when you were helplessly falling? A dull
rage stirred him. He had been pushed about like
a lay figure long enough; it was time he began to
act. If they wanted violence let them have
violence. The secretary stirred uneasily under
his gaze. He put his hand in his pocket where

the revolver lay; presumably he had fetched it
when he went out to speak to the Ambassador.

The detective read, 'I can't stand this any
longer. To-night he said we would both go away
for ever.' He explained, 'She kept a diary, you
see. Very well written, too.' It wasn't: it was
atrocious—like the magazines she read, but D.
could hear the tone of voice, the awkward
phrases stumbling on the tongue. He swore
hopelessly to himself: somebody has got to die.
That was what he had sworn when his wife was
shot, but nothing had come of it. 'To-night,' the
detective read, 'I thought he loved another, but
he said No. I do not think he is one of those men
who flit from flower to flower. I have written to
Clara to tell her of our plan. She will be sad, I
think.' The detective said with emotion,
'Wherever did she learn to write like that? It's as
good as a novel.'

'Clara,' D. said, 'is a young prostitute. You
ought to be able to find her easily enough.
Presumably the letter will explain what all this
means.'

'It sounds clear enough what's written here.'

'Our plan,' D. went on dully, 'was simply
this: I was going to take her away to-day from
the hotel.'

'Below the age of consent,' the detective said.

'I am not a beast. I asked Miss Cullen to find
her a job.'

The detective said, 'Would it be right to say

that you had got her to agree to go away with you, promising her employment?'

'Of course it wouldn't.'

'It's what you said. And what about this woman called Clara? Where does she come in?'

'She had invited the child to come and be her maid. It didn't seem to me—suitable.'

The detective began to write: 'She had been offered employment by a young woman, but it did not seem to me suitable, so I persuaded her to come away with me . . .'

D. said, 'You don't write, do you, as well as she did.'

'This isn't a joking matter.'

Rage grew in him slowly like a cancer. He began to remember phrases—'Most of the boarders like kippers,' turns of the head, her fear at being left alone, the appalling immaturity of her devotion. 'I'm not joking. I'm telling you there was no question of suicide. I charge the manageress and Mr. K. with deliberate murder. She must have been pushed . . .'

The detective said, 'It's up to us to do the charging. The manageress has been questioned—naturally. She was very upset. She admits she's been cross with the child, for slatternly ways. As for Mr. K., I've never heard of him. There's no one of that name in the hotel.'

He said, 'I'm warning you. If you don't do the job I will.'

'That's enough now,' the detective said. 'You won't be doing anything more in *this* country. It's time we moved.'

'There's not enough evidence to arrest me.'

'Not on this charge there isn't—yet. But the gentleman here says you are carrying a false passport...'

D. said slowly, 'All right. I'll come with you.'

'We've got a car outside.'

D. stood up. He said, 'Do you put on handcuffs?' The detective mellowed a little. He said, 'Oh, I don't think that will be necessary.'

'Will you need me?' the secretary asked.

'I'm afraid you'll be wanted down at the station, sir. You see, we haven't any right here—it's your country. In case there's questions asked by some of these politicians we'll need a statement that you called us in. I suppose there may be more charges to come. Peters,' he said, 'go and see if the car's outside. We don't want to stand about in this fog.'

It was apparently the absolute end—not only the end of Else but of thousands at home ... because there would be no coal now. Her death was only the first, and perhaps the most horrible because she was alone; the others would die in company in underground shelters. Rage slowly ate its way ... he had been pushed around.... He watched Peters out of the room. He said to the detective, 'That's my birthplace over there; that village under the mountains.' The detective turned and looked at it. He said, 'It's very picturesque,' and D. struck—right on the secretary's Adam's apple just where the high white collar ended. He went down with a whistle of pain, scrabbling for his gun. That helped. D. had it in his hand before the detective moved. He said quickly. 'Don't make the mistake of thinking I won't shoot. I'm on active service.'

'Now,' the detective said, holding up his hand as coolly as if he were on point duty, 'don't act wild—what we've got on you won't put you away for more than three months.'

D. said to the secretary, 'Get over to that wall. I've had a gang of traitors after me ever since I came across. Now I'm going to do the shooting.'

'Put away that gun,' the detective said in a gentle reasonable voice. 'You've got overwrought. We'll look into your story when we get to the station.'

D. started to move backwards towards the door. 'Peters,' the detective called sharply. D. had his hand on the handle: he began to turn it, but met resistance. Somebody outside wanted to get in. He dropped his hand and stood back against the wall with the gun covering the detective. The door swung open, hiding him. Peters said, 'What is it, Sarge?'

'Look out!' But Peters had advanced into the room. D. turned the gun on him. 'Back against the wall with the others,' he said.

The elderly detective said, 'You are acting very silly. If you do get out of here, you'll be picked up in a few hours. Drop that gun and we'll say no more about it.'

D. said, 'I need the gun.'

The door was open. He went backwards slowly and slammed the door to. He couldn't lock it. He called, 'I'll fire at the first one who opens the door.' He was in the hall, among tall old portraits and marble consoles. He heard Rose say, 'What are you doing?' and swung round, the gun in his hand. Forbes was beside her. He said, 'No time to talk. That child was murdered. Somebody's going to die.'

Forbes said, 'Drop that gun, you fool. This is London.'

He took no notice of him at all. He said, 'My name *is* D.' He felt that much of an avowal was due to Rose; he wasn't likely to see her again: he didn't want her to believe that she was always double-crossed by everyone. He said, 'There must be some way of checking up...' She was watching the gun with horror: she was probably not listening. He said, 'I once gave a copy of my book to the Museum—inscribed to the reading-room attendants—in thanks.' The handle began to turn. He called out sharply, 'Let go or I'll fire.' A man in black carrying a portfolio came running lightly down the wide marble steps. He exclaimed, 'I say!' seeing the gun and stood stock still. They made quite a crowd in the hall

154

now, waiting for something to happen. D. hesitated: he had a belief that she would say something, something important like 'Good luck' or 'Be careful,' but she was silent, staring at the gun. It was Forbes who spoke. He said in a puzzled voice, 'You know there's a police car just outside.' The man on the stairs said, 'I say!' again, incredulously. A bell tinkled and was silent. Forbes said, 'Don't forget they've got the telephone in there.'

He had forgotten it. He backed quickly, then by the glass doors of the hall thrust the gun in his pocket and walked quickly out. The police car was there, against the kerb. If Forbes called to the others he hadn't ten yards' start. He walked as fast as he dared: the driver gave him a sharp look—he had forgotten that he had no hat. In the fog it was possible to see for about twenty yards: he dared not run.

Perhaps Forbes hadn't called—he looked back; the car was obscured—he could see the tail light, that was all. He started to run on his toes—behind there was suddenly a clash of voices, the starting of an engine. They were after him. He ran—but there was no exit. He hadn't noticed that the embassy was in a square to which there was only one entrance—he had turned the wrong way and had three sides to cover. There wasn't time. . . . He could hear the car whine into top. They were not wasting time by turning—they were driving straight round the square.

Was this the end again? He nearly lost his head, running down the railings in what was now the direction of the car. Then his hand missed the railing: there was a gap: the head of basement stairs. He ran to the bottom and crouched close under the wall and heard the car go by above. He was saved for the moment by fog: they couldn't be sure that he wasn't all the time just ahead. They couldn't be certain he hadn't turned when they started and outrun them to the street.

But they weren't taking chances. He could hear a whistle blowing and presently footsteps coming slowly round the square: they were looking in the areas. One must be going round one way, one the other: the car probably blocked the street and they were getting more men. Had they lost their fear of his gun, or had they arms of their own in the police car? He didn't know how these things went in England. They were coming close.

There wasn't a light on. That alone was dangerous: they wouldn't expect to find him in an occupied basement. He peered through the window; he couldn't see much—the corner of what looked like a divan. It was probably a basement flat. There was a notice on the door: 'No milk till Monday'; he tore it down; a little brass plate beside the bell: Glover. He tried the door: hopeless: bolted and double-locked. The footsteps came nearer, very slowly. They must be searching thoroughly. There was only one chance: people were careless. He took out a knife and slipped it under the catch of the window, levered it: the pane slid up. He scrambled through and fell—silently—on the divan. He could hear somebody working up the square the other way; he felt weak and out of breath, but he daren't rest yet. He closed the window and turned on the light.

The place was stuffy with the smell of *potpourri* from a decorated pot on the mantelpiece; a divan covered with an art needlework counterpane: blue-and-orange cushions: a gas fire. He took it quickly in to the home-made water-colours on the walls and the radio set by the dressing-table. It spoke to him of an unmarried ageing woman with few interests. He heard steps coming down into the area: on no account must the place seem empty. He looked for the switch, plugged in the radio. A bright feminine voice said, 'But what is the young housewife to do if her table only seats four? To borrow from a neighbour at such short notice may be difficult.' He opened a door at random and found himself in the bathroom. 'Why not put two tables of the same height on end? The join will not be visible under the cloth. But where is the cloth to come from?' Somebody—it could only be a policeman—rang the area bell. 'Even this need not be borrowed if you have a plain counterpane upon your bed.'

Rage dictated his movements—they were pushing him around still: his turn had got to come. He opened a cupboard door, found what he wanted—one of the tiny razors women use for their armpits, and a stick of shaving soap, a towel. He tucked the towel into his collar, lathered over his moustache and the scar on his chin. The bell rang again. A voice said, 'That was Lady Mersham in the second talk of a series, Hints to the Young Housewife.'

D. moved slowly to the door, opened it. A policeman stood outside. He had a crumpled piece of paper in his hand. He said, 'Seeing as this said "No Milk till Monday," I thought the flat might be empty and the light left on.' He peered at D. closely. D. said, pronouncing his words carefully as if he had to pass an examination in English, 'That was last week.'

'You haven't seen any stranger about?'

'No.'

'Good morning,' the man said and moved reluctantly away. Suddenly he came back and said sharply, 'Funny sort of razor you use.'

D. realised that he was holding the woman's razor in his hand. He said, 'Oh, it's my sister's. I lost my own. Why?'

It was a young man. He lost his poise and said, 'Oh well, sir. We got to keep our eyes open.'

D. said, 'You'll excuse me. I am in rather a

158

hurry.'

'That's all right, sir.' He watched the man climb up into the fog. Then he closed the door and went back into the bathroom. The trapdoor had opened and let him out. He cleared the soap away from his mouth: no moustache. It made a difference, an enormous difference. It took ten years off his age. Rage was like vitality in his veins. Now they were going to have some of their own medicine: he had stood up to the watcher, the beating, the bullet: now it was their turn. Let them stand up to it equally well if they could. He thought of Mr. K. and the manageress and the dead child, and moving back into the stuffy female room which smelt of dead roses he swore that from now on he would be the hunter, the watcher, the marksman in the mews.

PART TWO

THE HUNTER

I

A HOLLOW B.B.C. voice said: 'Before we turn you over to the Northern Regional for a cinema organ recital from the Super-Palace, Newcastle, here is an SOS from Scotland Yard: "Wanted by the police: an alien passing under the name of D. who was arrested this morning at the request of the — Embassy and made his escape after assaulting the Ambassador's secretary. Aged about forty-five, five feet nine inches in height, hair dark inclined to grey, a heavy moustache, a scar on the right side of his chin. He is believed to carry a revolver."'

The waitress said, 'That's funny. You got a scar too. Don't you go and get into trouble.'

'No,' D. said, 'no. I must be careful, mustn't I?'

'The things that happen,' the waitress said. 'It's awful, isn't it? I was just going down the street, an' there was a crowd. Somebody committed suicide, they said, out of a window. Of course I stopped an' watched, but there wasn't anything to see. So at lunchtime I go round to the hotel—to see Else an' ask what it was all about. When they said it was Else—you could've knocked me down with a feather.'

'You and she were friends?'

'Oh, she hadn't got a better.'

'And of course you're upset?'

'I can't hardly believe it yet.'

'It doesn't seem likely, does it, a girl of that age? You don't think it was—perhaps—an accident.'

'Oh, it couldn't a' been. If you ask me, it's a case of still waters—I know more than most people, an' I think she was crossed in love.'

160

'You do?'

'Yes—with a married man living in Highbury.'

'Have you told the police that?'

'I'm to be called at the inquest.'

'Did *she* tell you that?'

'Oh no. She was a quiet one. But you pick up things.' He watched her with horror: this was friendship. He watched the small brown heartless eyes while she invented things even as she talked. There wasn't a man at Highbury— only in that romantic and squalid brain. Was it she who had lent Else those novelettes which had conditioned her speech? She said, 'I think it was the children was the difficulty.' There was a kind of gusto of creation in the voice. Else was safely dead; she could be reconstructed now to suit anybody at all. 'Else was mad about him. It was a proper spell.'

He laid the money down beside his plate. He said, 'Well, it was interesting to hear about your—adventure.'

'It'll be a long while before I forget it. I tell you—you could've knocked me down . . .'

He went out into the icy evening; it had been just chance which had led him to that café—or the fact that it was only two blocks from the hotel, and he wanted to make up his mind on the spot. The story was in all the papers now— 'Gunman in Embassy' stared at him from a poster. They had his description, the charge—

entering the country with a false passport, and one of the papers had routed out from somebody the fact that he had been staying in a hotel where a maid had committed suicide that morning. The fact was printed with a hint at a mystery, at developments to follow.... Well, there were going to be developments.

He moved boldly down the road towards the hotel. The fog had nearly lifted now. He felt like a man exposed by the drawing back of a curtain. He wondered if they would have posted a policeman at the hotel; he came cautiously along the railings, holding an evening paper in front of his face, reading.... There was nobody about; the door stood open, as usual. He went quickly in, through the glass inner door, closing it behind him. The keys hung on their hooks; he took down his own. A voice—it was the manageress's—called down from the first floor, 'Is that Mr. Muckerji?'

He said, 'Yes,' hoping that Mr. Muckerji had no pet phrase ... two foreign intonations were much alike. She seemed satisfied. He heard no more. The whole place was oddly quiet: as if death had touched it. No clatter of forks from the dining-room—no sound from the kitchen. He trod softly up the carpeted stairs. The door of the manageress's room was half shut; he went by and up the wooden stairs. What window had she dropped from? He put the key into his door and softly opened it. Somewhere out of sight somebody was coughing—cough, cough, cough. He left the door ajar behind him; he wanted to listen. Sooner or later he would hear Mr. K. He had marked down Mr. K. as the simplest to deal with; he would break quicker than the manageress when the screw was turned.

He turned into the dim room: the curtains were drawn for death. He reached the bed and realised with a shock that *she* was there—laid out ready for burial. Did they have to wait for the inquest? Presumably it was the only vacant room—her own would already have been filled—life goes on. She lay there stiff, clean and unnatural; people talked as if death were like sleep: it was like nothing but itself. He was reminded of a bird discovered at the bottom of a cage on its back, with the claws rigid as grape stalks: nothing could look more dead. He had seen people dead in the street after an air raid; but they fell in curious humped positions—a lot of embryos in the womb. This was different—a unique position reserved for one occasion. Nobody in pain or asleep lay like this.

Some people prayed. That was a passive part: he was anxious to express himself in action. Lying there the body seemed to erase the fear of pain; he could have faced the chauffeur now on any lonely road. He felt fear like an irrelevancy. He didn't speak to it: it couldn't hear—it was no longer she. He heard steps on the stairs, voices.... He went behind the curtain, sat back on the sill to keep his feet off the floor. Light came into the room. The manageress's voice said, 'I could have sworn I locked that door. There! That's her.'

A girl's voice said with avid emotion, 'She looks lovely.'

'She often talked of you, Clara,' the manageress said heavily.

'The dear ... of course she did. Whatever made her, do you think. . . ?'

'We never know—do we?—another person's heart.' He could see one of them now through a crack between the curtains—a girl with a coarse amiable pretty face a little smudged with facile tears. She asked 'Was it here?' in a tone of awe.

'Yes. Through that window.'

This window: but why hadn't she struggled? he wondered. Why were there no marks for the police to see?

'That very window?'

'Yes.'

They began to move across the room. Were they going to examine the scene a little more closely and discover him? Feet came towards him, paused as Clara spoke.

'If she'd come to me, it wouldn't have happened.'

'She was all right here,' the manageress said, 'before *he* came.'

'He's got something on his conscience all right. Though when she wrote to me she was

164

going away with him, I never thought she meant *this* way.' He thought: then even that letter doesn't help. She had been, poor child, incurably vague to the last with her novelette phrases.

The mangeress said, 'If you don't mind I'll bring up Mr. Muckerji. He was most anxious to see her—for the last time.'

'It's only right,' Clara said. He heard the manageress go. Through the crack he could see Clara making up—the dab of powder, the lipstick—a man was on his way. But she didn't touch the tears—they too were only proper.

The manageress returned. She was alone. She said, 'It's very odd. He's not in his room.'

'Perhaps he's not come in.'

'I heard him, though. He was in the hall taking his key. I called out to him and he answered.'

'Perhaps he's in—you know—the place.'

'Oh no. I tried the door.' She was ill at ease. She said, 'I can't understand. Somebody came in.'

Clara said, 'It sort of makes you think of ghosts, doesn't it, this sort of thing.'

'I think I'll go upstairs,' she said, 'and see how things are going. We have to get the room ready, you know, for the new maid.'

'Else wasn't much—was she?—for cleanness. Poor dear. I don't suppose she'd 'ave suited me. You want things just so when you have

165

gentlemen friends.' She was framed for a moment in the crack of the curtain, looking complacently down at the invisible dead. 'Well, I must be going now. A gentleman has an appointment for eight sharp. And he doesn't like to be kept.' She moved out of sight. The manageress's voice said, 'You don't mind if I don't come down with you, dear, do you? There's things . . .'

He put his hand upon his gun, waiting. The light went out. The door shut. He heard the lock turn; the manageress must have her master-key with her. He gave her a small start and then came out from behind the curtain. He didn't look at the body again: it had no interest now that it had no voice, no brain. . . . If you believed in God, you could also believe that it had been saved from much misery and had a finer future. You could leave punishment, then, to God . . . just because there was no need of punishments when all a murderer did was to deliver. . . . But he hadn't that particular faith. Unless people received their deserts, the world to him was chaos, he was faced with despair. He unlocked the door.

The manageress was on the floor above, talking. He closed the door behind him very softly; he didn't lock it—let them be haunted by the inexplicable. Suddenly he heard K.'s voice, 'You just forgot, I suppose. What else could it be?'

'I don't forget things,' the mangeress said. 'And, anyway, who answered me if it wasn't Mr. Muckerji?'

'He may have gone out again.'

'It isn't like him to pop in and out.'

There was a strong smell of paint. D. slowly mounted. He could see into the room now: the light was on, while he bowed in obscurity on the dark stairs. Mr. K. was standing by the window with a paintbrush—of course D. saw it now—it was from her own window she had fallen; there *had* been scratches, but there were no scratches any more. The room was redecorated for the next maid—the whole place whitened and freshened and free from crime. But Mr. K. had been awkward with the brush—they had been afraid to use a handyman—he had green paint on his jacket: it had even got on to his steel-rimmed spectacles. He said, 'Who could it have been, anyway?'

'I thought of D.'

'He'd never dare.' He asked sharply, for reassurance, 'Surely he'd never dare?'

'You can't tell what a man will dare when he hasn't anything to lose.'

'But he doesn't *know*. You don't really believe he's here—now—somewhere in the house? Perhaps—with *her*.' His voice broke a little. 'What could he want here?'

'He might be wanting us.'

It was a pleasure to D. to watch Mr. K.'s face,

puckered behind the steel rims. Unquestionably he'd break under pressure. He said, 'O God, the radio says he has a gun . . .'

'Better not talk so loud. He may be listening. We can't tell where he is. I'm sure I locked that door.'

Mr. K. screamed at her. 'You can tell—can't you—if he has the key.'

'Shsh!' She wasn't easy herself—the big spotty face was pastier than ever. 'To think he may have been there with me and Clara.'

D. began to move back down the stairs. He heard Mr. K. call sharply, 'Don't leave me alone,' and her contemptuous reply, 'We've got to be sure. I'll just go down and see if the key's there on the rack for his room. If it's not, we can always dial the police,' she added, doubtfully.

D. went quickly down, risking a creaking stair, risking the Indian on the second floor—perhaps he'd packed and gone: people don't like suicide in the house—everything was very quiet. He hung up his key: no need for the police to interfere in this vendetta: then stood inside the dining-room door and listened. He heard the manageress come cautiously down into the hall, heavily breathing, and then call out, 'The key's here.' Mr. K. could be heard on the stairs; he was moving very quickly, the paint slopped up and down in its pot. She called out encouragingly, 'It must have been a mistake. Just feel the door as you go by.'

'I don't like to.'

'Go on, you fool. I locked it only a minute ago.'

He panted down to her, 'It's not locked now.'

D. could see her face in a mirror over the aspidistra: it showed more than fear—calculation, listening ... it occurred to him that she mightn't want to call the police while the paint was still wet upstairs and the smell of it about the house: the less they had to explain the better. Mr. K. was in the hall now. He said anxiously, 'You must have thought you turned the key. He wouldn't dare.'

'And the voice?'

'Of course it was Mr. Muckerji...'

'Well,' she said, 'here he is, isn't he? You can ask him now—for yourself.' The hall door opened. In the mirror he could see her eyes ... absorbed, planning.... She said, 'You're late, Mr. Muckerji. I thought I heard you ten minutes ago...'

'Not me, madam. I have been busy, very busy ... among the neighbours.'

'O God,' Mr. K. said, 'then it was...'

'What have you been busy about, Mr. Muckerji?'

'Well—you will not be offended—you have a phrase, "The show goes on," haven't you? and when that poor child committed suicide, it seemed an occasion—of anthropological importance. You know how it is, Mrs. Mendrill,

169

we mass observers are always on duty.'

What was that? D. wondered. He could make no sense of it.

'So I have been collecting data. All the many reasons for her death—a married man in Highbury, a boy in Lambeth—all untrue, of course, but it shows the working of *their* minds. *We* know, of course, that the foreign gentleman . . .'

'Listen,' Mr. K. said, 'listen. I won't stay here. Get the police.'

Mr. Muckerji said reprovingly, 'There has been a lot of hysteria, too. And this will interest you, Mrs. Mendrill. There was somebody who said she saw the child fall. But she didn't.'

'No?'

'No. Because she told me the wrong window. Everything else was right—but she had read the papers, you see, so she filled in—about your being there, trying to hold her back . . . the scream . . . all of it. But she got the window wrong. That is very interesting. I think.'

'What do you do,' the manageress said, 'with all this information?'

'I type it out on my little Corona and send it to the organisers.'

'Do they print it?'

'They file it—for reference. Perhaps one day in a big book—without my name. We work,' he said regretfully, 'for science.'

Mr. K. said, 'You've got to send for the

police.'

'Don't be a fool,' the manageress said sharply. She explained, 'He sees that man—you know, the one who drove her to it—he sees him everywhere.'

Mr. Muckerji said automatically, 'That is interesting.' He sniffed. 'Ah, repainting. That is very interesting, too. Are you being practical—to eliminate traces—or superstitious?'

'What do you mean—traces?' Mr. K. said, excitedly.

'Oh, I mean untidiness, stains . . . things you do not want in an elegant hotel, which you were planning to re-do in any case. Or is it superstition? Because there has been a death. You see, there are tribes in West Africa who behave like that. They will even destroy the hut, the clothes, everything of the dead person. They want quite to forget that there has been a death. I am anxious to discover if your desire to put a new coat of paint over your hotel belongs to that category.'

Mr. K. said, 'I'm going. I can't stand this. If you want any help . . .'

Suddenly D. realised that he, too, was visible to the manageress in the same mirror. Their eyes had met. The manageress said slowly, 'I shall be all right. With Mr. Muckerji. It's you who had better be careful.' She said, 'Didn't you want to see the body, Mr. Muckerji?'

'Yes. If it is convenient. I have brought a few

flowers.... That is superstition, but it is also practical. Because of the scent...'

'I don't like flowers in a bedroom as a rule, but in this case I don't suppose it matters, does it?'

D. watched her narrowly and she returned his look—at second-hand. There were people, he thought, who could shoot like that. At shows. With the help of a mirror.

Mr. K. said, 'I'm going, Marie,' as if he expected something more than this heartless warning. It was as though, in the mirror, she were encouraging D. to do his worst. She was strong, all right; she would be the last to break: square and spotty and determined, she surrendered him, as it were, one victim....

Mr. Muckerji said, 'A moment. I left my glasses, I think, in the dining-room at breakfast-time.' D. drew the gun from his pocket and waited.

'Oh, no, Mr. Muckerji,' the manageress said, 'you'll find them in your room. We always clear away.' She led him up the stairs with a hand on his arm. He was carrying a few untidy flowers wrapped in newspaper. It was extraordinary how the whole world could alter after a single violent act. They had thought they would put him safely away, but it was he now who was safe ... because he had nothing to think about now but punishment: no duties ... and it was they who welcomed the presence of Mr. Muckerji

172

. . . as he had done only that morning.

The hall door shut; he followed Mr. K. into the street. Mr. K. walked fast without looking behind him, carrying an umbrella. They went rapidly down towards the Gray's Inn Road—D. twenty paces behind. He made no effort to disguise his pursuit; it seemed improbable that Mr. K. would really have the nerve to call a policeman. Suddenly, desperately, Mr. K. came to bay—on the pavement, by a bus stop: he must have heard the footsteps behind him, crossing the road when he crossed, pausing when he paused. He turned and watched D. approach. He had a cigarette in his hand: it wobbled. He said, 'Excuse me. Might I have a light?'

'Certainly.' D. struck the match and held it, so that it lit the scared short-sighted eyes. They peered at him with haunted relief: no recognition. It was astonishing what difference a moustache made. He had to steady the cigarette with his own fingers. K. said, 'I see you've got an evening paper in your pocket. Might I see?' He was the kind of man who always borrowed if he could: he saved a match and saved a paper.

'You can have it,' D. said. They had had only two interviews together, he and K., but something about the voice worried the man. He looked up sharply and then down at the paper again. He wasn't sure. A bus drew up. He said, 'Thank you,' climbing on board. D. followed—

up to the top deck. They swayed forward one behind the other. Mr. K. took the front seat: D. was just behind. Mr. K. looked sharply up and saw D.'s face reflected in the glass. He sat there, not reading the paper, thinking, hunched in his seat; his old and seedy overcoat registered sickness like a cat's fur.

The bus turned into Holborn: the queue was going into the Empire: big windows full of office furniture lined the street: a milk bar, then more furniture. The bus moved west. D. watched Mr. K.'s face in the window. Where did he live? Had he the courage to go home? They crossed St. Giles's Circus into Oxford Street; Mr. K. looked out and down with a kind of nostalgia at the policeman on point duty, the Jews outside the Astoria. He took off his spectacles and rubbed the glass; he wanted to see clearly. The paper was open on his knee at the story of the gunman in the Embassy. He began to read the description—as if he could trust that more than his own memory. Once again he took a quick snaky look at D.'s face; his eyes were on the scar this time. He said sharply, 'Oh!' before he could stop himself.

'Did you speak to me?' D. said, leaning forward.

'Me? Oh no,' Mr. K. said. He coughed with a dry throat—hack, hack, hack. He got on his feet, swaying with the bus.

'Do you get out here?'

'Me? Yes. Yes.'

'So do I,' said D. 'You look ill. Do you want a hand?'

'No, no. I'm quite all right.'

He made for the stairs, and D. followed at his heels.

They were side by side on the pavement, waiting for the traffic lights to change. D. said, 'Things have changed for the better, haven't they?' He felt himself shaken by a restless and malicious mirth.

'What do you mean?' Mr. K. said.

'I mean the weather. This morning there was so much fog.'

The traffic lights turned green and they crossed the entrance of Bond Street, side by side. He could see Mr. K. taking quick looks in the plate-glass windows at his companion, but he couldn't see—his eyes were spoilt by poverty and too much reading, and he daren't speak directly. It was as if, so long as D. did not declare himself, he wasn't D.

He suddenly turned into a doorway, into a dark passage, and almost ran towards the electric globe at the far end. The passage was somehow familiar; D. had been too absorbed to notice where they had come. He followed after Mr. K.: an old lift wheezing down towards his victim. Mr. K. suddenly said, in a voice pitched high to go up the lift shaft to the rooms above, 'You are following me. Why are you following me?'

D. said gently, 'Surely you ought to be speaking Entrenationo—to a pupil.' He laid his hand confidingly on Mr. K.'s sleeve. 'I should never have believed a moustache made all that difference.'

Mr. K. pulled the lift door open. He said, 'I don't want any more to do with you.'

'But we're on the same side, surely?'

'You were superseded.'

D. pushed him gently backwards and shut the lift gates. He said, 'I forgot. This is the night of the soirée, isn't it?'

'You ought to be on your way home by now.'

'But I've been prevented. You must know that.' He touched the emergency button and they stopped between two floors.

Mr. K. said, 'Why did you do that?' He leant against the lift wall, blinking, blinking behind the steel rims. Somebody was playing a piano upstairs rather badly.

D. said, 'Did you ever read Goldthorb's detective stories?'

'Let me out of here,' Mr. K. said.

'School-teachers generally read detective stories.'

'I shall scream,' Mr. K. said. 'I shall scream.'

'It wouldn't be good manners at a soirée. By the way, you've still got some of that paint on your coat. That's not clever of you.'

'What do you want?'

176

'It was so lucky that Mr. Muckerji found the woman who *saw* it happen—from the other window.'

'I wasn't there,' Mr. K. said. 'I know nothing.'

'That's interesting.'

'Let me out.'

'But I was telling you about Goldthorb's detective story. One man killed another in a lift. Rang the lift down. Walked up the stairs. Rang the lift up and—before witnesses—discovered the body. Of course, luck was on his side. You have to have a fortunate hand for murder.'

'You wouldn't dare.'

'I was just telling you Goldthorb's story.'

Mr. K. said weakly, 'There's no such man. The name's absurd.'

'He wrote in Entrenationo, you see.'

Mr. K. said, 'The police are looking for you. You'd better clear out—quickly.'

'They have no picture and the description's wrong.' He said mildly, 'If there were a way of dropping you down the lift-shaft. To make the punishment, you know, fit the crime . . .'

Suddenly the lift began to move upwards. Mr. K. said triumphantly, 'There. You see. You'd better run for it.' It wheezed and shook very slowly beyond the second floor—the offices of *Mental Health*.

D. said, 'I shouldn't speak if I were you. You read about the revolver.'

'It's not me you need be afraid of,' Mr. K. said. 'I bear you no malice—but Miss Carpenter or Dr. Bellows . . .'

There wasn't time to finish; the lift stopped, and Dr. Bellows came out of the big waiting-room to greet them; a faded woman in brown silk got into the lift, waving a hand thick with art jewellery like barnacles, squeaking a mysterious phrase which sounded like 'Nougat.' Dr. Bellows said, 'Bona nuche. Bona nuche,' and smiled at them happily.

Mr. K. glared at him and waited; D. had his hand upon his pocket—but Dr. Bellows seemed oblivious of anything wrong. He took a hand of each and shook them warmly. He said, 'To a new pupil I may perhaps be allowed to speak a few words in English.' He added in a slightly puzzled way, 'You are a new pupil, surely. I *thought* I knew you . . .'

D. said, 'You are looking for my moustahce.'

'Of course. That's it.'

'I told myself—for a new language a new face. Have you by any chance seen the evening paper?'

'No,' Dr. Bellows said, 'and please, please don't tell me. I never read the daily press. I find that in a good weekly paper fact has been sifted from rumour. All the *important* news is there. And so much less distress.'

'It's an admirable idea.'

'I recommend it. Miss Carpenter, my

secretary—you know her—adopted it and has been so much happier ever since.'

'It must make for everyone's happiness,' D. said. Mr. K., he noticed, had slipped away. 'I must speak to Miss Carpenter about it.'

'You'll find her presiding over the coffee. For these soirées rules are a little relaxed. We hope people will speak Entrenationo if possible—but the great thing is to get together.' He led D. into the waiting-room. There was a big urn on the counter and plates of rock cakes. Miss Carpenter waved to him from behind the steam: she was still wearing her blue-wool jumper with the bobbles. 'Bona nuche,' she called to him, 'Bona nuche.' A dozen faces turned to look at him; it was like one of those illustrations in a children's encyclopædia which show the races of the world. There were a good many Orientals wearing glasses. Mr. K. stood with a rock bun in his hand not eating.

'I must introduce you,' Dr. Bellows said, 'to our Siamese.'

He pressed D. gently onwards towards the far wall. 'Hi es Mr. D.—Dr. Li.'

Dr. Li looked at him inscrutably through very thick lenses. 'Bona nuche.'

'Bona nuche,' D. said.

Conversation went on among the leather arm-chairs spasmodically; little bursts of conversation rose up in corners and then withered away for want of nourishment. Miss

Carpenter poured out coffee, and Mr. K. stared at his rock bun. Dr. Bellows moved here and there erratically like love: the smooth white hair, the weak and noble face.

D. said, 'An idealist.'

'Qua?'

'I'm afraid,' D. said, 'I am a new pupil. I cannot yet speak much Entrenationo.'

'Qua?' Dr. Li said sternly. He watched D. narrowly through the thick glasses like portholes as if he suspected him of rudeness. Mr. K. began edging towards the door, still carrying his rock bun.

Dr. Li said sharply, 'Parla Entrenationo.'

'Parla Anglis.'

'No,' Dr. Li said firmly and angrily. 'No parla.'

'I am sorry,' D. said. 'Un momento.' He crossed the room rapidly and took Mr. K.'s arm. He said, 'We mustn't leave yet. It would look strange.'

Mr. K. said, 'Let me go. I implore you. I know nothing. I am feeling ill.'

Dr. Bellows appeared again. He said, 'How did you get on with Dr. Li? He is a very influential man. A professor at Chulalankarana University. It gives me great hopes of Siam.'

'I found it a little difficult,' D. said. 'He seems to speak no English.' He kept his hand through Mr. K.'s arm.

'Oh,' Dr. Bellows said, 'he speaks it

180

perfectly. But he feels—quite rightly, of course—that the only object of learning Entrenationo is to speak it. Like so many Orientals he is a little intransigent.' They all three looked at Dr. Li, who stood in an island of silence with his eyes half closed. Dr. Bellows went across to him and began to talk earnestly in Entrenationo. Silence spread around the room; it was a privilege to hear the inventor speak his own language: he gave the impression of gliding rapidly among the cases like a skater.

Mr. K. said rapidly, 'I can't stand this. What are you trying to get out of me?'

'A little justice,' D. said gently. He felt no pity at all: the odd occasion—the surroundings of office coffee and home-made cakes, of withered women in old-fashioned evening dresses which had had too little wear, and of Orientals shrewd and commercial behind their glasses—only lifted Mr. K. further out of the category of human beings who suffer pain and exact sympathy. Dr. Bellows was back again. He said, 'Dr. Li asked me to say that he would be pleased to meet you another time—when you have learned rather more Entrenationo.' He smiled feebly. 'Such a firm character,' he said. 'I have not met such faith—no, not in all Israel.'

'Mr. K. and I,' D. said, 'were just regretting that it was nearly time for us to leave.'

'So soon? And I did so much want to introduce you to a Rumanian lady—oh, I see

181

that she is talking to Dr. Li.' He smiled across the room at them as if they were a young couple whose timid courtship he was encouraging and superintending. He said, 'There! That is what I mean. Communication instead of misunderstanding, strife...' It seemed unlikely, D. thought, that Rumania and Siam were ever likely to come into serious conflict ... but Dr. Bellows was already off again, forging his links between the most unlikely countries, and Miss Carpenter stood behind the coffee urn and smiled and smiled.

D. said, 'It's time for us to move.'

'I won't move. I am going to see Miss Carpenter home.'

D. said, 'I can wait.'

He went over to the window and looked down: the buses moved slowly along Oxford Street like gigantic beetles. Across the top of the opposite building a skysign spelt out slowly the rudimentary news: 2 goals to one. Far away, foreshortened on the pavement, a squad of police moved in single file towards Marlborough Street. What next? The news petered out and began again. 'Another advance reported ... 5,000 refugees ... four air raids...' It was like a series of signals from his own country—what are you doing here? Why are you wasting time? When are you coming back? He felt homesick for the dust after the explosion, the noise of engines in the sky. You have to love your home for something—if only for its pain and violence. Had L. come to terms, he wondered, with Benditch? The deal was closed to him; no credentials would avail him now in this respectable country—a man wanted on suspicion of murder. He thought of the child screaming at the window, scratching with her nails at the paint, breaking through the fog, smashed on the pavement: she was one of thousands. It was as if by the act of death she had become naturalised to his own land—a country-woman. His territory was death: he could love the dead and the dying better than the living. Dr. Bellows, Miss Carpenter—they were robbed of reality by their complacent safety. They must die before he could take them seriously.

He moved away from the window and said to Miss Carpenter, 'Is there a telephone, I could use?'

'Oh, certainly. In Dr. Bellows' office.'

He said, 'I hear Mr. K. is seeing you home?'

'Oh, but that's sweet of you, Mr. K. You really oughtn't to bother. It's such a long way to Morden.'

'No trouble,' Mr. K. muttered; he still held the rock bun—like an identification disc—they would be able to recognise his body by it.

D. opened the door of the office and quickly apologised. A middle-aged man with a shaven Teutonic skull was sitting out with an angular

183

girl on Dr. Bellows' desk. There was a slight smell of onions—one of them must have been eating steak. 'I am so sorry. I came to telephone.' The angular girl giggled; she was singularly unattractive, with a large wrist-watch and a lapel pin in the shape of an Aberdeen dog.

'Not at all. Not at all,' the German said. 'Come Winifred.' He bowed stiffly to D. from the doorway. 'Korda,' he said. 'Korda.'

'Korda?'

'Entrenationo—for the heart.'

'Ah yes, yes.'

'I have a great passion,' the German frankly explained, 'for the English girls.'

'Yes?' The German kept Winifred's bony hand in a tight grip; she had bad teeth and mouse-coloured hair—she carried with her a background of blackboards and chalk and children asking permission to leave the room—and Sunday walks in ruined fields with dogs.

'They have so much innocence,' the German said, and bowed again and closed the door.

D. rang up Lord Benditch's house. He said, 'Is Miss Cullen there?'

'Miss Cullen doesn't live here.' Luck favoured him; it was a woman—not the manservant—who might have remembered his voice. He said, 'I can't find her in the telephone book. Would you give me her number?'

'Oh, I don't know that I can do that.'

'I am a very old friend. Only over in England

184

for a day or two.'

'Well . . .'

'She will be very disappointed. . . .'

'Well . . .'

'She particularly asked . . .'

'It's Mayfair 301.'

He dialled again and waited. He had to trust Miss Carpenter to keep a grip on Mr. K.; he knew very well how convention can be stronger than fear—especially when the fear is still a little vague and unbelievable: you have to learn to fear successfully. He said, 'Is Miss Cullen there?'

'I don't think so. Hold on.' Even if he couldn't get the coal himself, there must be some way of stopping L. If only he could prove that the murder . . . was a murder. . . .

Rose's voice suddenly said, 'Who's that?'

He said, 'The name is Glover.'

'What do you want? I don't know a Glover.'

'I live,' he said, 'at 3, Chester Gardens—nearly next door to the Embassy.'

There was silence at the other end. He said, 'Of course, if you believe that story—of the suicide pact—you can send the police round to-night. Or if you believe that I am not D. at all.'

She made no reply; had she rung off? He said, 'Of course, the girl was murdered. It was ingenious, wasn't it?'

She replied suddenly in a tone of fury, 'Is that all you care?'

He said, 'I shall kill whoever did it. . . . I am not sure yet . . . I want the right person. One can't afford to kill more than one . . .'

'You're crazy. Can't you get out of the country, go home?'

'They would probably shoot me. Not that that matters. But I shouldn't like L. . . .'

She said, 'You're too late. They've signed.'

'I was afraid . . .' He said, 'Do you know what the contract is? I don't see how they can hope to get the coal out of the ports. There's the neutrality agreement.'

She said, 'I'll ask Furt.'

'Has he signed, too?'

'Yes, he's signed.' Somebody was playing the piano again and singing; it seemed to be an Entrenationo song: the word Korda, Korda came in a lot. Presently she said, 'He couldn't do anything else.' She excused him, 'When all the others signed . . . the shareholders . . .'

'Of course.' He felt an odd prick of jealousy because she had taken the trouble to defend Forbes. It was like feeling painfully returning to a frozen hand. He didn't love, he was incapable of loving anyone alive, but nevertheless the prick was there. . . .

She said, 'Where are you? I keep on hearing the oddest sounds . . .'

'At a soirée,' he said. 'That's what they call it. Of the Entrenationo School.'

'You're such a fool,' she said despairingly.

'Don't you realise there's a warrant out for you? Resisting arrest. Forged passport. God knows what else.'

He said, 'It seems safe here. We are eating rock buns.'

'Why be such a fool?' she said. 'You're old enough—aren't you—to look after yourself.'

He said, 'Will you find out for me—from Forbes?'

'You didn't mean that, did you, about killing . . .'

'Yes, I meant that.'

The voice came fiercely and vividly out of the vulcanite: she might have been standing at his elbow, accusing him. 'So you did love the little bitch?'

'No,' he said. 'Not more than all the others. There have been four raids to-day. I daresay they've killed fifty children besides her . . . one has to get one's own back a little.' He suddenly realised how absurd it all was. He was a confidential agent employed in an important coal deal on which the fate of a country might depend; she was a young woman, the daughter of a peer whose coal he wanted, and the beloved, apparently, of a Mr. Forbes who also controlled several mines and kept a mistress in Shepherd's Market (that was irrelevant); a child had been murdered by the manageress or Mr. K.— acting, presumably, on behalf of the rebels, although they were employed by his own

187

people. That was the situation: a strategical and political—and criminal—one. Yet here they were talking to each other down the telephone like human beings, jealous of each other, as if they were in love, as if they had a world at peace to move about in, and the whole of time.

She said, 'I don't believe it. You must have loved her.'

'She was only fourteen I should think.'

'Oh, I daresay you've reached the age when you like them young.'

'No.'

'But you can't do anything of that kind here— killing, I mean—don't you understand? They'll hang you. Only the Irish try that on here—and they are always hanged.'

'Oh well . . .' he said vaguely.

'Oh God,' she said. 'The door's been open all the time.' There was silence; then she said, 'I've probably given you away. They'll have guessed—after the newspapers. Probably Scotland Yard's listening in now. They could have dialled 999 on the downstairs 'phone.'

'Who are they?'

'Oh, the maid or my friend. You can't trust anyone. Get away from there—wherever you are.'

'Yes,' he said. 'It's time to move on. Bona nuche.'

'What on earth's that?'

'Entrenationo,' he said, and rang off.

He opened the door into the waiting-room: there were fewer people about, less buns, the coffee was cooling in the urn. Mr. K. stood against the counter grasped firmly in the conversational hold of Miss Carpenter. D. made for them and Mr. K. wilted—it occurred to D. that he didn't look like the kind of man you killed. On the other hand he was a traitor and somebody had got to die. It was unsporting, perhaps, but Mr. K. might be the easiest—he would be a warning to other traitors. He said to Miss Carpenter, 'I'm afraid I've got to tear away your escort,' drawing on a pair of gloves he must be careful not to take off again.

'I won't go,' Mr. K. said, and Miss Carpenter pouted delightedly and set a wool bobble swinging.

'It's really important,' D. said, 'or, of course, I would never take him.'

'I don't see,' Miss Carpenter said playfully, 'that it could be so important.'

'I have been on to my Embassy,' D. said. His imagination was unbridled, he feared nobody: it was his turn to be feared—and he felt exhilaration like laughter in his brain. 'We have been discussing the possibility of setting up an Entrenationo centre at home.'

'What's that?' Dr. Bellows said. He appeared at the buffet with a dark middle-aged woman in pink cretonne. The mild eyes gleamed excitedly. 'But how—in the middle of a war?'

'It's no good fighting,' D. said, 'for a particular civilisation if we don't—at the same time—keep it alive behind the lines.' He felt a very slight horror at his own appalling fluency, a very little regret at the extravagant hopes he had aroused beside the coffee urn, in the dingy office. The old liberal eyes were full of tears. Dr. Bellows said, 'Then some good may come of all the anguish.'

'So you'll understand if I and my countryman here—we must rush away.' It was the wildest story, but no story is too wild for a man who hopes. . . . Everyone in this room lived in an atmosphere of unreality: high up above Oxford Street in an ivory tower, waiting for miracles. Dr. Bellows said, 'I never thought when I got up this morning . . . so many years . . . this is the birthday of my life. That was what one of our poetesses wrote.' He held D.'s hand: everybody was watching: Miss Carpenter wiped the corner of her eye. He said, 'God bless you, all of you.'

Mr. K. said, 'I will not go. I will not go,' but nobody paid him any attention. He was hustled out beside D. towards the lift by the lady in cretonne, hauled on his road. . . . In his fear he lost his English altogether—he began to beseech them all to wait and listen in a language only D. could understand. He looked ill, beaten . . . he sought in Entrenationo to express something, anything. He said, 'Mi Korda, Mi Korda,' white about the lips, but nobody else was

190

talking Entrenationo now, and they were together in the lift going down. Dr. Bellows' face disappeared: his waistcoat buttons: his boots—he wore boots. Mr. K. said, 'There's nothing you can do. Nothing.'

D. said, 'You've got nothing to fear if you weren't concerned in her death. Keep close beside me. Don't forget I have that revolver.' They walked side by side into Oxford Street: suddenly Mr. K. side-stepped, somebody came in between: they were separated by shop-window gazers. Mr. K. began to dart down the pavement, zig-zagging. He was a small man and agile, but short-sighted; he bumped into people and went on without apology. D. let him go: it was no good pursuing him through the crowd. He called a taxi and said to the driver, 'Go as slow as you can. There's a drunk friend of mine just in front—I've lost him in the crowd. He needs a lift before he gets in any trouble.' Through the window he could watch Mr. K.: he was wearing himself down: it all helped.

Mr. K. bounded from right to left and back again; people turned round and stared at him. A woman said, 'Ought to be ashamed,' and a man said, 'Guinness ain't so good for *him*.' His steel spectacles had slipped halfway down his nose, and every now and then he looked backwards: his umbrella got between people's legs, and a child howled at the sight of his little scared red eyes. He was creating a sensation. At the corner of South Audley Street he ran full tilt into a policeman. The policeman said kindly, 'Hi! You can't behave like that here.' Mr. K. stared up at him, his eyes blind above his glasses.

'Now go home quietly,' the policeman said.

'No,' Mr. K. said suddenly, 'no.'

'Put your head under the tap and go to bed.'

'No.' Mr. K. suddenly put his head down and rammed it at the policeman's stomach—ineffectually: a big gentle hand diverted him. 'Do you want to come to the station?' the policeman asked mildly. A small crowd collected. A man with a high hollow voice in a black hat said, 'You've no reason to interfere: he was doing no harm.'

'I only said . . .' the policeman began.

'I heard what you said,' the stranger retorted quickly. 'On what charge, may I ask, do you intend . . .'

'Drunk and disorderly,' the policeman said.

Mr. K. watched with an appearance of wild hope: he forgot to be disorderly.

'Nonsense,' the stranger said. 'He's done nothing. I'm quite prepared to stand in the witness-box . . .'

'Now, now, now,' the policeman said indignantly. 'What's all the fuss about? I only told him to go home to bed.'

'You suggested he was drunk.'

'He is drunk.'

'Prove it.'

192

'What's it to do with you, anyway?'

'This is supposed to be a free country.'

The policeman said plantively, 'What I want to know is—what have I *done*?'

The man in the black hat produced a card and said to Mr. K., 'If you want to charge this constable with slander, I am quite prepared to give evidence.' Mr. K. held the card as if he didn't understand. The policeman suddenly flung his arms above his head and shouted at the crowd, 'Get on there. Move on.'

'Do nothing of the kind,' the stranger said sharply. 'You are all witnesses.'

'You'll make me lose my patience,' the policeman said with a breaking voice. 'I warn you.'

'What of? Speak up now. What of?'

'Interfering with an officer in the performance of his duty.'

'Duty!' the stranger said sarcastically.

'But I am drunk,' Mr. K. said suddenly, imploringly, 'I am disorderly.' The crowd began to laugh. The policeman turned on Mr. K., 'Now you've started again,' he said. 'We aren't concerned with you.'

'Oh yes, we are,' the stranger said.

A look of agony crossed the policeman's face. He said to Mr. K., 'Now why don't you get quietly into a taxi and go home?'

'Yes. Yes. I'll do that,' Mr. K. said.

'Taxi!'

193

The taxi drew up beside Mr. K. and he grabbed thankfully at the handle, opened the door. D. smiled at him and said, 'Step in.'

'An' now,' the policeman said, 'for you—whatever your name is.'

'My name is Hogpit.'

'No more back answers,' the policeman said.

Mr. K. backed on the pavement. He said, 'Not that taxi. I won't take that taxi.'

'But my name *is* Hogpit.' Several people laughed. He said angrily, 'It's no funnier than Swinburne.'

Mr. K. struggled to get by.

'Moses!' the policeman said. 'You again.'

'There's a man in that taxi . . .' Mr. K. said.

D. got out and said, 'That's all right, officer. He's a friend of mine. He *is* drunk—I lost him up the road at the "Carpenters' Arms."' He took Mr. K.'s arm and led him firmly back. Mr. K. said, 'He'll kill me,' and tried to flop on the pavement. 'Would you mind giving me a hand, officer?' D. said. 'I'll see he's no more trouble.'

'That's all right, sir. I'm glad to be rid of him.' He bent and lifted Mr. K. as if he were a baby and piled him on the floor of the taxi. Mr. K. cried weakly, 'I tell you he's been following me . . .' The man whose name was Hogpit said, 'What right have you to do that, constable? You heard what he said. How do you know he's not telling the truth?'

The constable slammed the door and turned.

He said, 'Because I use my judgment ... an' now are *you* going to go quietly?...' The taxi drove on. The group slipped backwards gesticulating. D. said, 'You only made yourself look a fool.'

'I'll break the window. I'll scream,' Mr. K. said.

'If the worst came to the worst,' D. said in a low voice, as if he meant to confide a secret, 'I'd shoot.'

'You couldn't get away. You wouldn't dare.'

'That's the kind of argument they use in stories. It doesn't apply any more in these days. There's a war on: it's not likely that any of us will "get away," as you call it, for long.'

'What are you going to do?'

'I'm taking you home, for a talk.'

'What do you mean, "home"?' But D. had no more to say, as they bumped slowly on across the Park. The soap-box orators talked in the bitter cold at Marble Arch with their mackintoshes turned up around their Adam's apples, and all down the road the cad cars waited for the right easy girls, and the cheap prostitutes sat hopelessly in the shadows, and the blackmailers kept an eye open on the grass where the deeds of darkness were quietly and unsatisfactorily accomplished. This was technically known as a city at peace. A poster said: 'Bloomsbury Tragedy Sensation.'

# II

THE fight was out of Mr. K. He left the taxi
without a word and went on down the basement
steps. D. turned up the light in the little bed-
sitting-room and lit the gas; bent over the fire
with the match between his fingers, he
wondered whether he was really going to
commit a murder. It seemed hard luck on
Glover—whoever she might be: a person's home
had a kind of innocency. When a house front
gave way before an explosion and showed the
iron bed, the chairs, the hideous picture and the
chamber-pot, you had a sense of rape: intrusion
into a stranger's home was an act of lust. But
you were driven always to copy what your
enemy did. You dropped the same bombs: you
broke up the same private lives. He turned with
sudden fury on Mr. K. and said, 'You've asked
for this.'

Mr. K. backed against the divan, sat down.
Above his head was a small bookshelf with a few
meagre books in limp morocco bindings—the
inconsiderable library of a pious woman. He
said, 'I swear to you, I wasn't there.'

'You don't deny—do you?—that you and she
planned to get my papers.'

'You were superseded.'

'I know all that.' He came close up to him;

196

this was the moment for the blow in the face, the worked-up rage: they had shown him the other day how a man was beaten up. But he couldn't do it. To touch K. at all was to start a relationship . . . his mouth quivered in distaste. He said, 'Your only chance of getting out alive is to be frank. They bought you both, didn't they?'

Mr. K.'s glasses dropped on the divan: he felt for them over the art needle-work cover. He said, 'How were we to know you had not sold out?'

'There was no way, was there?' D. said.

'They didn't trust you—or why should we have been employed? . . .'

He listened with his fingers on the gun. If you were the jury as well as the judge—the attorney too—you had to give every chance: you had to be fair even if the whole world was biased. 'Go on.'

Mr. K. was encouraged. His pink-rimmed eyes peered up, trying to focus; he moved the muscles of his mouth into a testing smile. He said, 'And then, of course, you did behave oddly—didn't you? How could we tell that you wouldn't sell at a price?'

'True.'

'Everyone has to look after himself. If you had sold—we should have got nothing.'

It was a rather dreadful revelation of human depravity. Mr. K. had been more bearable when he was frightened, cringing. . . . Now his courage was coming back. He said, 'It's no good being left behind. After all, there's no hope.'

'No hope?'

'You've only to read the paper to-night. We are beaten. Why, you know yourself how many Ministers have ratted. You don't think they are getting nothing, do you?'

'I wonder what you got.'

Mr. K. found his glasses and shifted on the divan. Fear had almost entirely left him; he had a look of old and agile cunning. He said, 'I thought sooner or later we'd come to that.'

'It would be best to tell me everything.'

'If you want a cut,' Mr. K. said, 'you won't get it. Not even if I wanted . . .'

'Surely you haven't been foolish enough to sell for credit?'

'They knew better than to offer—to a man like me—money.'

D. was at a loss. He said incredulously, 'You mean—you've got nothing out of it?'

'What I've got's in writing. Signed by L.'

'I never thought you were quite such a fool. If it were only promises you wanted, you could have had as many from us.'

'This isn't a promise. It's an appointment. Signed by the Chancellor. You know L.'s the Chancellor now. That would be since your time.' He sounded positively at ease again.

'Chancellor of what?'

'The University, of course. I have been made a professor. I am on the Faculty. I can go home again.'

D. laughed, he couldn't help it; but there was disgust behind the laughter. This was to be the civilisation of the future, the scholarship of the future.... He said, 'It's a comfort to think, if I kill you, I'm killing Professor K.' He had a hideous vision of a whole world of poets, musicians, scholars, artists—in steel-rimmed spectacles with pink eyes and old treacherous brains—the survivals of an antique worn-out world teaching the young the useful lessons of treachery and dependence. He took out the secretary's gun. He said, 'I wonder who they'll appoint in your place.' But he knew they had hundreds to choose from.

'Don't play about with a gun like that. It's dangerous.'

D. said, 'If you were at home now, you would be put on trial by a military court and sentenced. Why do you think you ought to escape here?'

'You're joking,' Mr. K. said, trying to laugh.

D. opened the revolver: there were two shots in it.

Mr. K. said frantically, 'You said if I hadn't killed the girl, I'd be safe...'

'Well?' He closed the breach again.

'I didn't kill her. I only telephoned to Marie...'

199

'Marie? Oh yes, the manageress. Go on.'

'L. told me to. He rang me up from the Embassy. He said, "Just tell her—do what you can."'

'And you didn't know what that meant?'

'Not exactly. How could I? I only knew she had a plan ... to get you deported. She never meant it to look like murder. It was when the police read the diary ... it all fitted in. There was what you said—about taking her away.'

'You know a lot.'

'Marie told me—afterwards. It all came to her like a revelation. She had meant to frame a robbery. And then the girl, you see, was—insolent. She just thought she'd give her a scare—and then she lost her temper. You know she has an awful temper, and no control. No control at all.' He tried again that testing smile. 'It's only one girl,' he said, 'out of thousands. They die every day at home. It's war.' Something in D.'s face made him add too quickly, 'That was how Marie argued it.'

'And what did you say?'

'Oh, I was against it.'

'Before it happened—you were against it?'

'Yes. No, no, I mean ... afterwards. When I saw her afterwards.'

D. said, 'It won't hold water. You knew all right all along.'

'I swear I wasn't there ...'

'Oh, I believe you. You wouldn't have the

200

nerve. That was left to her.'

'It's *her* you want.'

'I've got a prejudice,' D. said, 'against killing women. But she'll suffer all right, when you are found dead.... She'll be left wondering, I daresay ... listening to sounds.... Besides, I've only two bullets. And I don't know how to get more.' He put up the safety catch.

'This is England,' the little grey man shrieked as if he wanted to convince himself. He started to his feet and knocked a book off the shelf—it fell open upon the divan—a little book of devotional verse with 'God' in capital letters. Certainly it was England—England was the divan, the waste-paper basket made out of old flower prints, the framed Speed map and the cushions: the alien atmosphere plucked at D.'s sleeve, urged him to desist. He said furiously, 'Get off that divan.'

Mr. K. got up tremulously. He said, 'You'll let me go.'

Years of academic life might make one a good judge: it didn't make one a good executioner.

'Why not L.?' Mr. K. implored him.

'Oh, I'll deal with L. one day. But he isn't one of us.' The distinction was real: you couldn't feel the same rage towards a museum piece.

Mr. K. thrust out his ink-stained hands with an air of pleading. He said, 'You couldn't blame me if you knew. The life I've had. Oh, they write books about slavery.' He began to cry.

'You pity *her*, but it's me,' he said, 'it's me...'
Words failed him.

'Get back through that door,' D. said. The bathroom couldn't be seen from outside. It had ventilation but no window. The hand which held the gun shook with the impending horror. They had pushed him around ... it was his turn now, but fear was returning—the fear of other people's pain, their lives, their individual despairs. He was damned like a creative writer to sympathy.... He said, 'Go on. Hurry,' and Mr. K. began to stumble back. D. raked his mind for any heartless joke—'We haven't got a cemetery wall...' but it petered out. You could only joke about your own death. Other people's deaths were important.

Mr. K. said, 'She hadn't lived through what I had ... fifty-five years of it.... And then to have only six months more, and no hope at all.'

D. tried not to listen, didn't in any case understand. He followed Mr. K. with the gun held before him with revulsion.

'If you had only six months, wouldn't you choose a little comfort..?' The glasses slipped off his nose and smashed. He said 'respect' with a sob. He said, 'I always dreamt one day ... the university.' He was in the bathroom now, staring blindly where he supposed D. to be, backing towards the basin. 'And then the doctor said six months...' He gave a yelp of mournful anguish like a dog ... 'die in harness ... with that fool in Oxford Street ... "bona matina," "bona matina" ... cold ... the radiator's never on.' He was raving now—the first words which came into his head as if he had a sense that as long as he talked he was safe; and any words which emerged from that tormented and embittered brain couldn't help but carry the awful impress of the little office, the cubicle, the cold radiator, the roller picture on the wall: 'un famil gentilbono.' He said, 'The old man creeping round on rubber soles ... I'd get the pain ... had to apologise in Entrenationo ... or else the fine ... no cigarettes for a week.' With every word he came alive ... and the condemned must not come alive: he must be dead long before the judge passes ssntence. 'Stop!' D. said. Mr. K.'s head switched round like a tortoise's. The blind eyes had got the direction wrong. 'Can you blame me?' he said. 'Six months at home ... a professor...' D. shut his eyes and pressed the trigger: the noise took him by surprise and the enormous kick of the gun: glass smashed, and somewhere a bell rang.

He opened his eyes: he had missed: he must have missed. The mirror of the basin was smashed a foot away from Mr. K.'s old head. Mr. K. was on his feet blinking, with a look of perplexity ... somebody was knocking on the door. One bullet gone.

D. said, 'Don't move. Don't make a sound. I

won't miss twice,' and shut the door. He was alone by the divan again, listening to the knock, knock on the area door. If it were the police what was he to do with his only bullet? There was silence again everywhere else. The little book lay open on the divan:

> 'God is in the sunlight,
> Where the butterflies roam,
> God is in the candlelight,
> Waiting in your home.'

The absurd poem was like a wax impress on his brain; he didn't believe in God, he had no home: it was like the incantation of a savage tribe which has an effect on even the most civilised beholder. Knock! Knock! Knock! and then a ring again. Was it one of the owner's friends, the owner herself? No, she would have a key. It must be the police.

He moved slowly across the room, gun in hand. He had forgotten the gun just as he had forgotten the razor. He opened the door like a doomed man.

It was Rose.

He said slowly, 'Of course. I forgot. I gave you my address, didn't I?' He looked over her shoulder as if he expected to see the police—or Forbes.

She said, 'I came to tell you what Furt said.'

'Oh yes, yes.'

She said, 'You haven't done anything, have you—wild?'

'No.'

'Why the gun?'

'I thought you might be the police.'

They came into the room and shut the area door. He had his eye on the bathroom: it was no good, he knew now he would never shoot. He might be a good judge, but he would never make an executioner. War toughened you but not to that extent: he carried around his neck like a dead albatross the lectures in Romance, the Song of Roland, the Berne MS.

She said, 'My dear—how strange you look! Younger.'

'The moustache . . .'

'Of course. It suits you like that.'

He said impatiently, 'What did Furt say?'

'They've signed.'

'But it's against your own law.'

'They haven't signed a contract direct with L. You can always get round the law. The coal will go by Holland . . .'

He had a sense of complete failure; he wasn't even capable of shooting a traitor. She said, 'You'll have to go. Before the police find you.' He sat on the divan with the gun hanging between his knees. He said, 'And Forbes signed too?'

'You can't blame him.' Again he felt the odd prick of jealousy. She said, 'He doesn't like it.'

'Why?'

She said, 'You know he's honest, in a way. You can trust him when the wind's blowing east.'

He said thoughtfully, 'I've got another shot.'

'What do you mean?' She sounded scared. She was looking at the gun.

'Oh,' he said. 'I didn't mean that. I mean the miners. The unions. If they knew what this really meant, mightn't they...?'

'What?'

'Do something.'

'What could they do?' she said. 'You don't know how things are here. You've never seen a mining village when all the pits are closed. You've lived in a revolution—you've had too much cheering and shouting and waving of flags.' She said, 'I've been with my father to one of these places. He was making a tour—with royalty. There's no spirit left.'

'Do you care, then?'

She said: 'Of course I care. Wasn't my grandfather...'

'Do you know anybody there among the workers?'

She said: 'My old nurse is there. She married a miner. But my father gives her a pension. She's not as badly off as some.'

'Anybody would do for a start.'

'You still don't understand. You can't go making speeches. You'd be in gaol at once.

You're wanted.'

'I'm not going to give up yet.'

'Listen. We can smuggle you out of here somehow. Money will do a lot. From one of the small ports. Swansea . . .'

He looked carefully up at her, 'Would you like that?'

'Oh, I know what you mean all right. But I like a man alive—not dead or in prison. I couldn't love you for a month if you were dead. I'm not that sort. I can't be faithful to people I don't see. Like you are.' He was playing absentmindedly with the revolver. She said, 'Give me that thing . . . I can't bear . . .'

He handed it across to her without a word. It was his first action of trust.

She said, 'Oh God! that's the smell. I thought there was something wrong. You've used it. You *have* killed . . .'

'Oh no. I tried to, but it wouldn't work. I'm a coward, I suppose. All I hit was the mirror. That's bad luck, isn't it?'

'Was it just before I rang?'

'Yes.'

'I heard something. I thought it was a car backfiring.'

He said, 'Luckily nobody in this place knows the *real* sound.'

'Where is he, then?'

'In there.'

She pulled the door open. Mr. K. must have

been listening hard; he came forward into the room on his knees. D. said gloomily, 'That's Professor K.' Then he slumped over and lay with his knees drawn up on the floor. D. said, 'He's fainted.' She stood over Mr. K. and looked at him with disgust. She said, 'You are sure you missed?'

'Oh yes, I missed all right.'

'Because,' she said, 'he's dead. Any fool can see that.'


### III


MR. K. was laid carefully out on the divan: the pious book lay by his ear. 'God is in the candlelight, waiting in your home.' He looked excessively unimportant with a red rim across the bridge of his nose where the spectacles had rubbed it. D. said, 'His doctor had given him six months. He was afraid he was going to end— suddenly—teaching Entrenationo. They paid him two shillings an hour.'

'What are we going to do?'

'It was an accident.'

'He died because you shot at him—they can call that murder.'

'Technically murder?'

'Yes.'

'It's the second time. I should like to be

charged with an honest malice-aforethought murder for a change.'

'You always joke when it's you who are concerned,' she said.

'Do I?'

She was in a rage again about something. When she was angry she was like a child, stamping and raging against authority and reason. Then he could feel an immense tenderness for her because she might have been his daughter. She made no demands on him for passionate love. She said, 'Don't stand there as if nothing had happened. What are we going to do with him—it?'

He said gently, 'I've been thinking about that. This is Saturday night. The woman who has this flat put out a notice—"No Milk till Monday." That means she won't be back before to-morrow night at the earliest. It gives me twenty-four hours—I can get to the mines by the morning, can't I, if I catch a train now.'

'They'll pick you up at the station. You're wanted already. Besides,' she said furiously, 'it's a waste of time. I tell you they haven't got any spirit left. They just live, that's all. I was born there. I know the place.'

'It's worth a try.'

She said, 'I don't mind your being dead. But I can't bear your dying.' She had no sense of shame at all—she acted and spoke without reserves. He remembered her coming down the foggy platform with the buns. It was impossible not to love her—in a way. After all, they had something in common. They had both been pushed around, and they were both revolting against the passive past with a violence which didn't really belong to them. She said, 'It's no good saying—for my sake—like they do in stories. I know that.'

'I'd do a lot,' he said, 'for your sake.'

'Oh God!' she said, 'don't pretend. Go on being honest. That's why I love you—that and my neuroses, Œdipus complexes, and the rest.'

'I'm not pretending.' He took her in his arms; it wasn't this time such a failure: everything was there except desire. He couldn't feel desire. It was as if he had made himself a eunuch for his people's sake. Every lover was, in his way, a philosopher: nature saw to that. A love had to believe in the world, in the value of birth. Contraception didn't alter that. The act of desire remained an act of faith, and he had lost his faith.

She wasn't furious any more. She said sadly, 'What happened to your wife?'

'They shot her accidentally.'

'How?'

'They took her as a hostage for the wrong man. They had hundreds. I expect, to the warders, they all looked much alike.' He wondered whether it would seem odd to quiet people, this making love with a dead wife on the tongue and a dead man on the divan. It wasn't very successful, anyway. A kiss gives away too much . . . it is far more difficult to falsify than a voice. The lips when together expressed a limitless vacancy.

She said, 'It seems odd to me, this loving someone who's dead.'

'It happens to most people. Your mother . . .'

'Oh, I don't love her,' she said. 'I'm a bastard. Legitimised by marriage, of course. It oughtn't to matter, ought it, but in a curious way one resents having been unwanted—even then.'

It was impossible to tell what was pity and what was love, without a trial. They embraced again beside Mr. K. Over her left shoulder he could see Mr. K.'s open eyes, and he let her go. He said, 'It's no use. I'm no good to you. I'm not a man any longer. Perhaps one day when all the killing has stopped . . .'

She said, 'My dear, I don't mind waiting . . . as long as you're alive.'

It was, in the circumstances, an enormous qualification.

He said, 'You'd better go now. Make sure nobody sees you when you go out. Don't take a taxi within a mile of this place.'

'What are you going to do?'

'Which station?'

She said, 'There's a train from Euston somewhere near midnight. . . . God knows when it gets there on a Sunday morning ... you'd have to change.... They'll recognise you, anyway.'

'Shaving off the moustache made a difference.'

'The scar's still there. That's what people look for.' She said, 'Wait a moment,' and when he tried to speak she interrupted him. 'I'll go. I'm going to be sensible, do anything that you say, let you go—anywhere. There's no point in not being sensible. But wait just a moment.' She disappeared into the bathroom; her feet crunched on Mr. K.'s spectacles. She returned very quickly. 'Thank God,' she said, 'she's a careful women.' She had some cotton-wool in her hand and some plaster. She said, 'Stand still. No one's going to see that scar.' She laid the cotton-wool over his cheek and stuck it down with the plaster. 'It looks convincing,' she said, 'like a boil.'

'But it's not over the scar.'

'That's the cunning. The plaster's over the scar. The cotton-wool's right up on your cheek. Nobody's going to notice that you are covering something on your chin.' She held his head between her hands and said, 'I'd make a good confidential agent, don't you think?'

'You're too good for that.' he said. 'Nobody trusts a confidential agent.' He suddenly felt a tremendous gratitude that there was somebody in the warring crooked uncertain world he could trust besides himself, It was like finding, in the awful solitude of a desert, a companion. He said, 'My dear, my love's not much good to anyone now—but it's all yours—what's left of it,' but while he spoke he could feel the steady tug of a pain which united him to a grave.

She said gently, as if she were speaking in terms of love, 'You've got a chance. Your English is good—but it's terribly literary. Your accent's sometimes queer—but it's the books you've read which really give you away. Try to forget you were ever a lecturer in the Romance languages.' She began to put her hand up to his face again when the bell rang.

They stood motionless in the middle of the little female room: it was like a legend where death interrupts love. The bell rang again.

He said, 'Isn't there somewhere where you can hide?' But of course there wasn't. He said: 'If it's the police you must accuse me straight away. I won't have you mixed up in things.'

'What's the use?'

'Go and open the door.' He took Mr. K. by the shoulders and turned him over to face the wall. He pulled the counterpane up round him. He was in shadow; you couldn't very easily see the open eyes: it was just possible to believe that he was asleep. He heard the door open: a voice said, 'Oh, excuse me. My name's Fortescue.'

The stranger came timidly and penetratingly in: an old-young man with receding hair and a double-breasted waistcoat. Rose tried to bar his way. She said, 'Well?' He repeated 'Fortescue' with weak good humour.

'Who the hell are you?'

He blinked at them. He had no hat or coat. He said, 'You know I live up above. Isn't Emily—that is Miss Glover—here?'

D. said, 'She's away for the week-end.'

'I knew she meant to go—but when I saw a light...' He said, 'Good God, what's that?'

'That,' Rose said, 'as you so winningly put it, is Jack—Jack Owtram.'

'Is he ill?'

'He will be—he's passed out. We've been having a party.'

He said, 'How very extraordinary. I mean Emily—Miss Glover—'

'Oh, call her Emily,' Rose said. 'We're all friends here.'

'Emily never has parties.'

'She lent us the flat.'

'Yes. Yes. So I see.'

'Do you want a drink?'

That's going too far, D. thought: this flat can't supply everything; we may be wrecked, but this isn't a schoolboy wreck which supplies the right thing to Crusoe at the right time.

'No, no, thank you,' Fortescue said. 'As a matter of fact, I don't—drink, I mean.'

'You must. Nobody can live without drinking.'

'Oh, water. I drink water, of course.'

'You do?'

'Oh yes, undoubtedly.' He looked nervously again at the body on the bed, then at D. like a sentry beside it. He said, 'You've hurt your face.'

'Yes.' Silence was present: it was the most prominent thing there, like the favoured guest who outwaits all the others. Fortescue said, 'Well, I must be getting back.'

'Must you?' Rose said.

'Well, not literally. I mean, I don't want to interrupt a party.' He was looking round—for the bottles and glasses: there were things about this room he obviously couldn't understand. But the awful fact was beyond his suspicion; his world didn't contain horror. He said, 'Emily didn't warn me...'

'You seem to see a lot of Emily.'

He blushed. He said, 'Oh, we're good friends. We're both Groupers, you see.'

'Gropers?'

'No, no. Groupers. Oxford Groupers.'

'Oh yes,' Rose said. 'I know—house parties, Brown's Hotel, Crowborough...' She reeled off a string of associations which were incomprehensible to D. Was she going to be hysterical?

Fortescue brightened. His old-young face was like a wide white screen on which you could project only selected and well-censored films for the family circle. He said, 'Have you ever been?'

'Oh no. It wouldn't suit me.'

He began to penetrate back into the room towards the divan; he had a liquid manner; you had to be very careful how you tilted the conversation or he would flow all over the place. He said, 'You ought to try. We have all kinds of people—business men, Blues—we once had the Under-Secretary for Overseas Trade. And of course there's always Frankie.' He was almost up to the divan explaining ardently, 'It's religion—but it's practical. It helps you to get on—because you feel *right* towards people. We've had an enormous success in Norway.'

'That's fine,' Rose said, trying to tilt him the other way.

He said, with his rather protuberant eyes upon the head of Mr. K., 'And if you feel bad about things—you know what I mean—there's nothing clears the air like sharing . . . at a house party. The other fellows are always sympathetic. They've been through it too.' He leant a little forward and said, 'He does look ill . . . are you quite sure?'

It was a fantastic country, D. thought. Civil war provided nothing so fantastic as peace. In war life became simple—you didn't worry about sex or international languages or even getting on: you worried about the next meal and cover from high explosives. Fortescue said, 'Wouldn't he feel better if—well—you know—if he

216

brought it up?'

'Oh no,' Rose said, 'he's better as he is—just lying quiet.'

'Of course,' he said meekly, 'I don't know much about these things. Parties, I mean. I suppose he doesn't hold his drink very well. He oughtn't to do it—ought he?—it can't be good for him. And such an old man too. Forgive me—if he's a great friend . . .'

'You needn't mind,' Rose said. D. wondered: will he never go? Only the warmest heart could have failed to be frozen by Rose's manner.

'I know I must sound prejudiced. You see in the Group we learn to be ascetic—in a reasonable way.' He said, 'I suppose you wouldn't care to step upstairs to my place . . . I've got a kettle boiling now for tea. I was going to ask Emily . . .' He leant suddenly forward and said, 'Good heavens, his eyes are open . . .' This is the end, D. thought.

Rose said slowly, 'You didn't think—did you?—he was asleep."

You could almost see a terrible surmise come up behind the eyes, then fall again for the mere want of foothold. There was no room for murder in his gentle and spurious world. They waited for what he would say next: they had no plan at all. He said in a whisper, 'How dreadful to think that he heard everything I said about him.'

Rose said harshly and nervously, 'Your kettle

will be all over the floor.'

He looked from one to the other of them—something was wrong. 'Yes, it will be, won't it? I hadn't meant to stay.' Back and forth from one to the other as if he wanted reassurance—tonight he would have bad dreams. 'Yes, I must be going. Good night.'

They watched him climbing up the area steps into the safe familiar reassuring dark. At the top he turned and waved his hand to them, tentatively.

PART THREE

# THE LAST SHOT

## I

It was still dark over the whole quiet Midland countryside. The small unimportant junction lay lit up like a centre-piece in a darkened shop window: oil lamps burned beside the General Waiting Room, an iron footbridge straddled across towards another smoky flame, and the cold wind took the steam of the engine and flapped it back along the platform. It was Sunday morning.

Then the tail-light of the train moved on like a fire-fly and was suddenly extinguished in some

218

invisible tunnel. D. was alone except for one old porter hobbling back from where the luggage van had stood: the platform sloped down past a lamp into the indecipherable wilderness of lines. Somewhere not far away a cock crew, and a light which hung in mid-air changed from red to green.

'Is this right for the Benditch train?' D. called out.

'It'll be right,' the porter said.

'Is it a long wait?'

'Oh, it'll be an hour ... if it's on time.'

D. shivered and beat his arms against his body for warmth. 'That's a long time,' he said.

'You can't expect different,' the porter said. 'Not on a Sunday.'

'Don't they have any through trains?'

'Ah, they used to when the pits was working—but no one goes to Benditch now.'

'Is there a restaurant here?' D. said.

'A restaurant!' the porter exclaimed, peering closely up at him. 'What call would there for a restaurant at Willing?'

'Somewhere to sit?'

'I'll open the waiting-room for you—if you like,' the porter said. 'It's cold in there, though. Better to keep moving.'

'Isn't there a fire?'

'Well, it might've kept in.' He took a monstrous key out of his pocket and opened a chocolate-coloured door. 'Ah well,' he said, 'it's

219

not so bad,' switching on the light. There were old faded photographs all round the walls of hotels and resorts, fixed benches round the walls, two or three hard movable chairs and an enormous table. A faint warmth—the memory of a fire—came out of the grate. The porter picked up a black ornamental cast-iron scuttle and shook a lot of coal-dust on to the dying embers. He said, 'That'll keep it in.'

D. said, 'And the table. What's the table for?'

The porter looked at him with sharp suspicion. He said, 'To sit at. What d'you think?'

'But the benches won't move.'

'That's true. They won't.' He said, 'Darn it, I've been here twenty years an' I never thought of that. You're a foreigner, ain't you?'

'Yes.'

'They're sharp, foreigners.' He stared moodily at the table. 'Most times,' he said, 'they sit on it.' Outside there was a cry, a roar, a cloud of white steam, wheels pounding past and fading out, a whistle again and silence. He said, 'That'll be the four-fifty-five.'

'An express?'

'Fast goods.'

'But not for the mines?'

'Oh no—for Woolhampton. Munitions.'

D. bent his arms for warmth and walked slowly round the room. A tiny pillar of smoke fumed upwards in the grate. There was a

photograph of a pier: a gentleman in a grey
bowler and a Norfolk jacket was leaning over a
handrail talking to a lady in a picture hat and
white muslin—there was a perspective of
parasols. D. felt himself touched by an odd
happiness, as if he were out of time altogether
and already belonged to history with the
gentleman in the bowler: all the struggle and
violence over, wars decided one way or another,
out of pain. A great Gothic pile marked
'Midland Hotel' stared out across some tramlines, the statue of a man in a leaden frock-coat,
and a public lavatory. 'Ah,' the porter said,
giving the coal-dust a stir with a broken poker.
'What you're looking at's Woolhampton itself.
I was there in 1902.'

'It looks a busy place.'

'It is busy. An' that hotel—you won't find a
better in the Midlands. We 'ad a Lodge dinner
there—in 1902. Balloons,' he said, 'a lady sang.
An' there's Turkish baths.'

'You miss it, I daresay.'

'Oh, I don't know. There's something to be
said for any place—that's how I look at it. Of
course at Christmas time I miss the panto. The
Woolhampton Empire's famous for its panto.
But on the other 'and—it's 'ealthy here. You can
see too much of life,' he said, poking at the coal-
dust.

'I suppose this was quite an important station
once.'

'Ah, when the mines was working. I've had Lord Benditch waiting in this very room. *And* his daughter—the Honourable Miss Rose Cullen.'

D. realised that he was listening—avidly, as if he were a young man in love. He said, 'You've seen Miss Cullen?' and an engine whistled somewhere over the waste of rails and was answered, like a dog calling to other dogs in the suburb of a city.

'Ah, that I have. The last time I saw her here, it was only a week before she was presented—at the Court—to the King an' Queen.' It filled him with sadness—the vast social life going on all round her in which he had no part at all. He felt like a divorced man whose child is in another's custody—somebody richer and abler than himself; he has to watch a stranger's progress through the magazines. He found he wanted to claim her. He remembered her on the platform at Euston. She had said, 'We are unlucky. We don't believe in God. So it's no use praying. If we did I could say beads, burn candles—oh, a hundred things. As it is, I can only keep my fingers crossed.' In the taxi, at his request, she had given him back his gun. She had said, 'For God's sake be careful. You are such a fool. Remember the Berne MS. You aren't Roland. Don't walk under ladders . . . or spill salt.'

The porter said, 'Her mother came from these parts. There's stories . . .'

222

Here he was: shut out for a little while from the monstrous world. He could see—from the security and isolation of this cold waiting-room—just how monstrous it was. And yet there were people who talked of a superintending design. It was a crazy mixture—the presentation at Court, his own wife shot in the prison yard, pictures in the *Tatler* and the bombs falling; it was all hopelessly jumbled together by their mutual relationship as they had stood side by side near Mr. K.'s body and talked to Fortescue. The accomplice-to-be of a murderer had received an invitation to a Royal Garden Party. It was as if he had the chemical property of reconciling irreconcilables. After all, even in his own case it might have seemed a long way from his lectures on Romance to the blind shot at K. in the bathroom of a strange woman's basement flat. How was it possible for anyone to plan his life or regard the future with anything but apprehension?

But he had to regard the future. He came to a stop in front of a beach scene—bathing huts and sand-castles and all the dreary squalor of a front reproduced with remarkable veracity—the sense of blown newspapers and half-eaten bananas. The railway companies had been well advised to leave photography and take to art. He thought: if they catch me, of course, there *is* no future—that was simple. But if, somehow, he evaded them and returned home, *there* was the problem.

She had said, 'It's no good shaking me off now.'

The porter said, 'When she was a little thing she used to give away the prizes—for the best station garden in the county. That was before her ma died. Lord Benditch, he always overmarked for roses.'

She couldn't come back with him to his sort of life—the life of an untrusted man in a country at war. And what could he give her, anyway? The grave held him.

He went outside; it was still pitch dark beyond the little platform, but you were aware that somewhere there was light. Beyond the rim of the turning world, a bell, as it were, had rung in warning ... perhaps there was a greyness.... He walked up and down, up and down: there was no solution except failure. He paused by a slot machine: a dry choice of raisins, chocolate creams, matches and chewing-gum. He inserted a penny under the raisins, but the drawer remained stuck. The porter appeared suddenly behind him and said accusingly, 'Did you try a crooked penny?'

'No. But it doesn't matter.'

'Some of them are so artful,' the man said, 'you can't trust them not to get two packets with one penny.' He rattled the machine. 'I'll just go an' get the key,' he said.

'It's doesn't matter. It really doesn't matter.'

'Oh, we can't have that,' the porter said, limping away.

A lamp lit each end of the platform; he walked from one to the other and back again. The dawn came with a kind of careful and prepared slowness. It was like a ritual—the dimming of the lamps, the cocks crowing again, and then the silvering of the sky. The siding loomed slowly up with a row of trucks marked 'Benditch Collieries,' the rails stretched out towards a fence, a dark shape which became a barn and then an ugly blackened winter field. Other platforms came into sight, shuttered and dead. The porter was back, opening the slot machine. 'Ah,' he said, 'it's the wet. They don't care for raisins here. The drawer's rusty.' He pulled out a greyish paper carton. 'There,' he said, 'there you are.' It felt old and damp to the fingers.

'Didn't you say it was healthy here?'

'That's right. The 'ealthy Midlands.'

'But the damp . . .'

'Ah,' he said, 'but the station's in the holler—see?' And sure enough the dark was shredding off like vapour from a long hillside. The light came drably up behind the barn and the field, over the station and the siding, crept up the hill. Brick cottages detached themselves; the stumps of trees reminded him of a battlefield; an odd metallic object rose over the crest. He said, 'What's that?'

'Oh, that,' the porter said, 'that's nothing. That was just a notion they got.'

225

'An ugly-looking notion.'

'Ugly? You'd say that, would you? I don't know. You get used to things. I'd miss it if it weren't there.'

'It looks like something to do with oil.'

'That's what it is. They had a fool notion they'd find oil here. We could've told 'em—but they were Londoners. They thought they knew.'

'There was no oil?'

'Oh, they got enough to light these lamps with, I daresay.' He said, 'You won't have so long to wait now. There's Jarvis coming down the hill.' You could see the road now as far as the cottages; there was a little colour in the east, and all the world except the sky had the blackness of frost-bitten vegetation.

'Who is Jarvis?'

'Oh, he goes into Benditch every Sunday. Week-days too, sometimes.'

'Works at the mines?'

'No, he's too old for that. Says he likes the change of air. Some says his old woman's there—but Jarvis, he says he's not married.' He came plodding up the little gravelled drive to the station—an elderly man in corduroys with bushy eyebrows and dark evasive eyes and a white stubble on the chin. 'How's things, George?' the porter said.

'Aw—might be worse.'

'Going in to see the old woman?'

Jarvis gave a sidelong and suspicious glance and looked away.

'This gentleman's going to Benditch. He's a foreigner.'

'Ah!'

D. felt as a typhoid-carrier must feel when he finds himself among the safe and inoculated: these he couldn't infect. They were secured from the violence and horror he carried with him. He felt an enormous inanition as if at last, among the frost-bitten fields, in the quiet of the deserted junction, he had reached a place where he could sit down, rest, let time pass. The voice of the porter droned on beside him—'Bloody frost killed every one of the bloody . . .'; every now and then Jarvis said, 'Ah!' staring down the track. Presently a bell rang twice in a signal box; one noticed suddenly that unobtrusively the night had quite gone. In the signal box he could see a man holding a teapot; he put it down out of sight and tugged a lever. A signal— somewhere—creaked down and Jarvis said, 'Ah!'

'Here's your train,' the porter said. At the far end of a track a small blob of steam like a rose advanced, became an engine, a string of vibrating carriages. 'Is it far to Benditch?' D. asked.

'Oh, it wouldn't be more than fifteen miles, would it, George?'

'Fourteen miles from the church to the "Red

Lion.'''

'It's not the distance,' the porter said, 'it's the stops.'

A row of frosty windows split up the pale early morning sun like crystals. A few stubbly faces peered out into the early day; D. climbed into an empty carriage after Jarvis and saw the porter, the general waiting-room, the ugly iron foot-bridge, the signalman holding a cup of tea, go backwards like peace. The low frosty hills closed round the track: a farm building, a ragged wood like an old fur toque, ice on a little ditch beside the line—it wasn't grand, it wasn't even pretty, but it had a quality of quiet and desertion. Jarvis stared out at it without a word.

D. said, 'You know Benditch well?'

'Ah!'

'You might know Mrs. Bennett?'

'George Bennett's wife or Arthur's?'

'The one who was nurse to Lord Benditch's girl.'

'Ah!'

'You know her?'

'Ah!'

'Where does she live?'

Jarvis gave him a long suspicious look from his blue pebbly eyes. He said, 'What do you want *her* for?'

'I've got a message for her.'

'She's one door up from the "Red Lion."'

The woods and meagre grass gave out as they

pottered on from stop to stop. The hills became rocky a quarry lay behind a halt and a rusting single line led out to it: a small truck lay overturned in the thorny grass. Then even the hills gave out and a long plain opened up dotted with strange erratic heaps of slag—the height of the hills behind. Short unsatisfactory grass crept up them like gas flames, miniature railways petered out, going to nowhere at all, and right beneath the artificial hills the cottages began— lines of grey stone like scars. The train no longer stopped; it rattled deeper into the shapeless plain, passing halts under every slag-heap dignified by names like Castle Crag and Mount Zion. It was like a gigantic rubbish heap into which everything had been thrown of a whole way of life—great rusting lift-shafts and black chimneys and Nonconformist chapels with slate roofs and hopeless washing darkening on the line and children carrying pails of water from common taps. It was odd to think the country lay only just behind—ten miles away the cocks were crowing outside the junction. The cottages were continuous now, built up against the slag and branching out in narrow streets towards the railway: the only division the tracks to each black hill. D. said, 'Is this Benditch?'

'Naw. This is Paradise.'

They ground over a crossing under the shadow of another heap. 'Is *this* Benditch?'

'Naw. This is Cowcumberill.'

'How do you tell the difference?'

'Ah!'

He stared moodily out—had he got an old woman here or was it for the change of air he came? He said at last very grudgingly—as if he had a grievance, 'Anyone can tell Cowcumberill ain't Benditch.' He said, 'There's Benditch,' as another slag-heap loomed blackly up and the long grey scar of houses just went on. 'Why,' he said, working himself up into a kind of gloomy and patriotic rage, 'you might as well say it was like Castle Crag—or Mount Zion, come to that. You've only got to look.'

He did look. He was used to ruin, but it occurred to him that bombardment was a waste of time. You could attain your ruined world as easily by just letting go.

Benditch had the honour of a station—not a halt. There was even a first-class waiting-room, bolted, with broken glass. He waited for the other to get down, but Jarvis outwaited him, as if he suspected he was being spied on. He gave an effect of innocent and natural secrecy; he distrusted, as an animal distrusts, the strange footstep or the voice near the burrow.

When D. left the station the geography of his last stand stood plainly before him—one street ran down towards the slag-heap and another street crossed it like a T, pressed up under the black hill. Every house was the same: the uniformity was broken only by an inn sign, the

230

front of a chapel, an occasional impoverished shop. There was an air of rather horrifying simplicity about the place, as if it had been built by children with bricks. The two streets were curiously empty for a working-class town, but then, there was no work to go to: it was probably warmer to stay in bed. D. passed a Labour Exchange and then more grey houses with the blinds down in the windows. Once he got a glimpse of horrifying squalor in a backyard where a privy stood open. It was like war, but without the spirit of defiance war usually raised.

The "Red Lion" had once been a hotel. This must have been where Lord Benditch stayed: it had a courtyard and a garage and an old yellow A.A. sign. A smell of gas and privies hung about the street. People watched him—a stranger—through glass, without much interest: it was too cold to come out and exchange greetings. Mrs Bennett's house was just the same grey stone as all the rest, but the curtains looked cleaner; there was almost a moneyed air when you looked in through the window to the little unused and crowded parlour. D. beat the knocker; it was of polished brass, in the shape of a shield and a coat of arms—the Benditch arms?—a mysterious feathered animal seemed to be holding a leaf in its mouth. It looked curiously complicated in the simple town—like an algebraic equation, it represented an abstract set of values out of place in the stony concrete street.

An elderly woman in an apron opened the door. Her face was withered and puckered and white like old clean bone. 'Are you Mrs. Bennett?' D. asked

'I am.' She barred the way into the house with her foot like a doorstop on the threshold.

'I have a letter for you,' D. said, 'from Miss Cullen.'

'Do you know Miss Cullen?' she asked him with disapproval and incredulity.

'You will read it all there.' But she wouldn't let him in until she had read it, very slowly, without spectacles, holding the paper up close to the pale obstinate eyes. 'She writes here,' she said, 'that you're her dear friend. You'd better come in. She says I'm to help you ... but she doesn't say how.'

'I'm sorry it's so early.'

'It's the only train on a Sunday. You can't be expected to walk. Was George Jarvis on the train?'

'Yes.'

'Ah!'

The little parlour was crammed with china ornaments and photographs in tortuous silver frames. A round mahogany table, a velvet-covered sofa, hard chairs with twisted backs and velvet seats, newspaper spread on the floor to save the carpet—it was like a scene set for something which had never happened, which would never happen now. Mrs Bennett said sternly with a gesture towards a silver frame, 'You'll recognise that, I suppose?' A white plump female child held a doll unconvincingly. He said, 'I'm afraid . . .'

'Ah!' Mrs Bennett said with a kind of bitter triumph. 'She hasn't shown you everything, I dare say. See that pin-cushion?'

'Yes.'

'That was made out of her presentation dress—what she wore to meet Their Majesties. Turn it over and you'll see the date.' It was there—picked out in white silk—that was the year he had been in prison waiting to be shot. It was one of the years in her life too. 'And there,' Mrs. Bennett said, 'she is—in the dress. You'll know *that* picture.' Very formal and absurdly young and recognisably Rose, she watched him from a velvet frame. The little room seemed full of her.

'No,' he said, 'I have never seen that either.'

She glared at him with satisfaction. She said, 'Oh well, old friends are best, I daresay.'

'You must be a very old friend.'

'The oldest,' she rapped out at him. 'I knew her when she was a week old. Even His Lordship didn't see her then—not till she'd passed her first month.'

'She spoke of you,' D. lied, 'very warmly.'

'She had cause,' Mrs. Bennett said, tossing her white bony head. 'I did everything for her—

after her mother died.' It's always odd, learning the biography of someone you love at second-hand—like finding a secret drawer in a familiar desk full of revealing documents.

'Was she a good child?' he inquired with amusement.

'She had spirit. I don't ask for more,' Mrs. Bennett said. She went agitatedly around, patting the pin-cushion, pushing the photographs a little this way and that. She said, 'Nobody expects to be remembered. Though I don't complain of His Lordship. He's been generous. As was only proper. I don't know how we'd manage otherwise with the pits closed.'

'Rose told me she writes to you—regularly. So *she* remembers you.'

'At Christmas,' Mrs. Bennett said. 'Yes. She doesn't say much—but, of course, she hasn't time in London with parties and so on. I thought she might have told me what His Majesty said to her . . . but then . . .'

'Perhaps he said nothing.'

'Of course he said something. She's a lovely girl.'

'Yes. Lovely.'

'I only hope,' Mrs. Bennett said, looking daggers across the china ornaments, 'she knows her friends.'

'I don't think she'd be easy to deceive,' he said, thinking of Mr. Forbes and the private detectives and the whole dreary background of distrust.

'You don't know her like I do. I remember once—at Gwyn Cottage—she cried her eyes out. She was only four and that boy Peter Triffen— deceitful little monkey—he'd got a clockwork mouse.' The old face flushed with ancient battle, 'I'll be sworn that boy never came to any good.' It was strange to think that—in a way— this woman had made her. Her influence had probably been as real as the mother's who had died; perhaps the old bony face sometimes bore expressions he could detect in Rose—if he knew her better. The old woman said suddenly, 'You're a foreigner, aren't you?'

'Yes.'

'Ah!'

He said, 'Miss Cullen will have told you that I'm here on business.'

'She didn't write *what* business.'

'She thought you could tell me a few things about Benditch.'

'Well?'

'I wondered who was the local union leader.'

'You don't want to see *him*, do you?'

'Yes.'

'I can't help you,' Mrs. Bennett said. 'We don't mix with *their* kind. An' you can't tell me Miss Cullen wants anything to do with that lot. Socialists.'

'After all . . . her mother . . .'

'We know what her mother was,' Mrs.

Bennett said sharply, 'but she's dead now, an' what's dead's forgotten.'

'Then you can't help me at all?'

'Won't's the word.'

'Not even his name?'

'Oh, you'll find that out soon enough. For yourself. It's Bates.' A car went by outside; they could hear the brakes go on. 'Now who,' Mrs. Bennett said, 'would be stopping at the "Red Lion"?'

'Where does he live?'

'Down Pit Street. We had royalty once,' Mrs. Bennett said, with her face against the window, trying to see the car. 'Such a pleasant-spoken young man. He came into this house and had a cup of tea—just to show him there was miners' folk who kept their homes clean. He wanted to go into Mrs. Terry's, but they told him she was sick. Oh, she was furious when she heard a child say. "Is it a Dook?" He wondered that she's got anything to clean. Everything's popped. It's as bare as a bone at Terry's. That's why, of course. It wouldn't have been nice for him.'

'I must be going.'

'You can tell her from me,' Mrs. Bennett said, 'that she's got no business with Bates.' She spoke with bitter and wavering authority—the manner of one who could at one time have commanded anything— 'Change your stockings. No more sweets. Drink up that medicine,' but is now afraid that things have

236

changed.

Luggage was being carried into the "Red Lion," and the street had come alive. People stood in knots, defensively, as if ready to retreat, watching the car. He heard a child say: 'Is it a Dook?' He wondered whether Lord Benditch was already acting; it was quick work: the contract had been signed yesterday. Suddenly a rumour began; you couldn't tell where it started. Somebody called out, 'The pit's opening.' The knots, converged together, became a small crowd; they stared at the car as if on its polished and luxurious body they could read definite news. A woman raised a feeble cheer which died out doubtfully. D. said to a man, 'Who is it?'

'Lord Benditch's agent.'

'Can you tell me where Pit Street is?'

'Turn left at the end of the road.'

People were coming out of their houses now all the way along: he walked against a growing tide of hope. A woman called up to a bedroom window, 'The agent's at the "Red Lion," Nell.' He was reminded of an occasion when in the hungry capital a rumour spread that food had arrived: he had watched them swarming down on to the quay, just like this. It hadn't been food but tanks, and they had watched the tanks unloaded with angry indifference. Yet they had needed tanks. He stopped a man and said, 'Where's Bates?'

237

'Number seventeen—if he's there.'

It was just beyond the Baptist chapel, a grey stony symbol of religion with a slate roof. A "Wayside Thought" said enigmatically, "The Beauty of Life is only Invisible to Tired Eyes."

He knocked on the door of No. 17 again and again; nobody answered, and all the time the people went by—the old mackintoshes which wouldn't keep out the cold, the shirt too often washed for any warmth to be left in the thinned flannel. They were the people he was fighting for—and he had a frightening sense now that they were his enemies: he was here to stand between them and hope. He knocked and knocked and knocked without reply.

Then he tried No. 19, and the door came open at once before he expected it. He was off his guard. He looked up and there was Else.

She said, 'Well, who do you want?' standing there like a ghost in the stone doorway, harried and under-nourished and too young. He was shaken: he had to look closely before he saw the differences—the gland scar on the neck, a missing tooth. Of course it wasn't Else. It was only somebody out of the same mould of injustice and bad food.

'I was looking for Mr. Bates.'

'He's next door.'

'I can't make anyone hear.'

'He'll have gone up to the "Red Lion," then—most like.'

'There seems to be a lot of excitement.'

'They say the pit's starting.'

'Aren't you going up?'

'Somebody,' she said, ' 'as got to light the fire, I suppose.' She looked at him with faint curiosity, 'You the foreigner that came in the train with George Jarvis?'

'Yes.'

'He said you wasn't up to any good.' He thought, with a touch of fear, that he hadn't been much good to her double. Why carry this burden of violence into another country? Better be beaten at home, perhaps, than involve others—that was undoubtedly heresy. His party were quite right, of course, not to trust him. She said kindly, 'Not that anyone pays attention to George. What do you want Bates for?'

Well, he wanted everyone to know: this, after all, was a democracy; he'd got to begin sometime—why not here? He said, 'I wanted to tell him where the coal's going—to the rebels in my country.'

'Oh,' she said wearily, 'you're one of that lot, are you?'

'Yes.'

'What's it to do with Bates?'

'I want the men to refuse to work the pits.'

She looked at him with amazement. 'Refuse? Us?'

'Yes.'

'You're off your nut,' she said. 'What's it got

to do with us where the coal goes?'

He turned away: it was hopeless—he felt it now as a conviction. Out of the mouths of children.... She called after him, 'You're crazy. Why should we care?' He went stubbornly back up the street; he had to go on trying until they shut him up, hanged him, shot him, stopped his mouth somehow and relieved him of loyalty and let him rest.

They were singing now outside the "Red Lion": events must be moving fast. There must have been some definite announcement. Two songs were fighting for supremacy—both old ones. He had heard them both when he was working in London years ago. The poor were extraordinarily faithful to old tunes. 'Pack Up Your Troubles' and 'Now Thank We All Our God'—the crowd swayed between the two, and the secular song won. More people knew it. He could see papers being handed from hand to hand—Sunday papers. There seemed to be loads of them on the back seat of the car. D. caught a man's arm and said urgently, 'Where's Bates?'

'He's upstairs with the agent.'

He struggled through the crowd. Somebody stuck a paper into his hand. He couldn't help seeing the head-lines— 'Foreign Coal Deal. Pits to Reopen.' It was a staid Sunday paper of limited imagination which carried conviction. He ran into the lounge of the hotel; he felt an urgent need to do something now—before the hope was too strong. The place was empty—big stuffed fish hung on the walls in glass cases—there must have been a time when people came to the district for sport. He went upstairs—nobody about. They were cheering now outside; something was happening. He threw open a big door marked "Drawing Room" and immediately faced his own image in a tall gilt mirror—unshaven, with cotton-wool hanging out of the plaster dressing. A big french window was open; a man was speaking. There were two men at a table with their backs to him. The place smelt of musty velvet.

'All the stokers, lift-men, mechanics are wanted at once—first thing in the morning. But don't be afraid. There'll be work for every man jack of you in less than a week. This is the end of *your* depression.' He said, 'You can ask your Mr. Bates in here. This isn't a four-day week for you—it's a three-hundred-and-sixty-five-day year.' He lifted himself up and down on his toes in the window, a little dark astute man in gaiters who looked like an estate agent.

D. came across the room behind him. He said, 'Excuse me—may I have a word with you?'

'Not now. Not now,' the little man said, without turning round. He said, 'Now go home and have a good time. There'll be work for everyone before Christmas. And in return we hope—'

241

D. said to the two backs, 'Is one of you Mr. Bates?'

Both men turned. One of them was L.

'That you'll put your backs into it. You can trust the Benditch Colliery Company to help *you*.'

'I'm Bates,' the other said.

He could tell that L. hadn't quite recognised him. He was looking puzzled.... D. said, 'Well, I see you've met the General's agent, then. It's time I had a word.' Then L.'s face cleared. He gave a tiny smile of recognition, an eyelid twitched....

The orator turned from the window and said, 'What's all this?'

D. said, 'This coal contract—it's said to be for Holland—it's nothing of the kind.' He had his eye on Bates, a youngish man with a melodramatic shock of hair and a weak mouth. He said, 'What's this got to do with me?'

'The men trust you, I suppose. Tell them to keep away from the pit.'

'Look here. Look here,' Benditch's agent said.

D. said, 'Your unions declared they'd never work for them.'

'This is for Holland,' Bates said.

'That's cover. I came over to buy coal for the Government. That man there had my credentials stolen.'

'He's cuckoo,' the agent said with conviction,

lifting himself up and down on his toes. 'That gentleman's a friend of Lord Benditch.'

Bates shifted uneasily. 'What can I do?' he said. 'It's a Government matter.'

L. said gently, 'I do know this man. He's a fanatic—and he's wanted by the police.'

'Send for a constable,' the agent said.

'I've got a gun in my pocket,' D. said. He kept his eye on Bates. He said, 'I know this means a year's work to your people. But it's death to ours, Why, it's been death to yours too if you only knew.'

Bates suddenly broke out furiously. He said, 'Why the hell should I believe a story like that? This is coal for Holland.'

He had an uncertain night-school accent; he had risen—you could see that—and the marks of his rising he had tucked away with shame. He said, 'I've never heard such a story.' But D. knew that he half-believed. His weak mouth carried his shock of hair like a disguise, suggesting a violence, a radicalism which wasn't his at all.

D. said, 'If you won't speak to them, I will.' The agent started for the door. D. said, 'Sit down. You can call the police when I've done. I'm not trying to escape, am I? You can ask that man there—how many charges: I begin to forget. False passport, stealing a car, carrying firearms without a licence. Now I'm going to add incitement to violence.'

He went to the window and called out, 'Comrades!' At the back of the crowd he could see old Jarvis watching him sceptically. There were about a hundred and fifty people outside; a good many had already gone to spread the news. He said, 'I've got to speak to you.' Somebody called out, 'Why?' He said, 'You don't know where this coal's going.'

They were hilarious and triumphant. A voice said, 'The North Pole.' He said, 'It's not going to Holland...' They began to drift away; he had been a lecturer once, but he had never been a public speaker: he didn't know how to hold them. He said, 'By God! you've got to listen.' He picked up an ash-tray from the table and smashed the window with it.

'Here,' Bates said in a shocked voice, 'that's hotel property.'

The sound of breaking glass brought the crowd round. D. said, 'Do you want to dig coal to kill children with?'

'Aw, shut up,' a voice said.

He said, 'I know this means a lot to you. But it means everything to us.' Glancing sideways he saw in the mirror L.'s face—complacent, unmoved, waiting for him to finish. Nothing would make any difference. He shouted, 'Why do they want *your* coal? Because the miners at home won't work for them. They shoot them, but they won't work....' Over the heads of the crowd he could see old George Jarvis, keeping a little apart, secretive, not believing a word about anything. Somebody called out, 'Let's hear Joe Bates,' and the cry was taken up here and there. 'Joe Bates! Joe!'

D. said, 'Here's your chance,' turning back into the room towards the union secretary.

The little man like an estate agent said, 'I'll see you get six months for this.'

'Go on,' D. said.

Bates went unwillingly to the window. He had a mannerism learned from his leaders of tossing back his unruly hair—it was the only unruly thing, D. thought, about him. He said, 'Comrades! You've heard a very serious charge.' Was it possible, after all, that he was going to act?

A woman's voice shouted, 'Charity begins at 'ome.'

'I think the best thing we can do,' Bates said, 'is to ask a definite assurance from Lord Benditch's agent that his coal is going to Holland—and only Holland.'

'What's the good of an assurance?' D. said.

'If he gives us that, why, we can go to work tomorrow with a clear conscience.'

The little man in gaiters bustled forward. He said, 'That's right. Mr. Bates is right. And I give you the assurance in Lord Benditch's name . . .' What he said was drowned in cheers. D. found himself alone with L. as the cheers went on and the two men moved from the window. L. said, 'You should have taken my offer, you know. You're in a very awkward situation. . . . Mr. K. has been found.'

'Mr. K.?'

'A woman called Glover came home late last night. She told the police she had psychic feelings. It's in the papers this morning.'

The agent was saying, 'As for this man, he's wanted by the police for fraud . . . and theft . . .'

L. said, 'They want to interview a man who was seen in the flat with a young woman—by a man called Fortescue. He had a bandaged cheek, but the police seem to think that may have hidden a scar.'

Bates said, 'Let the constable pass, men.'

'You'd better go, hadn't you?' L. said.

'I've a bullet left.'

'You mean me—or yourself?'

'Oh,' D. said, 'I wish I knew just how far you'd go.' He wanted to be driven to shoot—to know that L. had given the orders for the child's death: to hate him, despise him and shoot. But L. and the child hadn't belonged to the same world—it was unbelievable that he could have given any order . . . you had to have something in common with people you killed, unless death was dealt out impersonally from a long-range gun or a plane.

'Come up here, constable,' Lord Benditch's agent called out of the window to somebody below. He had the simple faith of his class that one constable could deal with an armed man.

L. said, 'Almost any distance ... to get back...' It was unnecessary to say what or where: a whole way of life behind the quiet unfrightened voice—long corridors and formal gardens and expensive books, a picture gallery, a buhl desk and old servants who admired him. But would it be "getting back" to have a ghost tagged for ever at your side as a reminder?... D. hesitated—with the gun pointed through his pocket. L. said, 'I know what you're thinking ... but that woman was mad—literally mad.'

D. said, 'Thank you. In that case...' He felt a sudden lightening of the heart as if madness had brought a kind of normality into his world. It even eased his own responsibility a little. He made for the door.

Lord Benditch's agent turned from the window and said, 'Stop him!'

'Let him go,' L. said. 'The police...'

He ran down the stairs: the police constable, an elderly man, was coming into the hall. He looked sharply at D. and said, 'Hi, sir! have you seen...'

'Up the stairs, officer.'

He turned towards the yard at the back; Lord Benditch's agent squealed over the banisters, 'That's him, officer. That's him.'

D. ran. He had a few yards' start: the yard looked empty. He heard a shout and a crash behind him—the constable had slipped. A voice said, 'This way mate,' and he swerved automatically into an outside lavatory. Things were going too fast. Somebody said, 'Give him a leg up,' and he found himself being propelled over a wall. He fell heavily on his knees beside a rubbish can, and a voice whispered, 'Quiet.' He was in a tiny back garden—a few square feet of thin grass, a cinder track, a piece of ragged coconut hanging on a broken brick to attract birds. He said, 'What are you doing? What's the good?' This must be Mrs. Bennett's, he wanted to explain; what was the good? She'd only call the police ... but everybody had gone. He was alone like something you throw over a wall and forget. There was a lot of shouting in the street. He knelt exhausted, like a garden image, while thoughts raced this way and that—he might have been holding a bird-bath. He felt sick and angry; he was being pushed around again. What was the good? He was finished. A prison cell attracted him like quiet. Surely he'd tried enough. He put his head between his knees to cure his dizziness. He remembered he had had nothing to eat since a rock bun at the soirée.

A voice whispered to him urgently, 'Get up.'

He looked up and focused on three young faces. He said, 'Who are you?'

They watched him with glee—the oldest couldn't have been more than twenty. They had soft, unformed, anarchic faces. The oldest said,

'Never mind who *we* are. Come into the shed.'

He obeyed them dreamily. In the little dark box there was just room for the four of them: they squatted on the coke- and coal-dust and the bits of old boxes torn up for firewood. A little light came in through the knots in the planks which someone had poked out with a finger. He said, 'What's the good of this? Mrs. Bennett...'

'The old woman won't carry coal on a Sunday. She's strict.'

'What about Bennett?'

'He's properly boozed.'

'Somebody must have seen?'

'Naw. We've scouted.'

'They'll search the houses.'

'How can they without a warrant? Magistrate's in Woolhampton.'

He gave it up and said wearily, 'Well, I suppose I ought to thank you.'

'Stow the thanks,' the oldest boy said. 'You got a gun, ain't you?'

'Yes.'

The boy said, 'The Gang want that gun.'

'They do, do they? Who are the Gang? You?'

'We're the—exexetive.'

They squatted round him watching greedily. He said evasively, 'What happened to the constable?'

'The Gang saw to 'im.'

The youngest boy rubbed his ankle

thoughtfully.

'It was smart work.'

'We're organised, you see,' the oldest boy said.

'An' we've got—scores.'

'Joey 'ere,' the oldest boy said, 'got the birch once.'

'I see.'

'Six strokes.'

'That was before we organised.'

The oldest boy said, 'An' now we want your gun. You don't need it any more. The Gang's looking after you.'

'It is, is it?'

'We got it arranged. You stay here—an' when it's dark—when you hear seven strike—you go along up Pit Street. They'll all be at tea then. Those that aren't in Chapel. There's an alley up by Chapel. You wait there for the bus. Crikey'll be on the watch for you.'

'Who's Crikey?'

'He's one of the Gang. He punches tickets. He'll see you get over to Woolhampton safe.'

'You've got it all planned. But what do you want the gun for?'

The oldest boy leant close. He had a pale thick skin: his eyes had the blankness of a pit pony's. There was no enthusiasm anywhere—no wildness; anarchy was just an absence of certain restraints. He said, 'We was listening to you. You don't want that pit worked. We'll stop them for you. It's all the same to us.'

'Don't your fathers work there?'

'That don't worry us.'

'But how?'

'We know where they keep the dynamite. All we got to do is bust the shed open an' pitch the sticks down. They won't be able to work that pit for months.'

The boy's breath smelt sour. He felt revulsion. He said, 'Is nobody working there?'

'There's nobody up there at all.'

It was his duty, of course, to take the chance, but he was reluctant. He said, 'Why the gun?'

'We'll shoot out the lock.'

'Do you know how to use one?'

'Of course we do.'

He said, 'There's only one bullet...' They were all cramped together in the little shed: hands were against his hands: sour breath whistled in his face. He felt as if he were surrounded by animals—who belonged in the dark and had senses adjusted to the dark, while he could see only in the light.... He said, 'Why?' and an uninterested boy's voice came back, 'Fun.' A goose went winging by somewhere above his grave—where? He shivered. He said, 'Suppose there *is* someone up there...'

'Oh, we'll be careful. We don't want to swing.' But they wouldn't swing. That was the trouble—they had no responsibility: they were

251

under age. But all the same, he told himself, it was his duty ... even if there should be an accident ... you couldn't count strangers' lives in the balance against your own people's. When war started the absolute moral code was abolished: you were allowed to do evil that good might come.

He took the gun out of his pocket and immediately the scaly hand of the oldest boy dropped on it. D. said, 'Throw the gun down the pit first. You don't want finger-marks.'

'That's all right. You can trust us.'

He kept his fingers on it—reluctant to let it go: it was his last shot. The boy said, 'We shan't squeal. The Gang never squeals.'

'What are they doing in the town now? The police, I mean?'

'There's only two of 'em. One of them's got a bike. He's fetching a warrant from Woolhampton. They think you're in Charlie Stowe's—an' Charlie won't let them in to look. Charlie's got a score, too.'

'You won't have long—after you've shot the lock—to throw the sticks and get away.'

'We'll wait to dark.' The hand disengaged the gun—immediately it disappeared in someone's pocket. 'Don't forget,' the leader said. 'Seven—at Chapel—Crikey'll be watchin' out.'

When they had gone he remembered that he might at least have asked them for a little food.

Without it the hours went all the more slowly;

252

he opened the door of the shed a crack; but all he could see was a dry shrub, a few feet of cinder path, the piece of coconut on its dirty string. He tried to plan ahead, but what was the good when life took you like a high sea and flung you . . . ? If he got to Woolhampton, would it be any use trying the station . . . or would it be watched? He remembered the bandage on his cheek: that was no longer any good; he tore it off. It had been bad luck that the woman should have found Mr. K.'s body so soon. But he had been pursued by bad luck ever since he landed—he saw Rose again, coming down the platform with the bun. If he had not taken a lift from her, would everything have been different? He would not have been beaten up, delayed. . . . Mr. K., perhaps, would not have suspected him of selling out and become determined to sell out himself first . . . the manageress . . . but she was mad, L. said. What exactly had he meant by that? Whichever track he took seemed to begin with Rose on the platform and end with Else lying dead on the third floor.

A small bird—he didn't know the names of English birds—was sitting on the coconut. It pecked very quickly and pecked again: it was having a good meal. Suppose he got to Woolhampton, should he aim at getting back to London—or where? That had been the idea when he said good-bye to Rose, but things had changed now . . . if he were wanted for Mr. K.'s murder, too. The hunt would be far more serious than before. He didn't want to mix her up more than he had already done. It would be so much simpler, he thought wearily, if a policeman now just walked in. ...The bird suddenly took off from the coconut: there was a sound on the cinder path like somebody walking on tiptoe. He waited patiently for capture.

But it was only a cat. It looked in at him, black and tailored, from the bright winter daylight—regarded him, as it were, on an equality, as one animal by another, and moved again out of sight, leaving behind a faint smell of fish. He thought suddenly: the coconut ... when it's dark enough I can get the coconut.But the hours went by with appalling slowness; at one time there was a smell of cooking, at another high words came down to him from an upper window ... the phrase 'bringing disgrace' and 'drunken brute': Mrs. Bennett was probably trying to get her husband out of bed. He thought he heard her say, 'His Lordship,' and then a window slammed, and what went on after that went on without the neighbours knowing, in the dreadful secrecy of a home—man's castle. The bird returned to the coconut, and he watched it jealously; it used its beak like a labourer does a pick; he was tempted to scare it away. The afternoon light flattened over the garden.

What troubled him now more than all was the

fate of the gun. Those boys were not to be trusted. Probably the whole story of the explosives shed was false, and they just wanted the weapon to play with. Anything might happen at any moment. They might let it off in mere devilry—not that you could think of high spirits in relation to those pasty and unwanted faces. Once he was startled by what might have been a shot—until it was repeated. It was probably the agent's car. At last the dark did fall. He waited until he couldn't see the coconut before he ventured out. He found his mouth was actually watering at the prospect of that dry bird's-leaving. His foot crunched over-loudly on the cinder track, and a curtain in the house was drawn aside. Mrs. Bennett glared out at him. He could see her plainly—dressed up to go out, flattening her nose against the kitchen window, beside the cooker, the jealous heartless bony face. He waited motionless; it seemed impossible that she shouldn't see him, but the garden was dark and she let the curtain fall.

He waited a while, and then went on—to the coconut.

It wasn't, after all, much of a feast; he found it tough and dry in the throat. He crouched in the shed and ate it in small shreds: he hadn't got a knife and he wore down his finger-nails scraping off the hard white food. At last even the longest wait is over; he had thought of everything—of Rose, the future, the past, the boys with the gun—until there was no more to think about at all. He had tried to remember the poem he had copied out into the notebook which L.'s chauffeur had stolen. . . . 'The beat . . . something of thy heart and feet, how passionately and irretrievably . . .' He gave it up. It had seemed at the time to mean a great deal. He thought of his wife: it represented all the ignobility of life that he felt the tie weakening between him and the grave. People should die together, not apart. A clock struck seven.


## II

HE came carefully out of the shed with what was left of the coconut in his pocket. He realised suddenly that the boys had never told him how he was to get out of this back garden. That was like a child: the immense organised plan and the small practical detail forgotten. It was madness to trust them with a gun. He supposed they had gone themselves over the wall—the way they had come. But he wasn't young; he was a weak, hungry, middle-aged man. He put his hands up: he could reach the top of the wall, but he hadn't the strength in the arms to raise himself. He tried again and again, each time more weakly. A very young voice from the lavatory whispered,

'That you, mate?'

So they hadn't forgotten the detail.

He whispered, 'Yes.'

'There's a loose brick.'

He felt along the wall until he found it. 'Yes.'

'Come over quick.'

He landed on his feet where his escape had begun. A small dirty urchin watched him critically. 'I'm the lookout,' he said.

'Where are the others?'

He jerked his head up towards the dark background of slag which hung like a storm cloud above the village. 'They'll be at the pit.' He felt the sense of apprehension grow: it was like the five minutes between the warning and the first bombs; he had a feeling of merciless anarchy let loose like thunder on the hill.

'You go an' wait for Crikey,' the minute and grubby creature commanded him harshly.

He obeyed: there wasn't anything else to do. The long grey street was badly lighted, and the Gang seemed to have chosen their time correctly—there was nobody about at all. He might have been going through a deserted town—a relic shown to tourists of the Coal Age, if it had not been for the light in the Chapel windows. He felt very tired and very sick, and every step he took his apprehensions gathered. He felt a physical shrinking from the sudden noise which at any moment now would tear across this quiet. In the north-west sky there was a glow of light cast by Woolhampton, like a city on fire.'

A narrow passage ran up between the Baptist Chapel and the next house—it gave it a spurious detached dignity in the crammed village. He waited there with his eyes on the street for Crikey and the Woolhampton bus. The only policeman left was presumably keeping an eye on Charlie Stowe's while he waited for the search warrant. Straight up at the back rose the mountains of slag, and somewhere in the dark the boys were gathering round the explosives shed. Inside the Chapel the tuneless voices of women were singing 'Praise to the Holiest in the Height . . .'

A thin rain began to fall, blowing from the north across the hills of slag. It was impregnated with dust—it streaked the face like diluted paint. A man's voice, rough and tender and assured, said distinctly, close to his elbow. 'Let us all pray,' and the impromptu prayer began to roll magnificently on its way: 'Fountain of all goodness and truth . . . we bless thee for all thy gifts so freely bestowed . . .' The cold seeped through his mackintosh and lay like a wet compress on his breast. Was that the sound of a car? It was. He heard it backfiring furiously down the street, and he came cautiously to the entrance of his burrow, hoping for Crikey.

But he started quickly back into the dark: it wasn't the bus—it was a motor-bicycle ridden by a policeman. He must have got back from Woolhampton with the warrant; they would soon discover that he wasn't at Charlie Stowe's. How long would the bus be? They'd search it, surely ... unless the Gang had thought of that, too, and got a plan. He flattened himself against the Chapel wall, presenting as little surface as he could to the penetrating rain, and heard the prayer going on and imagined the big bare lighted interior with the pitch-pine panels and the table instead of an altar and the hot radiator and all the women in their Sunday best ... Mrs. Bennett.... 'We pray thee for our torn and tortured world ... we would remember before thee the victims of war, the homeless and destitute...' He smiled grimly, thinking: they are praying for me if they only knew it; how would they like that? They began to sing a hymn; the words came erratically and obscurely out from their prison of stone and flesh: 'In heavenly love abiding, no change my heart shall fear...'

He was flung right across the passage and fell with the back of his head against a stone, glass flew like shrapnel. He had a sense that the whole wall above him was caving in to fall upon his face, and he screamed and screamed. He was aware of violence and not of noise—the noise was too great to be heard. You became conscious of it only when it was over, and there were only barking dogs and people shouting and the soft sifting of dust from a broken brick. He put his hands over his face to protect his eyes and screamed again: people ran along the street: not far away a harmonium began defiantly to play, but he didn't hear it, he was back in the foundations of a house with a dead cat's fur touching his lips.

A voice said, "That's him.' They were digging him out, but he couldn't move to avoid the edge of a spade or the point of a pick: he sweated with fear and called out in his own language. Somebody's hand was passing over him—and his mind went flick! flick! and he was back on the Dover Road and the chauffeur's large and brutal hands were touching him. He said fiercely, 'Take your hands off.'

'Has he got a gun?'

'No.'

'What's that in his right pocket?'

'Well now, isn't that a funny thing? It's a piece of coconut.'

'Hurt?'

'I don't think so,' the voice said. 'Just scared, I reckon.'

'Better put on the cuffs.'

He came back down the long track which led from the dead cat to Benditch village by way of the Dover Road. He felt his hands gripped and his eyes were uncovered. The wall still stood above him and the thin rain came steadily down: there was no change. Violence had passed, leaving only a little broken glass. Two policemen stood over him and a small dismal crowd had collected at the entrance of the alley and watched avidly. A voice said, 'The Scripture lesson is taken from . . .'

'It's all right,' D. said. 'I'm coming.' He got up painfully: the fall had strained his back. He said, 'I'd be glad to sit down, if you don't mind.'

A policeman said, 'You'll have plenty of time for that.'

One of them took his arm and led him out into the dingy street. A little way off stood a bus marked Woolhampton; a youth with a satchel slung across his shoulder watched him with poker face from the step.

He asked, 'What are the charges?'

'There'll be plenty,' the policeman said, 'don't you worry.'

'I think,' D. said, 'I have the right . . . looking at his cuffed hands.

'Using words likely to lead to a breach of the peace . . . an' being on enclosed premises with the purpose of committing a felony. That'll be enough to get on with.'

D. laughed. He couldn't help it. He said. 'Those are two fresh ones. They mount up, don't they?'

At the station they gave him a cup of cocoa and some bread and butter and locked him in a cell. He had not experienced such peace for a long time. He could hear them telephoning to

Woolhampton about him, but he couldn't hear what was said beyond a few words.... Presently the younger policeman brought him a bowl of soup. He said, 'You're quite a catch, aren't you?'

'Am I?'

'They want you up in London—and in a hurry, too.' He said with respect. 'They want to question you . . .'

'What about?'

'I couldn't tell you, but you've seen the paper, I suppose. You've got to go up by the midnight train. With me. I won't mind taking a look at London, I can tell you.'

D. said. 'Would you mind telling me—that explosion—was anybody hurt?'

The policeman said, 'Some kids set the explosive shed off up at the mine. But nobody was hurt—for a wonder. Except old George Jarvis—what he was doing up there no one knows. He complains of shock, but it would need an earthquake to shock old George.'

'Then the damage wasn't great?'

'There wasn't any damage—if you don't count the shed and some windows broken.'

'I see.'

So even the last shot had failed.

# PART FOUR

# THE END

## I

THE magistrate had thin white hair, and pince-nez, and deep lines around the mouth—an expression of soured kindliness. He kept on tapping his blotter impatiently with his fountain pen. It was as if the endless circumlocutions of police witnesses were at last getting his nerves frayed beyond endurance. 'We proceeded to so-and-so . . .' 'On information received . . .' He said with irritation, 'What you mean to say, is, I suppose . . .'

They had allowed D. to sit down in the dock. Where he sat he could see nobody but a few solicitors and policemen, the clerk at a table under the magistrate's dais, all strangers. But as he had stood at the entrance of the court waiting for his name to be called all sorts of familiar faces had been visible—Mr. Muckerji, old Dr. Bellows, even Miss Carpenter was there. He had smiled painfully towards them as he climbed into the dock before he turned his back. How puzzled they must be—except, of course, Mr. Muckerji, who was certain to have his theories. He felt inexpressibly tired.

It had been a long thirty-six hours. First the journey up to London with an excited police officer who kept him awake all night talking about a boxing match he might or might not get to at the Albert Hall. And then the questioning at Scotland Yard. At first he had been amused— it contrasted oddly with the sort of questioning he had had in prison at home with a club. Three men sat or strolled about the room; they were meticulously fair, and sometimes one of them would bring in tea and biscuits on a tray for him—very strong cheap tea and rather sweet biscuits. They also offered him cigarettes, and he had returned the compliment. They hadn't liked his black strong kind, but he noticed with secret amusement that they unobtrusively made a note of the name on the packet—in case it should come in useful later.

They were obviously trying to pin Mr. K's death on him—he wondered what had happened to the other charges, the false passport and Else's so-called suicide—not to speak of the explosion at Benditch. 'What did you do with the gun?' they said. That was the nearest they came to the odd scene at the Embassy.

'I dropped it in the Thames,' he said with amusement.

They pursued the point very seriously—they seemed quite prepared to employ divers, dredgers. . . .

He said, 'Oh, one of your bridges . . . I don't

264

know all their names.'

They had found out all about his visit to the Entrenationo soirée with Mr. K. and a man had come forward who said that Mr. K. had made a scene because he was being followed. A man called Hogpit. 'He wasn't being followed by me,' D. said. 'I left him outside the Entrenationo office.'

'A witness called Fortescue saw you and a woman . . .'

'I don't know anyone called Fortescue.'

The questioning had gone on for hours. Once there was a telephone call. A detective turned to D. with the receiver in his hand and said, 'You do know, don't you, that this is all voluntary? You can refuse to answer any questions without your solicitor being present.'

'I don't want a solicitor.'

'He doesn't want a solicitor,' the detective said down the 'phone and rang off.

'Who was that?' D. asked.

'Search me,' the detective said. He poured D. out his fourth cup of tea and asked, 'Two lumps? I always forget.'

'No sugar.'

'Sorry.'

Later in the day there had been an identification parade. It was rather disillusioning to a former lecturer in the Romance languages to see the choice of faces. This—it seemed to indicate—is what you're like to us. He looked with distress down a line of unshaven Soho types—they looked, most of them, like pimps, or waiters in undesirable cafés. He was amused to find, however, that the police had been only too fair. Fortescue suddenly came through a door into the yard, carrying an umbrella in one hand and a bowler hat in the other. He walked down the seedy parade like a shy young politician inspecting a guard of honour and hesitated a long while before a blackguard on D.'s right—a man who looked as if he would kill you for a packet of cigarettes. 'I think...' Fortescue said. 'No ... perhaps.' He turned pale earnest eyes towards the detective with him and said, 'I'm very sorry, but, you know. I'm short-sighted, and everything here looks so different.'

'Different?'

'Different, I mean to Emily's—I mean Miss Glover's flat.'

'You aren't identifying furniture,' the officer said.

'No. But then, the man I saw was wearing a plaster dressing ... none of these...'

'Can't you just imagine the dressing?'

'Of course,' Fortescue said with his eye on D.'s cheek, 'this one's got a scar ... he might have been...'

But they were very fair. They wouldn't allow that. They had led him out and brought in a man in a big black hat whom D. vaguely remembered having seen ... somewhere. 'Now, sir,' the detective said, 'can you see here the man you say was in the taxi?'

He said, 'If your man had paid proper attention at the time instead of trying to arrest him for drunkenness...'

'Yes, yes. It was a mistake.'

'And a mistake, I suppose, hauling me into court for obstruction?'

The detective said, 'After all, sir, we've apologised.'

'All right, then. Bring out these men.'

'They are here.'

'Oh, these, yes.' He asked sharply, 'Are they here willingly?'

'Of course. They get paid ... all except the prisoner.'

'And which is he?'

'Why, that's for you to say, sir.'

The man in the hat said, 'Yes, yes, of course,' and strode rapidly down the line. He stopped in front of the same scoundrelly-looking fellow as Fortescue and said firmly, 'That's your man.'

'Are you quite sure, sir?'

'Of course.'

'Thank you very much.' They hadn't brought anybody else in after that. Perhaps they felt they had so many charges against him that they had plenty of time ahead to pin on to him the most serious charge of all. He felt complete apathy; he had failed, and he contented himself with denying everything. Let them prove what they wanted. At last they left him alone again in a cell and he slept fitfully. The old dreams were returning with a difference. He was arguing with a girl up and down a river bank—she was saying the Berne manuscript was of much later date than the Bodleian one. They were fiercely happy, walking up and down by the quiet stream. He said, 'Rose...' There was a smell of spring, and over the river very far away the skyscrapers stood—like tombs. A policeman was shaking him by the shoulders. 'There's a solicitor to see you, sir.'

He hadn't really wanted to see the solicitor. It was too tiring. He said, 'I don't think you understand. I haven't got any money. That is to say—to be accurate, I have a couple of pounds and a return ticket.'

The solicitor was a smart agile young man with a society manner. He said, 'That's all right—that's being seen to. We're briefing Sir Terence Hillman. We feel that it's necessary, as it were, to show that you are not friendless, that you are a man of substance.'

'If you call two pounds...'

'Don't let's discuss the money now,' the solicitor said. 'I assure you *we* are satisfied.'

'But I must know, if I'm to consent...'

'Mr. Forbes is taking care of everything.'

'Mr. Forbes!'

'And now,' the solicitor said, 'to go into

details. They certainly seem to have chalked up a good few charges against you. Anyway, we've disposed of one. The police are satisfied now that your passport is quite correct. It was lucky you remembered that presentation copy at the Museum.'

D. thought, with a slight awakening of interest: good girl, trust her to remember the right thing and to go for it. He said, 'And that child's death . . .?'

'Oh, they never had any evidence there. And as it happens, the woman's confessed. She's mad, of course. She went off into hysterics. You see, an Indian living there had been going round among the neighbours asking questions. . . . No, we've got more serious things to guard against than that.'

"When did all this happen?"

'Saturday evening. It was in the last edition of the Sunday papers.' D. remembered how, driving across the Park, he had seen a poster—something about a sensation, a Bloomsbury sensation—a Bloomsbury tragedy sensation, the whole absurd phrase came back. If only he had bought a copy he might have let Mr. K. alone and all this trouble would have been saved. An eye for an eye—but one didn't necessarily demand two eyes.

The solicitor said, 'Of course in a way our chance lies in the number of charges.'

'Doesn't murder take precedence?'

'I doubt if they can charge you with that yet.'

It all seemed to D. abysmally complicated and not very interesting. They had got him, and they could hardly fail to get their evidence. He hoped that Rose would be kept safely out of it: it was a good thing she hadn't visited him. He wondered whether it was safe to send a message by the solicitor, and then decided that she had a lot of sense—enough sense to stay away. He remembered her candid statement, 'Don't think I'd love you if you were dead,' and he felt a slight unreasoning pain that you could depend on her now to do nothing rash.

She wasn't in court either. He was sure of that—one glance would have been enough to pick her out. Perhaps if she had been there he would have paid more attention to the proceedings. One tried to show off with quickness or bravado if one was in love—if he was in love.

Every now and then an elderly man with a nose like a parrot's got up to cross-examine a policeman. D. supposed he was Sir Terence Hillman. The affair dragged on. Then, quite suddenly, it all seemed to be over: Sir Terence was asking for a remand. His client had had no time to get his evidence together . . . there were issues which were not clear lying behind this case. They were not even clear to D. Why ask for a remand? Apparently he hadn't yet been charged with murder . . . surely the less time the police were given the better.

Counsel for the police said they had no objection. He smirked sardonically—an inferior little bird-like man—towards the distinguished K.C., as if he had gained an unexpected point through the other's stupidity.

Sir Terence was on his feet again, asking that bail should be allowed.

A prolonged squabble began in court which seemed to D. quite meaningless. He would really rather stay in a cell than a hotel room ... and, anyway, who would stand bail for so shady and undesirable an alien?

Sir Terence said, 'I do object, your Worship, to the attitude of the police. They drop hints about a more serious charge..... Let them bring it, so that we can see what it is. At present they've mustered a long array of very minor charges. Being in possession of firearms ... resisting arrest ... and arrest for what? Arrest on a false charge which the police hadn't taken the trouble to investigate properly.'

'Incitement to violence,' the bird-like man said.

'Political,' Sir Terence exclaimed. He raised his voice and said, 'Your Worship, a habit seems to be growing on the police which I hope you will be the means of checking. They will put a man in prison over some trivial offence while they try and get their evidence together on another charge—and if they fail—well, the man comes out again and we hear no more about those weighty reasons.... *He* has had no chance of getting his witnesses together....'

The wrangle went on. The magistrate said suddenly, impatiently, stabbing at his blotting paper, 'I can't help feeling, Mr. Fennick, that there's something in what Sir Terence says. Really there's nothing in these charges at present which would prevent me granting bail. Wouldn't it meet your objections if the bail were made a very substantial one? After all, you have his passport.' Then the arguments began over again.

It was all very fictitious; he had only two pounds in his pocket—not literally in his pocket because, of course, they had been taken way from him when he was arrested. The magistrate said, 'In that case I'll remand him for a week on bail in two recognisances of one thousand pounds each.' He couldn't help laughing—two thousand pounds! A policeman opened the door of the dock and plucked his arm. 'This way.' He found himself back in the tiled passage outside the court. The solicitor was there, smiling. He said, 'Well, Sir Terence was a bit of a surprise for them, wasn't he?'

'I don't understand what all the fuss was about,' D. said. 'I haven't the money—and, anyway, I'm quite comfortable in a cell.'

'It's all arranged,' the solicitor said.

'But who by?'

'Mr. Forbes. He's waiting for you now outside.'

'Am I free?'

'Free as the air. For a week. Or until they've got enough evidence to re-arrest.'

'I don't see why we should give them all that trouble.'

'Ah,' the solicitor said, 'you've got a good friend in Mr. Forbes.'

He came out of the court and down the steps; Mr. Forbes, in loud plus-fours, wandered restlessly round the radiator of a Packard. They looked at each other with some embarrassment, not shaking hands. D. said, 'I understand I've got you to thank—for somebody they call Sir Terence and for my bail. It really wasn't necessary.'

'That's all right,' Mr. Forbes said. He gave D. a long unhappy look as if he wanted to read in his face some explanation—of something. He said, 'Will you get in beside me? I've left the chauffeur at home.'

'I shall have to find somewhere to sleep. And I must get my money back from the police.'

'Never mind about that now.'

They climbed in and Mr. Forbes started up. He said, 'Can you see the petrol gauge?'

'Full.'

'That's all right, then.'

'Where are we off to?'

'I want to call in—if you don't mind—at

273

Shepherd's Market.' They drove in silence all the way—into the Strand, round Trafalgar Square, Piccadilly. ... They came into the little square in the middle of the market and Mr. Forbes sounded his horn twice, looking up at a window over a fishmonger's. He said apologetically, 'I won't be a minute.' A face came to the window, a little plump pretty face over a mauve wrap. A hand waved: an unwilling smile. 'Excuse me,' Mr. Forbes said and disappeared through a door next the fishmonger's. A large tom-cat came along the gutter and found a fish-head; he spurred it once or twice with his claws and then moved on: he wasn't all that hungry.

Mr. Forbes came out again and climbed in: they backed and turned. He gave a cautious look sideways at D. and said, 'She's not a bad girl.'

'No?'

'I think she's really fond of me.'

'I shouldn't wonder.'

Mr. Forbes cleared his throat, driving on down Knightsbridge. He said, 'You're a foreigner. You won't think it odd of me—keeping on Sally when—well, when I'm in love with Rose.'

'It's nothing to do with me.'

'A man must live—and I never thought I had a chance—until this week.'

'Ah!' D. said. He thought, I'm beginning to talk like George Jarvis.

'And it's useful, too,' Mr. Forbes said.

'I'm sure it is.'

'I mean—to-day, for instance. She is quite ready to swear that I spent the day with her if necessary.'

'I don't see why it should be.' They were silent through Hammersmith.

It wasn't until they were upon Western Avenue that Mr. Forbes said, 'I expect you're a bit puzzled.'

'A little.'

'Well,' Mr. Forbes said, 'you realise, of course, that you've got to leave the country at once—before the police get any more evidence to connect you with that unfortunate affair. The gun would be enough . . .'

'I don't think they'll find the gun.'

'You can't take any risks. You know, whether you hit him or not, it's technically murder. They wouldn't hang you, I imagine. But you'd get fifteen years—at the least.'

'I daresay. But you forget the bail.'

'I'm responsible for the bail. You've got to leave to-night. It won't be comfortable, but there's a tramp steamer with a cargo of food leaving for your place to-night. You'll probably be bombed on the way—that's your own affair.' There was an odd break in his voice; D. glanced quickly at the domed Semitic forehead, the dark eyes over the rather gaudy tie: the man was crying. He sat at the wheel, a middle-aged Jew

275

crying down Western Avenue. He said, 'Everything's been arranged. You'll be smuggled on board in the Channel after they've cleared the customs.'

'It's very good of you to take so much trouble.'

'I'm not doing it for you.' He said, 'Rose asked me to do my best.'

So he was crying for love. They turned south. Mr. Forbes said sharply, as if he had been accused, 'Of course I made my conditions.'

'Yes?'

'That she wasn't to see you. I wouldn't let her go to the court.'

'And she said she'd marry you—in spite of Sally?'

'Yes.' He said, 'How did you know she knew . . .?'

'She told me.' He said to himself: everything's for the best. I'm not in a condition for love: in the end she'll find that—Furt—is good for her. In the old days nobody ever married for love. People made marriage treaties. This was a treaty. There's no point in feeling pain. I must be glad—glad to be able to turn to the grave again without infidelity. Mr. Forbes said, 'I am going to drop you at a hotel near Southcrawl. They'll see you are picked up there by motor-boat. You won't be conspicuous—it's quite a resort—even at this time of year.' He added irrelevantly, 'Climate's as good as

276

Torquay.' Then they sat in gloomy silence, driving south-west, the bridegroom and the lover—if he were a lover.

It was well on into the afternoon, among the high bare downs of Dorset, that Mr. Forbes said, 'You know you haven't done so badly. You don't think there'll be—trouble—when you get home?'

'It seems likely.'

'But that explosion at Benditch—you know, it blew L.'s contract sky-high. That and K.'s death.'

'I don't understand.'

'You haven't got the coal yourself, but L. hasn't got it either. We had a meeting early this morning. We've cancelled the contract. The risk is too great.'

'The risk?'

'To reopen the pits and then find the Government stepping in. You couldn't have advertised the affair better if you'd bought the front page of the *Mail*. Already there's been a leading article—about political gangsters and the civil war being fought out on English soil. We had to decide whether to sue the paper for libel or cancel the contract and announce that we had signed in good faith under the idea the coal was going to Holland. So we cancelled.'

It was certainly half a victory: he thought grimly that it would probably postpone his death—he would be left to an enemy bomb, instead of reaching a solution of his problems quickly in front of the cemetery wall. On the crown of the hill they came in sight of the sea. He hadn't seen it since that foggy night at Dover with the gulls crying—the limit of his mission. Far away to the right a rash of villas began; lights were coming out, and a pier crept out to sea like a centipede with an illuminated spine.

'That's Southcrawl,' Mr. Forbes said. There were no ships' lights visible anywhere on the wide grey vanishing Channel. 'It's late,' Mr. Forbes said with a touch of nervousness.

'Where do I go?'

'See that hotel over on the left about two miles out of Southcrawl?' They cruised slowly down the hill; it was more like a village than a hotel as they came down towards it—or, nearer comparison still, an airport: circle after circle of chromium bungalows round a central illuminated tower—fields and more bungalows. 'It's called the Lido,' Mr. Forbes said. 'A new idea in popular hotels. A thousand rooms, playing fields, swimming pools . . .'

'What about the sea?'

'That's not heated,' Mr. Forbes said. He looked slyly sideways. 'As a matter of fact I've bought the place.' He said, 'We're advertising it as a cruise on land. Organised games with a secretary. Concerts. A gymnasium. Young people encouraged—no reception clerk looking down his nose at the new Woolworth ring. Best

278

of all, of course, no seasickness. And cheap.' He sounded enthusiastic; he said, 'Sally's very keen. She's great, you see, on physical fitness.'

'You take a personal interest?'

'I wish sometimes I could do more. A man must have a hobby. But I've got a fellow down now taking a look round the place. He's had a lot of experience with road-houses and things— if he likes the idea I'm putting him in complete charge at fifteen hundred a year and all found. We want to make it an all-the-year-round resort. You'll see—the Christmas season's beginning.'

A little way up the road Mr. Forbes stopped the car. He said, 'Your room's been booked for a night. You won't be the first in this place to slip away without paying the bill. We shall report it, of course, to the police—but I daresay you don't mind one more minor charge. Your number's 105$c$.'

'It sounds like a convict's.'

Mr. Forbes said, 'You'll be fetched from your room. I don't see that anything can go wrong. I won't come any further. You ask at the office for your key.'

D. said, 'I know there's no point in thanking you, but all the same...' He stood beside the car: he felt at a loss for the right words. He said, 'You'll give my love to Rose, won't you? And my congratulations, I do congratulate her...' He broke off: he had surprised a look on Mr. Forbes's face which was almost one of hate. It

279

must be a bitter thing to be accepted on such humiliating conditions—a dowry is less personal. He said, 'She couldn't have a better friend.' Mr. Forbes leant passionately forward and jabbed at the self-starter. He began to back: D. had a glimpse of the red-rimmed eyes. If it wasn't hate, it was grief. He left Mr. Forbes and walked down the road to the two neon-lighted pillars which marked the entrance of the Lido. Two enormous plum puddings in electric light bulbs had been set up on the pillars, but the wiring wasn't completed; they looked black, steely, unappetising.

The reception clerk occupied a little lodge just inside the grounds. He said, 'Oh yes, your room was booked by telephone last night, Mr.—' he took a look at the register, 'Davis. Your luggage, I suppose, is coming up?'

'I walked from Southcrawl. It should be here.'

'Shall I telephone to the station?'

'Oh, we'll give them an hour or two. One doesn't have to dress for dinner, I imagine?'

'Oh no. Nothing of that sort, Mr. Davis. Perfect liberty. May I send the sports secretary along to your room for a chat?'

'I think I'll just breathe the air for twenty-four hours first.'

He strolled round and round the big chromium circles—every room with a sun-bathing roof. Men in shorts, their knees a little blue with cold, were chasing each other hilariously in the dusk: a girl in pyjamas called out, 'Have they picked up for basket ball, Spot?' to a man with a bald head. 105*c* was like a cabin—there was even a sham port-hole instead of a window, and the washing basin folded back against the wall to make more room: you could almost imagine a slight smell of oil and the churning of the engines. He sighed. England, it appeared was to maintain a certain strangeness to the very end: the eccentricities of a country which had known civil peace for two hundred and fifty years. There was a good deal of noise, the laughter which is known technically as happy, and several radios were playing, plugged in to different stations; the walls were very thin, so that you could hear everything which went on in the neighbouring rooms—a man seemed to be flinging his shoes against the wall. Like a cabin the room was overheated; he opened a port-hole, and almost at once a young man put his head through. 'Hullo!' he said. 'Hullo in there!'

'Yes?' D. inquired wearily, sitting on the bed: it didn't seem likely that this was the summons he was waiting for. 'Do you want me?'

'Oh, sorry. I thought this was Chubby's room.'

'What is it, Pig?' a girl's voice said.

The young man's head disappeared. He whispered penetratingly on the gravel. 'It's a foreign bloke.'

281

'Let me take a look.'

'Don't be silly. You can't.'

'Oh, can't I?' A beaky girl with fluffy fair hair thrust her head through the window, giggled and disappeared again. A voice said, *'There's* Chubby. What've you been doing with yourself, you old rotter?'

D. lay on his back, thinking of Mr. Forbes driving back through the dusk to London: was he going to see Rose—or Sally? Somewhere a clock struck. This at last was the end: the sooner he was back now the better: he could begin to forget the absurd comic image which remained fixed in his mind of a girl tossing a bun into the fog. He fell asleep and woke again; half an hour had passed by his watch. How much longer? He went to the window and looked out; beyond the bar of lights from his own outer circle of steel bungalow there was nothing—just night and the sound of the sea washing up on shingle and withdrawing—the long sigh of a defeated element. In the whole arc of darkness not a light to show that any ship was standing in to shore.

He opened his door. There were no passages; every room opened immediately, as it were, on to the unsheltered deck. The clock tower, like the bridge of a ship, heaved among the clouds: a moon raced backwards through the marbled sky—a wind had risen, and the sea seemed very near. It seemed odd not to be pursued; for the first time since he landed nobody 'wanted' him:

he had the safe legal existence of a man on bail.

He walked briskly in the cold evening air past the little lighted overheated rooms. Music came up from Luxemburg. Stuttgart and Hilversum: radio was installed everywhere. Warsaw suffered from atmospherics, and National gave a talk on the Problem of Indo-China. Below the clock tower wide rubber steps led up to the big glass doors of the recreation centre. He walked in. Evening papers were laid out for sale on a central table—a saucer full of pennies showed that the trust system was in operation. There was a lot of boisterous laughter in one corner where a group of men were drinking whisky; otherwise the big draughty steel and glass room was empty—if you could talk of emptiness among all the small tables and club arm-chairs, the slot machines and boards for Corinthian bagatelle. There was even a milk bar, up beside the service door. D. realised that he hadn't a single penny in his pockets: Mr. Forbes had not given him time to get his money back from the police. It would be awkward if the ship didn't turn up.... He looked down at the evening papers; he thought, with so many crimes on my head, I may as well add petty larceny. Nobody was looking. He sneaked a paper.

A voice he knew said, 'It's a damned fine show.'

God, he thought, could only really be pictured as a joker—it was absurd to have come all this way only to encounter Captain Currie at the end of it. He remembered that Mr. Forbes had spoken of a man with experience of road-houses.... Well, it hardly seemed a moment for amicable greetings. He spread the paper open and sheltered himself behind it. A rather servile voice said, 'Excuse me, sir, but I think you've forgotten your penny.' A waiter must have come in under cover of that boisterous laughter—the trust system might be in operation, but they kept a careful watch on the number of pennies in the saucer. It didn't say much, he thought, for Chubby and Spot and the rest of Mr. Forbes's clientèle.

He said, 'Sorry. I haven't got any change.'

'Oh, I can give you change, sir.'

D. had his back to the drinkers now, but he had a sense that the laughter had stopped and that they were listening. He said with his hand in his pocket, 'I seem to have left my money in my other suit. I'll pay you later.'

'What room, sir?' If counting pennies made you rich, they deserved a fortune.

He said, '105c.'

Captain Currie's voice said, 'Well, I'm damned.'

It was no good trying to avoid the encounter. After all, he was on bail: there was nothing Currie could do. He turned and felt his poise a little shaken by Captain Currie's shorts—he had obviously been entering into the life of the place. D. said, 'I hadn't expected to meet you here.'

'I bet you hadn't,' Captain Currie said.

'Well, I'll be seeing you, I expect, at dinner.' Paper in hand he moved towards the door.

Captain Currie said, 'No, you don't. You stay where you are.'

'I don't understand.'

'This is the fellow I was telling you about, boys.' Two moony middle-aged faces stared at him with awe, a little flushed with Scotch.

'No!'

'Yes.'

'I'm damned if he wasn't pinching a paper,' one of them said.

'He's capable of anything,' Captain Currie said.

'Would you mind,' D. said, 'getting out of my way? I want to go to my room.'

'I daresay,' Captain Currie said.

One of his companions said timidly. 'Be careful, old man. He might carry a gun.'

D. said. 'I don't quite know what you gentlemen think you are doing. I'm not a fugitive from justice—isn't that the phrase? I happen to have been bailed, and there's no law which says I can't spend my time where I like.'

'He's a regular sea-lawyer,' one of the men said.

'You'd better take things quietly,' Captain Currie said. 'You've shot your bolt, man. You thought you'd get out of the country, I suppose—but you can't fool Scotland Yard. Best police force in the world.'

'I don't understand.'

'Why, man, you must know there's a warrant out. Look in the stop press. You're wanted for murder.'

D. looked: it was there. Sir Terence Hillman had not fooled the police for long; they must have decided to take out a warrant as soon as he'd left the court. They were looking for him— and Captain Currie had, triumphantly, found him, and now watched him firmly, but with a kind of respect. Murder wasn't like stealing a car. It was the English tradition to treat a condemned man kindly—the breakfast before the execution. Captain Currie said, 'Now, we are three to one. Take things quietly. It's no good making a scene.'


## II


D. SAID, 'Can I have a cigarette?'

'Yes, yes, of course,' Captain Currie said. 'Keep the whole packet.' He told the waiter, 'Ring up Southcrawl police station and tell them that we've got him.'

'Well,' one of his companions said, 'we may as well sit down.'

They had an air of embarrassment, standing between him and the door; they were obviously doubtful whether they ought not to pinion his arms or tie him up or something, but at the same time they had a horror of being conspicuous: the place was too public. They were obviously relieved when D. sat down himself; they pulled their chairs up around him. 'I say, Currie,' one of them said, 'there'd be no harm in giving the fellow a drink.' He added, rather unnecessarily it seemed to D., 'He's not likely to get another.'

'What will you have?' Currie asked.

'I think a whisky and soda.'

'Scotch?'

'Please.'

When the waiter came back, Currie said, 'A Scotch. Get that message off?'

'Yes, sir. They said they would be over in five minutes and you was to keep him.'

'Of course we'll keep him. We aren't fools. What do they think?'

D. said, 'I thought in England people are supposed to be innocent until they are proved guilty.'

'Oh yes,' Currie said, 'that's right. But of course the police don't arrest a man unless they've got the right dope.'

'I see.'

'Of course,' Captain Currie said, syphoning his whisky, 'it's a mistake you foreigners make. In your own country you kill each other and nobody asks questions, but if you do that sort of thing in England, well, you're for it.'

'Do you remember Blue?' one of the other men asked Currie.

'Tony Blue?'

'That's right. The one who played so badly in the Lancing-Brighton match in 'twenty-one. Muffed five catches.'

'What about Blue?'

'He went to Rumania once. Saw a man fire at a bobby in the street. So he said.'

'Of course, Blue was a stinking liar.'

D. said, 'Would you mind if I went to my room for my things? One of you could come with me.' It occurred to him that, once in his room, it might be possible ... when the messenger arrived. . . . They'd never find him here.

'Better wait for the police,' Blue's friend said. 'Mustn't take any risks.'

'Might hit and run.'

'I couldn't run far, could I?' D. said. 'You're an island.'

'I'm not taking any chances,' Currie said.

D. wondered whether whoever was fetching him had already gone to room 105c and found it empty.

Currie said, 'Would you two fellows mind keeping an eye on the door for a moment while I have a word with him alone?'

'Of course not, old man.'

Currie leant over his chair arm and said in a low voice, 'Look here, you're a gentleman, aren't you?'

'I'm not sure . . . it's an English word.'

'What I mean is—you won't say more than you need. One doesn't want a decent girl mixed up in this sort of thing.'

'I don't quite follow . . .'

'Well, there was that story of a woman with you in the flat when that fellow Forester . . .'

'I read 'Fortescue' in the papers.'

'Yes, that was it.'

'Oh, I imagine the woman—of course, I don't know anything about it—was some prostitute or other.'

'That's the idea,' Currie said. 'Stout fellow.'

He called out to the others, 'All right, you chaps. What about another Scotch all round?'

Blue's friend said, 'This one's on me.'

'No, you did the last. This is my turn.'

'As a matter of fact,' the third said, 'it's my turn.'

'No, you did the one before last.'

'Let's toss for it.'

While they argued D. stared out between the hopeless barrier of their shoulders to the big glass doors. The floodlights were on, so that beyond a few feet of grass outside nothing could be seen at all. The hotel was there for the world to look at, but the world itself was invisible. Somewhere in that invisibility the cargo ship

289

was passing—to his own country. He almost wished that he hadn't surrendered his gun to the gang of children in Benditch, even though they had, in a way, proved successful. The one shot would have put an end to a very boring and long drawn-out process.

A party of girls pushed in, bringing a little cold air into the overheated room. They were noisy and heavily made-up and rather unconvincing; they were trying to imitate the manner of a class more privileged than their own. They called out loudly, 'Hullo, there's Captain Curly.'

Currie blushed all down the back of his neck. He said, 'Look here, girls. Get yourselves drinks somewhere else. This is a private party.'

'Why, Curly?'

'We are talking important business.'

'I expect it's just dirty stories. Tell.'

'No, really, girls—I mean it.'

'Why do they call you Curly?' D. asked.

Currie blushed again.

'Introduce us to the fascinating stranger,' a fat girl said.

'No, no. It's impossible. Absolutely no go.'

Two men in mackintoshes pushed open the door and looked into the recreation room. One of them said, 'Is there anybody here called . . .?'

Captain Currie said, 'Thank God, are you the police?'

They watched him from the door. One of

them said, 'That's right.'

'Here's your man.'

'Are you D.?' one of them said.

'Yes.' D. stood up.

'We have a warrant for your arrest on the charge of . . .'

'Never mind,' D. said. 'I know what it's all about.'

'Anything you say . . .'

'Yes. Yes. Let's go.' He said to the girls who stood gaping by the table, 'You can have Curly now.'

'This way,' the detective said. 'We've a car at the gate.'

'No handcuffs?'

'I don't think they'll be needed,' the man said with a heavy smile. 'Come on. Get moving.'

One of them took him by the arm, unobtrusively. They might have been friends leaving after a few drinks. The English law, he thought, was remarkably tactful: everybody in this country hated a scene. The night embraced them. Floodlights drowned the stars in favour of Mr. Forbes's fantastic hobby. Far out at sea a light burned. Perhaps that was the ship in which he was supposed to leave—leave this country free from his infection and his friends free from embarrassment, from the dangerous disclosure and the untimely reticence. He wondered what Mr. Forbes would say when he read the morning papers and found he hadn't gone.

'Come on,' the detective said. 'We've not got all night.'

They led him out past the neon lights, saluting the clerk with a flick of the hand as they went. After all, the charge of leaving without paying his bill would not be added to the other misdemeanours. The car was up on the grass verge with the lights discreetly out. It would not have been good for the hotel, he supposed, if a police car had been too prominently on view. The taxpayer in this country was always protected. A third man sat at the wheel. He started up as soon as they appeared and switched on the lights. D. got into the back between the two others. They swerved out on to the road and drove down towards Southcrawl.

One of the men in the back began to wipe his forehead. 'God damn!' he said.

They swerved left down a by-road away from Southcrawl. He said, 'When they told me you were being taken care of, you could've knocked me down with a feather.'

'You're not detectives?' He felt no elation: everything was starting all over again.

'Of course we're not detectives. You gave me a turn in there. I thought you were going to ask for my warrant. Haven't you the sense?'

'You see, detectives are on the way.'

'Step on it, Joe.'

They ricocheted down the rough path towards the sound of the sea. It came more boisterously up at them now every minute: the noise of surf beating on the rocks. 'You a good sailor?' one of the men asked.

'Yes. I think so.'

'You need to be. It's a fierce night—and it'll be worse in the Bay.'

The car drew up. The headlights illuminated for a few feet a rough red chalk track and then ploughed on into nothing. They were at the edge of a low cliff. 'Come on,' the man said, 'we've got to hurry. It won't take them long to tumble to things.'

'Surely they can stop the ship—somehow.'

'Oh, they'll send us a wire or two. We radio back that we haven't seen you. You don't think they'll turn out the Navy, do you? You aren't all that important.'

They led the way down the steps cut in the cliff. In the little cove below a motor-boat bobbed at the end of a chain. 'What about the car?' D. said.

'Never mind the car.'

'Won't it be traced?'

'I dare say—back to the shop it was bought at this morning—for twenty pounds. Anyone who likes is welcome to it. I wouldn't drive a car like that again—not for a fortune.' But it seemed likely that a small fortune had been spent already—by Mr. Forbes. They puttered out of the cove and immediately met the force of the sea. It smashed at them deliberately like an

293

enemy. It was not like an impersonal force at all riding in long regular breakers: it was like a madman with a pickaxe, smashing at them now on this side, now on the other. They would be lured, as it were, into a calm trough, and then the blows would come one after another in rapid succession: then calm again. There wasn't much time or chance to look back; only once, as they bobbed up on what seemed the top of the world, D. caught a glimpse of the floodlit hotel foundering in the far distance, as the moon swept up the sky.

It took them more than an hour to reach the ship, a dingy black coaster of about three thousand tons flying a Dutch flag. D. came up the side like a piece of cargo and was immediately shipped below. An officer in an old jumper and dirty grey flannel trousers said, 'You keep below for an hour or two. It is better so.'

The cabin was tiny and close to the engine-room. Somebody had had the forethought to lay out an old pair of trousers and a waterproof: he was wet through. The port-hole was battened down, and a cockroach moved rapidly up the steel wall by the bunk. Well, he thought, I am nearly home. I am safe . . . if it was possible to think in terms of safety at all. He was safe from one danger and going back to another.

He sat on the edge of his bunk: he felt dizzy. After all, he thought, I am old—for this kind of life. He felt a sensation of pity for Mr. K. who had dreamed in vain of a quiet life in a university far behind the lines—well, at least he hadn't died in an Entrenationo cubicle in the presence of some sharp oriental like Mr. Li, who would resent the interruption of a lesson he had paid for in advance. And there was Else— the terror was over: she was secure from all the worse things which might have happened to her. The dead were to be envied. It was the living who had to suffer from loneliness and distrust. He got up; he needed air.

The deck was uncovered, and the wind whipped the sharp spray against his mouth. He leant over the side and saw the great creamy tops rise up against the galley lights and surge away down into some invisible abyss. Somewhere far off a light went on and off—Land's End? No, they couldn't be as far as that yet from London and Mr. Forbes driving through the dark, and Rose waiting—or Sally.

A voice he knew said, 'That'll be Plymouth.'

He didn't turn: he didn't know what to say: his heart had missed a beat like a young man's; he was afraid. He said, 'Mr. Forbes...'

'Oh, Furt,' she said, 'Furt turned me down.' He remembered the tears on Western Avenue, the look of hate on the hill above Southcrawl. 'He's sentimental,' she said, 'he preferred a gesture. Poor old Furt.' In a phrase she dismissed him; he moved back into the salt and noisy dark at ten knots.

He said. 'I'm an old man.'

'If I don't care,' she said, 'what does it matter what you are? Oh, I know you're faithful—but I've told you I shan't go on loving a dead man.' He took a quick look at her; her hair was lank with spray. She looked older than he had ever seen her yet—plain. It was as if she were assuring him that glamour didn't enter into *this* business. She said, 'When you are dead, she can have you. I can't compete then—and we'll all be dead a long, long time.'

The light went by astern: ahead there was only the splash, the long withdrawal, and the dark. She said, 'You'll be dead very soon: you needn't tell me that, but *now* . . .'

Photoset, printed and bound in Great Britain by REDWOOD BURN LIMITED, Trowbridge, Wiltshire